THE CANARD CASE

Book Four of the Artifactor

HONOR RACONTEUR

Raconteur House

Published by Raconteur House
Murfreesboro, TN

This is a work of fiction. Names, characters, places and incidents either are the product of the author's imagination or are used fictitiously, and any resemblance to actual persons, living or dead, business establishments, events or locales is entirely coincidental.

THE CANARD CASE
Book Four of the Artifactor

A Raconteur House book/ published by arrangement with the author

Copyright © 2019, 2016 by Honor Raconteur
Cover Design by Katie Griffin
Antique Clock Face by Vladimir Sazonov /Shutterstock
Chinese landscape watercolor painting by Baoyan/Shutterstock

All rights reserved.
No part of this book may be reproduced, scanned, or distributed in any printed or electronic form without permission. Please do not participate in or encourage electronic piracy of copyrighted materials in violation of the author's rights.
Purchase only authorized editions.
For information address: www.raconteurhouse.com

"If you can't do something, then don't. Focus on what you can do."
— Shiroe, *Log Horizon*

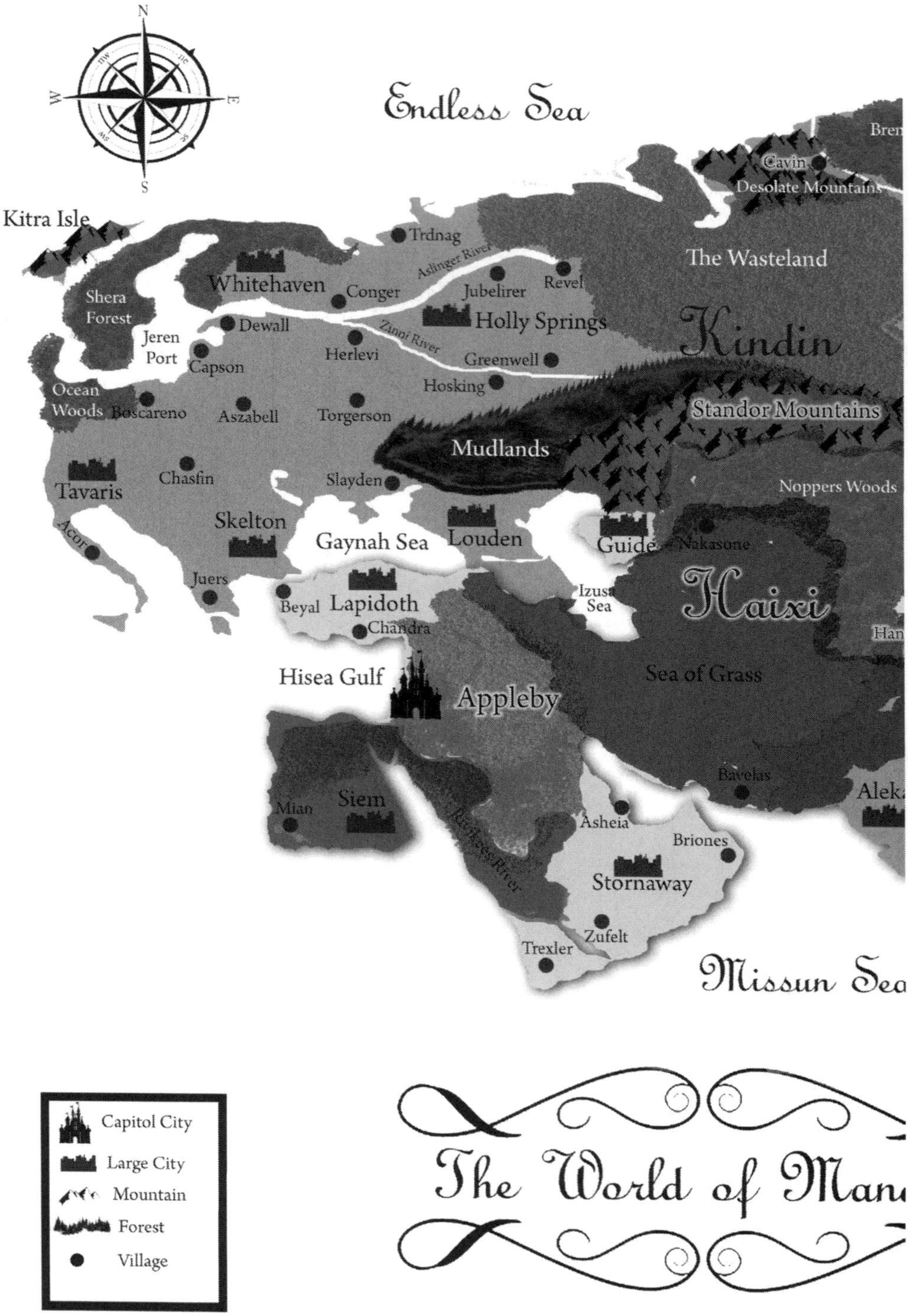

N
E
S
W
Endless Sea
Kitra Isle
Cavin
Desolate Mountains
Trdnag
The Wasteland
Aslinger River
Whitehaven
Conger
Jubelirer
Revel
Shera Forest
Holly Springs
Dewall
Zanni River
Jeren Port
Capson
Herlevi
Greenwell
Kindin
Ocean Woods
Boscareno
Aszabell
Torgerson
Hosking
Standor Mountains
Mudlands
Tavaris
Chasfin
Slayden
Noppers Woods
Acor
Skelton
Gaynah Sea
Louden
Guide
Nakasone
Juers
Beyal
Lapidoth
Izusa Sea
Haixi
Chandra
Hisea Gulf
Appleby
Sea of Grass
Mian
Siem
Bavelas
Asheia
Briones
Stornaway
Zufelt
Trexler
Missun Sea
Capitol City
Large City
Mountain
Forest
Village
The World of Man

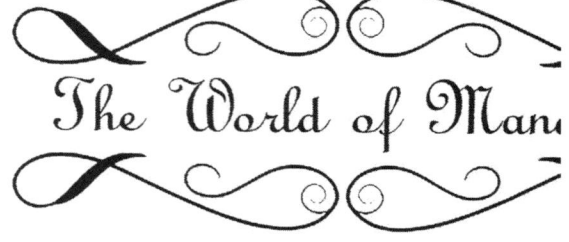

Shinogee Mountains
Lorin Woods
Nanashi Isle
Brennan Woods
Galyean
Holdaway
Windtower
Harkin
Tiburon
Kvenvold
Belen
Van Kamen
Noshiravan
Salazar
Thirdcastle
Stanger
Daelyn River
Bornemeier
Denniston Forest
Jendah Gulf
Nastase
Khoury
Stillwater
Essen
Stillwater Lake
Master Tashjian
Sondack
Winfield
Vanorman
Seaton
Tresvant
Gerrety
Critchlow
Vigil
Kingman
Windamere
Wilfong
Ence
Stamons
Klose
Nickerchen Ruins
Milby
Lockbright
Richins
Milby River
Hanford Mtns. (Big)
Hock
Lavella Harbor
Platt
Sanat Forest
Ries
Sa Kao
Tree-on-the-sea
Tea Amo
Zuria
Manalo
Nokoni
Tashjian
Thabit
Kamae Harbor
Shah
Kalel
Lansky Isle
Koch
Vash
Kesly Islands
Dragon Sea

Ailana's eyebrows nettled with intense focus, lips pursed, her expression more troubled than she likely meant it to be. Sevana watched the Fae Mother watch her, and Sevana did not like what she saw. That expression did not bode well for her.

Finally, Ailana sat back, the movement graceful, as every motion from her was. She blew out a soft breath that had an air of resignation to it. The active wisps of blue magic that flowed from her hands and around Sevana stilled and then dissipated like dust motes into the air.

"I fear I do not know what to do at this time."

Not the answer Sevana wanted. "Didn't you tell me that once my body was physically healed, my magic would do the same?"

"I did say that," Ailana admitted, becoming more troubled as she spoke, "and that is usually what happens. Your magical core was offset with Arandur's magic when he put his blood into you. We do share our Fae blood with our children, in very diluted forms, so his method is not unusual. We feared for your safety because he did not dilute his blood first, and with it at full potency, we anticipated it would be too much of a shock to a human system. But since you healed, we expected it to adapt to your body. And it has done so, admirably."

"Just not with my magical core." Sevana put a flat palm to her chest and tried not to have a breakdown right then and there. This state was beyond frustrating, so frustrating that she had caught herself almost crying angry tears more than once. She had taken nearly two months to physically heal from her ordeal. Her magic had been a little out of sorts, but then with everything that had happened, that was to be expected. Or so they had kept saying for the past month.

Sevana looked away, over the glen, watching a herd of children play some sort of game that involved a great deal of chasing and giggling. Even from here their half-Fae status was apparent, as their bodies gradually changed from their human makeup. "I guess," she said in a subdued tone, "I now understand why your lore instructs you to never try and turn a human with magic in them into Fae."

"It does seem to cause complications," Ailana agreed readily. "But at the same time, I'm not sure if we should leap to any conclusions. Sellion, we were deathly afraid that you would not survive the change at all, or be so damaged by it on a physical level that it would take considerable effort to right matters. Magical core aside, you are thriving. Your physical structure is much stronger and more capable than before."

That part was true. Sevana had done careful tests and measurements and discovered that her sight, hearing, and sense of smell had all improved significantly. It was at least a twenty percent increase in all three senses, which was unheard of. She felt like she was a cat, sometimes. And that didn't even mention that her aging process had slowed to an absolute crawl. Her timespan now was no longer human, not yet Fae, but in some limbo in between.

And Sevana had no idea what to think about that at all.

"The way that your body adapted tells me that our lore is not entirely correct," Ailana continued. "After all, it also tells us that we should never take a human child older than ten, that a change on a fully grown adult would be impossible. And yet here you sit, perfectly whole and hearty, even though you are mid-change."

True. That was also true. Sevana came out of her depression a little. "Do I look quasi-Fae to you?"

"Yes, it is very clear to my eyes that you are partially changed into Fae structure. I realize it would be difficult for you to see yourself with your own eyes, but has no one else said as much?"

Sevana gave a slow shake of the head. "No, not really." But then, everyone had more or less been focused on her magical dysfunctions.

Although come to think of it... "The Fae in Sanat said something about that. They were surprised at my appearance."

"As well they should be. You are not like anything we have seen before. Even our lore contains very little record of someone changed as you were." Ailana wasn't the sort to bite her nails and brood, but Sevana gathered the distinct impression that she was doing that on some level. "These mixed signals are very confusing for all of us. I will contact my sisters in the other areas, see if I can't find a lore master that might know more about this. We cannot leave you in this state."

On that, Sevana vehemently agreed. Her physical body was fine. Well, mostly fine. Sevana felt like she had a cold most of the time with the coughing, and the sneezing, and the slight ache in her joints. But considering that she had foreign Fae blood running around in her system, this was a remarkably mild reaction. If that was the only price to pay for this strange half-and-half state, she had no complaints, but her magical core absolutely had to be fixed soon. She'd melted half her workroom already because of magical flares, all caused by her unstable core. Taking on work from the outside had proven to be difficult at best. She had to outsource a good majority of it to either Master, Sarsen, or Aran. The Fae tracker had proven to be an invaluable friend to her during all of this, and rarely left her side for any length of time. She depended on his magic to get her through the rougher spots.

Ailana patted her on the hand, expression sympathetic. "Do not fret, Sellion. We will find the answer to this."

"You better find it soon," Sevana grumbled. "Otherwise I'll end up accidentally blowing up Big."

"For my information, tell me exactly how your magic is reacting," Ailana requested. "I must give particulars when I send out the letters."

Having just reported this to Aranhil, the words still lingered like a bitter aftertaste in the back of her mouth, and she didn't like repeating them. But Sevana also recognized that she needed to, and so forced them out. "There's little in the way of a pattern. It doesn't react strongly to any particular element, or tool, or specific type of magic.

Rather, it seems to be a matter of how much magic I'm drawing from my core. If it's a simple matter, like invoking a spell, then I have fifty-fifty odds of it working. A quick burst of magic from me doesn't seem to cause any conflagration. At least not regularly. It's sustained magic that gets me in trouble every time."

Ailana gave a slow, thoughtful nod. "This does not surprise me. How long can you sustain your magic before it causes problems?"

"Five seconds is my absolute max. Sometimes I can't even manage five seconds." Which meant that using any of her flying devices, or her Caller, or things of that nature were almost beyond her. Fortunately Aran was a quick student and he often channeled his magic into those devices on her behalf.

"This sounds like an incompatibility between Fae magic and human," Ailana stated thoughtfully. "But I would like to confer with others before making any assumptions."

Sevana understood that and didn't argue. "So for now, I suppose I go back to Big and try not to blow anything sky-high."

"Keep Arandur with you," Ailana instructed.

Snorting, Sevana parried, "You think I have a choice on that? The man's like my living shadow. I'm not sure if it's guilt or worry that makes him act like that."

"Perhaps a little of those emotions," Ailana responded with a distinct twinkle of amusement in her eyes. "But I do not think that is his prime motivation. In any case, keep him with you. You are highly vulnerable at the moment, Sellion, and I do not think it wise to step outside of Big until we have this resolved."

Sevana started shaking her head even before Ailana trotted that whole sentence out. "Emergencies don't stop and jobs don't cease to come in just because I'm a little off my game, Ailana. Granted, working right now is a challenge, and there are certain things I don't dare touch—" like a certain magical doohickey that Master had brought back for her from the evil magician's lair "—but it's not like I can halt everything altogether. I've managed now for three months, I can continue working until we get this imbalance of mine resolved."

1

"Can't you just magic up a solution?" Booker asked. No, more like demanded.

Sevana had been asked this question almost every hour on the hour since she'd arrived on the job, and hearing it again snapped what was left of her patience. "If you wanted a magical solution," she snarled at him, "you should have requested a sorcerer!"

He flinched back, hands rising as if ready to duck and cover.

Flinging a hand out, she pointed toward Stillwater Dam. "That is the largest dam in the whole of Mander. No Artifactor has the magical power of a sorcerer or sorceress—none of us could stop it alone! If you had called for me the minute that you knew there was a problem, perhaps I could have done that. Right now I don't have the time to devise a magical solution for you."

Everyone in the room fell eerily silent, as if all hope had drained out of them. Sevana blew out a breath, struggling to rein in her temper. "Oh, stop looking like I just danced on your graves. I didn't say I don't have a solution, it's just not magical."

The sole female engineer, Kira, dared to ask, "What's the solution?"

"Old fashioned human ingenuity." Sevana waved them in closer to the window so that she could point as necessary. The dam looked like it had pox, even from here. They were actually in the dam work shed, where they kept all of the necessary supplies and equipment to make repairs. The single table in the room had been cleared off so they had room to work if needed, but there were no chairs. Six people in the room made for cramped conditions, but it was the only building near the dam. 'Near' being a relative term, as the building was several hundred yards from it.

Rainfall for this year was at an unprecedented high, so much so that it had overflowed the banks of the Daelyn River and in turn caused the reservoir near Stillwater Dam to nearly flood. The dam had not been constructed to hold this much water weight, and it was slowly collapsing under the strain. They had opened up every emergency valve on either side of the dam, letting out what water they could into the lake, but it wasn't enough. One of the tunnels had collapsed under the force of the water and the other three weren't in much better shape. The dam was breaking apart in front of her eyes.

If the dam broke, it would destroy thousands of acres and homes, and Essen and Stillwater would likely be severely damaged. She really could not let the dam fall. Never mind the property damage, they wouldn't be able to evacuate everyone in time. The loss of life.... She shuddered as her mind calculated the odds of survival for the people in the nearby cities. It wasn't a pretty number.

"Artifactor?" Kira asked, a little timidly.

Sevana's mind switched gears. She had to think of solving the problem, not what would happen if she didn't. "I can't be in two places at once. We're going to have to divide the work." Pointing to the top of the dam, she ordered, "I need a work crew at the top of the dam. We're adding four feet of sheetwood, bracketed by steel beams, to the top. That should make sure that the reservoir doesn't spill over."

Booker shook his head in instinctive protest. "Artifactor, sheetwood is incredibly thin. Barely two inches thick! I know we have a lot of it stored in here, which makes it tempting to use, but it doesn't have the strength necessary to hold that kind of water weight."

"It won't be holding the full weight of the dam," she pointed out, striving to be patient. "It's only holding the water at the very top. That's a different weight. It would be about the same as, oh, a large pool. Don't believe me? Do the math."

No one believed her, except perhaps Kira, who silently muttered numbers to herself with growing enlightenment. She, at least, could do the math in her head. The men grabbed sheets of paper and the pencils from behind their ears and went to madly scribbling on any free space of the table they could reach. Two of the men reached the same conclusion at basically the same time and they looked stunned at the result.

"See?" Sevana grinned at them. It was so satisfying being right. "I'll draw up what it needs to look like, but you'll have to build it."

Yosef gave her a steady nod, bushy dark brows drawn together in a firm line of determination. "We can do that, Artifactor. While we work on the top, you'll repair the holes in the dam?"

She spread her hands. "It'll be patchwork at best. But I'll do what I can. We have to be quick, though, we're losing the light. And the storm overhead is mild compared to what's coming our direction." She strode to the table, forcing people to move aside, and flipped over the nearest paper before commandeering a pen and quickly drawing out the plans. As she drew, she issued orders. "Kira, there is a box in my *Jumping Clouds* that's blue, labeled climbing equipment. Grab that and give a belt to each worker. It'll keep them from falling off the top of the dam. Tell them not to try that theory out until I can set the perimeter, though. There is also one in there that is a dark blue belt with a rope attached—that one's mine, don't hand it out."

Kira gave her a quick curtsey and ran out the door in a flash, letting in sprinkles of rain to litter the floor.

Sevana took note of this. It meant the storm was picking up. Mentally swearing, she kept barking out commands. "Yosef, get these steel beams ready to weld. Do you have equipment that will work in this storm?"

"I do, Artifactor."

"Then move. If they fail you, tell me, I have an alternative."

He too left, although not as quickly as the younger and more spry Kira.

"Booker," she pointed toward the illustration, "you see how the sheets need to be fitted together?"

"I do, Artifactor, I'll get on it immediately."

"Make sure they overlap at least a foot on all sides, otherwise no single board will have the strength to hold it," and then they'd all be in trouble. Sevana especially, as she'd be dangling over the side of the dam. If it broke, she'd be swept away, magical climbing harness or no.

Oh how she wished she had Aran and his magic with her right now. The call for help had come in unexpectedly and she hadn't had the time to track him down. His Caller hadn't connected for some reason, which likely meant he was head-deep in some problem and wasn't paying attention to it. She'd had no other way to reach him and couldn't wait. As it was, she had no time to work.

Nothing for it. Sevana would do her best with her wonky magic. It either petered out and gave her the bare minimum, or went far above what she actually needed done. If it went overboard while patching the dam, so much the better. If it went the other direction, she'd spell the area twice.

She ran to the top of the dam and put the climbing restraints in place so the belt harnesses would know where their limits were. She had one man to help her with things, as she couldn't easily move from one section of the dam to other without climbing up, changing her anchor, and then moving again. With him operating a pulley system for her, the anchor could go the breadth of the dam without issue.

"Dougan, if I lift my hand straight out, go that direction. If I put a hand above my head, that means lower me. If both hands are up, I actually want to come up. Got that?"

Dougan was a senior dam worker who had been there for over twenty years. Even this dangerous situation didn't rattle him as much as it did the others, and he gave her a somber nod. "I do, Artifactor. Dam's made mostly from sand and concrete. You need supplies to patch with?"

"It wouldn't do any good to take normal supplies down with me," she denied, slipping her legs into the harness and pulling it on over her hips. "The water is gushing out of the holes at such force that nothing would harden, not even with magic. I've got magical seals that I can slap over it that can hold a charging elephant. I'll try those first."

"If those don't?"

"I have a backup plan." Unfortunately, she had less faith in her backup plan than in her first, but she wasn't about to tell him that. "Let me down, Dougan."

He let her down in easy stages to the first hole. Actually, it wasn't as much of a hole as some of the others, as it seeped more than gushed. Sevana reached into the pack strapped to her chest and pulled out a ready-made seal designed to detect the material it affixed to and duplicate its strength and permeability in a five-foot radius. Some of the holes in the dam were larger than that, so it would take more than one seal. Sevana started praying she had enough on her. If she didn't, they were in trouble—these took a week to make. Individually.

Because the heavens were not listening, and her magic was less than cooperative, the first seal barely had enough magic to activate with. But activate it did, strongly enough to hold back the water and keep anything else from seeping through. Phew, alright, it worked. Although why was the spell spluttering like that? It was almost like a magical hiccup happening in front of her eyes. To her relief, it only lasted a second, and then it settled down into an overall hum like it was supposed to. Still, that worried her. Sevana had never seen magic do that before.

"That do it?!" Dougan yelled down at her over the roaring sound of the water.

She didn't have the ability to yell back and be heard so she put both arms over her head in large circle, signaling an affirmative, then pointed to the next hole. Dougan pulled her the right direction, she put two seals on it (as her magic was still not cooperating), and then it was onto the next. And the next. Sevana had of course counted the holes before she ever got into the harness, but what she hadn't been able to calculate was how many seals it would take to close them all.

The skies overhead were also in an uncooperative mood. As the sun started to set, the rain came in harder than before. Worse, lightning started to flash overhead. Sevana felt half-drowned. She constantly wiped water out of her eyes, for all the good that did her. Today was becoming thoroughly rotten.

From her angle halfway down the dam, she had no way of

checking on the workers on top. She couldn't begin to see them from here. There was also no way for her to communicate with Dougan to ask. He could barely see her as it was, and if not for the head lamp on her hat, he wouldn't be able to at all. She had to trust the workers hadn't been fried by lightning and were still working. It was too much of a miracle to ask that they finished before the storm truly hit.

She ran out of seals before she could patch all of the holes, but the last two weren't actively gushing out water, so she felt it was safe enough to leave them alone. Tomorrow, after the storm had abated, she'd come back down here to check on things properly. Getting out of the way before lightning could strike her or she was swept away by a flood of water seemed like a higher priority.

Sevana gestured to Dougan to pull her up and he did so with commendable alacrity. When she got near the top, she found that Booker was helping him, and she thought a little better of the man because he had stayed behind on a dangerous ledge just to help her.

They spoke no words to each other. Sevana quickly shucked the harness and unclicked the main part of it to carry along with her. (The thing was expensive and difficult to make.) They didn't dare run on this slick, wet surface that was only two feet wide, but they moved at a fast walk and with many a worried glance toward the sky. The other eight workmen were already off, also anxious to get back onto land before lightning could strike them. She didn't breathe easily until they cleared the dam entirely and made it back to the work shed.

Kira handed her a towel the moment she came through the door, which Sevana took with heartfelt thanks. Drying her exposed skin and hair, she stepped through to see the result of their work.

The workers had managed to get all of the beams and sheetwood in place. It was just as well, too, as the water level continued to steadily rise. Already it was above the normal level of the dam. Without the boards in place, it would have spilled over before she could have gotten back onto solid ground. That had been too close for comfort.

Not a word passed between them as time ticked relentlessly by. There was a small brazier near the door of the shed, giving off some heat, but Sevana shivered while standing around in her wet clothes.

She wasn't willing to leave yet and try to find something warm, though. Any second, she might have to dash back out again and try some other fix to keep the dam intact.

Slowly, she realized that the storm was abating. Lightning had ceased to strike and the visibility had increased so that she was no longer straining to see the dam.

"It's not rising," Booker breathed, sounding as if he almost doubted his own words.

Sevana pulled out her glasses, choosing the telescope lenses to get a better look. She let out a low whistle. "Six inches from the top of the boards. That's cutting it close." Turning her head, she peered toward the direction of the river. "The water seems calmer now than it was before. There's no choppiness, at least."

Yosef let out a loud breath. "We might survive this night after all."

As he spoke, the storm died down to a sprinkling of raindrops. They all held their breath and waited to see if this change was permanent or just a break in the storm. Minutes ticked by and the storm stopped completely, leaving a cool and moist feeling to the air. Sevana grinned, relief mixing in with a heady sense of victory. "I think we did it."

The whole shed burst into a raucous outcry of celebration. Sevana laughed at their reaction and then joined in. They had beaten the odds getting it done. Truly, there were few jobs that could rival this one in gut-wrenching tension.

"I'll stay the night and watch it," Yosef volunteered readily. "I'll sound the alarm if the situation changes for the worst."

"Good idea," Booker agreed, clapping the man on the back. "Meanwhile, the rest of us should find our beds. We should get some sleep in case we need to be back at work."

Sevana had no idea what they would do if their patches failed. She hadn't the slightest inkling if her backup plan would have really worked or not—it was just the only other idea that she could think of to try. It was true, though, that they all needed rest. When she had arrived this morning, they'd already been up for one full day trying to fix the situation. Most of the people standing here had been awake for over fifty hours, which wasn't good. Tired people made mistakes.

"Artifactor," Kira motioned her toward the door, "there's a house nearby that has agreed to shelter you while you're here. They have a bed made up and waiting for you."

Now when had she found the time to see to that? "Let's go, then. The place is nearby?"

"Very close. We'll call you first if something happens."

Well enough. Sevana followed her out the door, but stopped by *Jumping Clouds* long enough to grab her bag. She wanted dry clothes to change into before trying to sleep.

The house was owned by an elderly couple that seemed oddly in awe of her. Sevana had no idea what part of her reputation made them react so, but enjoyed the stroke to her ego so did nothing to dissuade their over-the-top hospitality.

Still, it wasn't long before she was in dry clothes, in a country-style room, on a soft feather-tick mattress. Snuggling under two quilts, she expected it to take a few minutes to warm the bed up enough for her to get comfortable. Even longer for her to actually fall asleep. Her expectations were proved false, as she didn't even remember when her eyes closed.

Her sleep was deep, dreamless, revitalizing. A passing chill awoke her, and she reached for the blankets to draw them up closer to her chin, only for her hand to grasp empty air. Something poked her back and she realized that the comfortable mattress under her was gone. Eyes snapping open, she flailed upright in a panic.

Bed, room, house, everything was gone only to be replaced by forest.

A forest she didn't recognize.

Sevana stared straight ahead, heart still racing and sounding like a war drum in her ears, eyes locked on a group of three of the strangest people she had ever seen standing in front of her. Was this a dream? Surely not, it felt all too real to be a dream. Although this gathering of oddities in a forest setting certainly made it look like a dream.

A robust man with a round belly, oblong hat of silk, and droopy black mustache was shaking a finger to emphasize his point. "—not to be confused with any other Artifactor or magician. She is the one that has saved not just one royal family, but three!"

"She is known as a curse-breaker," a large...wait, what was he? His shape seemed to shift between a man and a large black bear, making it seem as if he were shifting from one to another in a constant transition. "There is no curse here to break. What good is she?"

"While I agree that her reputation does not give her the qualities we need, I am also inclined to think that she may be the most suitable to help us." The third and final member of the group was not human, not beast, but something that Sevana had only ever read about. This was a Qi-lin. It simply had to be. It resembled a dragon with scaly red skin and three horns on its forehead, but it was in the general shape of a deer, and had hefty manes of hair flowing out. They were not to be confused with a unicorn, even though their general body shape made one think they were a cousin of that race.

There was only one place in the world that the Qi-lins lived. "I'm on Nanashi Isle," she blurted out incredulously. How?! This place was at least a two day trip from Stillwater! How could she have possibly crossed that distance in one night?!

All three stopped and turned to look at her.

"You are," the mustached man confirmed. Well, the term 'man' was misleading. There was no way he was a regular man, not with the way he glowed. "Sevana Warren, stand and speak with us. We wish to see if you are adequate to the task."

He made this sound like a job interview instead of a kidnapping. Sevana stood, but did so crossly. After all, she was still in her nightclothes (although fortunately she had worn pants and a shirt as a precaution, since she had half-expected to be yanked out of bed) and didn't have any shoes on. If they imagined that she would meekly go along with whatever they wanted, they were sorely mistaken. She'd come up with suitable payback shortly, but first she had get the full scope of the situation. Making her way gingerly across the forested floor, she tried to avoid any fallen twigs or stones, and came to stand with them.

"First, who are you?"

They seemed taken aback at her brusqueness. The Qi-lin's mane actually huffed out like an enraged cat's. "You do not know who we are?"

"You are a Qi-lin," she riposted flatly. "So I'm assuming that I'm on Nanashi Isle, and you are the inhabitants, perhaps the minor deities of the Isle, but I want proper names. Who are you?"

The Qi-lin's golden eyes narrowed to mere slits. "I am Chi-lin."

Oh? Sevana's memory was a bit dusty, as she hadn't studied the Nanashi mythology in some time, but if memory served, if a Qi-lin took on a variation of the race's name, they were very highly ranked.

Without prompting, the bear/man took a half-step forward. His form settled more into that of a man, black hair, slanted dark eyes in round face. "I am Da-Yu."

"Cheng-Huang," the last man introduced himself, the only person to not have a challenge in his voice. He seemed more inclined to study her as she caught up. "You are correct. We are deities of Nanashi Isle."

At least she'd guessed that part right. They were likely not the only ones—her memory drew a blank on how many there actually were—but that was fine. She had enough to contend with at the moment with these three. "Why did you bring me here?"

Da-Yu gave a pointed look at Cheng-Huang. "I didn't."

"Artifactor Sevana Warren," Cheng-Huang faced her squarely, "there is a disaster facing our isle that will consume it utterly unless it is stopped."

In spite of her better judgment, she felt a flicker of intrigue. Sevana never could turn down a challenge. It was a failing of hers. "Three minor gods can't handle it, but you believe I can?"

"Your reputation precedes you," Cheng-Huang answered simply.

"She also solved two major problems for the Fae," Chi-Lin added, more toward Da-Yu than to her, "which is why I'm inclined to at least let her try. Our powers are not suitable to this task."

"Despite all of the prayers we've been getting," Cheng-Huang added sourly in a mutter.

Yes, this had to be good. Sevana didn't know what 'two' problems they were referring to. She had given children to the Fae, certainly, but that wasn't a 'solution' to her mind. She'd also helped magic-proof the Fae storerooms to prevent any more thefts, but that wasn't a 'solution' either, not really. It had barely been a problem to begin with, what with that evil prodigy dead. For the moment, she wouldn't argue either point. She wanted to hear what was so dire that they had brought her here. "So what is the problem?"

"You are aware that Nanashi has an active volcano on it?" Cheng-Huang inquired. At her nod, he continued, "It will explode soon. The pressure is rising quickly and there's little that we can do to stop it."

A volcano? Sevana's eyes threatened to pop out of her head. "You want me to *stop a volcano*?!"

"You have the ability to save kings and help the Fae," Cheng-Huang answered forthrightly. "This task is within your capabilities."

Sevana stared at him, completely flabbergasted. For the first time in her adult life, she felt like protesting that she couldn't do something. It was a rare moment, as she had been stumped before, many times, but not once had she felt like it was completely outside of her abilities. Was this how normal people felt?

Da-Yu snorted, bitterly satisfied. "Look at her expression. She has no idea how to help us."

That reaction put her back up so fast a few vertebrae snapped. "Stuff it, bear-man."

"B-bear!" he spluttered, hackles rising.

"First, boots," she ordered Cheng-Huang. "I'm not walking around this place barefoot. Then you'll show me this volcano before I make any decisions. Oh, and don't think you won't pay through the nose for dragging me here without my consent, because you will."

Chi-lin raised his head in a small jerk. "You think you can do something about this? When even we can't?"

"I've never turned down a challenge in my life and honestly this doesn't qualify as the hardest thing I've had to do." Although it was coming in a very close second. In her opinion, having to break Kip's curse would always be the hardest job she had ever taken on. "Show me the problem first. Then I'll be able to offer solutions." She pointed at her feet. "Boots."

Cheng-Huang gave an expansive wave of the hand and her boots arrived on her feet, laced up perfectly as if she had just put them on herself. Sevana was dying to know how he did that trick. "Anything else, Artifactor?"

"I'm not done having you summon things," she informed him, doubling back for her pack. "But for now, I need to see the volcano. Then I'll tell you what I need." He was also going to call home for her and inform people where she had gone, although he didn't know that yet. Forget Master or Sarsen's reactions when they discovered her missing. It was Aran's that she worried about. Aran would not take her disappearance well, and he was as likely to hunt her down himself as to inform Aranhil. And if her Fae King learned of this, he was just as likely to slaughter people first and put flowers on their graves afterwards.

Volcanic islands were not shaped like most islands. They were crafted from large amounts of magma all pushed upwards through the crust, so they always formed a rough cone shape. Nanashi Isle was no different. Shaped like a giant mountain, it had little in the way of flat land. There were trees, of course, vegetation of various sorts, thick and dense. Because of the severe slope of the mountain, Sevana was able to see some of the beach below, although tree limbs did obscure her view.

The inhabitants of the isle had wisely chosen to settle first along the beach, as that would be the easiest place to build and the only sensible location for trade. Growing things was the challenge here without any real flat land to work with, but the people here had adapted by carving out sections along the side of the mountain, creating narrow fields that went steadily up. From her high vantage point, she could see paths that wound in and around them. Her three guides did not lead her down the mountain but instead went up. Sevana quickly appreciated boots on her feet, as the climb became more and more rocky. Lava rock could be horrendously sharp, especially against bare skin.

Somewhat to her surprise, the area did not go straight upwards. Instead they reached a small plateau that went more or less flat for several hundred feet before rising sharply again. This area had limited vegetation, mostly grass and ferns, and the area ahead was even sparser. Sevana took one look at the volcano, saw steam and gases rising out of the top, and felt like swearing. "You've seen no sign of magma coming out? It's just bubbling and causing deformities?"

"This is the most we see coming from the top," Cheng-Huang responded. "In fact, the summit bulges a few feet upward a day but nothing overflows."

Sevana swore some more, louder this time.

Chi-Lin gave her a nod of grudging respect. "You know what that means."

"I do," she acknowledged grimly. "That volcano is on the edge of erupting. We have days at best to stop this thing." Her mind raced. What could she possibly do about this situation? Evacuating the inhabitants of the isle went without saying, of course, but this volcano was large. Large enough to impact the mainland. Belen would not be getting out free and clear if the volcano blew. It would likely impact the lives of tens of thousands of people for hundreds of miles around.

And no matter what these three thought, this was most definitely a job for the Fae. They were the ones that could sweet talk rocks into doing whatever they wanted.

Sevana dropped to her knees, slinging her pack around to the front, and frantically dug through it. But even though she searched three times, she could not find her Caller. Releasing it, she twisted around to demand of Cheng-Huang, "I need my Caller. It's a small statue that looks like a human. It should be on my flying device."

"I do not need to know where it is," he assured her. With a wave of the hand, it appeared, hovering just in front of her.

Sevana grabbed it and placed it on a flat palm. Now, calm down. Her magic would only let her sustain for about five seconds, which meant she only had that much time to give Master the information he needed to know. Last time, she had been in too much of a rush and her magic power had gotten all excited, accidentally overloading the Caller and burning it to a crisp. She could not afford to lose this one; it was the last one she had that was still intact. Taking a deep, calming breath, she tried to settle herself. When that didn't work, she tried another. Right, that was better. Forming what she needed to say in her head, she commanded, "Call Master."

There was a long pause and then the Caller adopted the features of her Master, raising his head, the outlines of his favorite tattered robe hanging off one shoulder. "*Sweetling! Now—*"

She didn't have time to let him talk, so cut in. "Master, I've been called by three deities about an active volcano. I could use some help, we don't have a lot of time. I'm in—" at that moment her unpredictable magic flared and sparked, arcing out over her hand. It shot through the Caller and melted it to the point that the ceramic crumbled into fine dust, trailing to the ground in waves. Sevana sank, head hanging between her shoulders, and screamed in the back of her throat.

So much for her five second rule.

"Why is your magic so unstable?" Da-Yu demanded of her. "You are like a novice."

Sevana shot to her feet, a snarl on her lips. "You try being infused with Fae magic without going through the proper rituals and see what happens!" Throwing what was left of the Caller to the ground, she snatched up her bag. "Do deities pray?"

"Why?" Chi-Lin asked, prancing in agitation, likely because of her attitude.

"Because if you do, you should start now. If Master doesn't figure out where I am, and then contact the Fae nation, you're going to get some very angry guests soon. And believe me, you don't want them upset with you."

Da-Yu at least didn't like this idea one bit. "You're not going to send them a message?"

"The only thing I have that will communicate with them is in a pile of burnt sand right now," she growled at him. "So no, I'm not. I'll work on the problem while I wait for Aran."

"He is Fae? How do you expect this Aran to know where you are?"

"Aran will find me." Just hopefully not with an army at his back.

Arandur tapped a quick hello on Big's walls as he entered. "Big. Where is our Sevana?"

The mountain shifted in agitation. *She was called away early yesterday morning. There was a dam near Stillwater that was being torn apart. They wanted her help patching it before it could fail.*

That stopped him in his tracks. He had been unexpectedly delayed on his way here by a lost Fae child that had wandered into an area he was not supposed to. It had taken Arandur the better part of the day to find him, negotiate his release, and take him back to two very distraught parents. By that point, he'd tried calling Sevana several times, but the Caller would never connect. He'd thought she'd accidentally broken her last one and so came this morning to talk to her in person.

"You've had no word from her since she left?"

No, the mountain responded, rocks shifting in an open fidget. *But Master spoke to Milly, asking her to look for Sevana. She's had no luck so far.*

Master had Milly searching for her? That didn't sound good at all. Aran did an about face and went for the reading room and the standing mirror that Sevana kept there. Leaning against the frame, he called, "Milly?"

It took several moments before the middle-aged spirit appeared in the mirror. She clasped a hand to her heart in open relief. "Arandur, I'm so glad you're here. I've been trying to find you. Sevana has gone missing."

His heart twisted and dropped. "How? When?"

"I'm not sure exactly when, but she was able to contact Master Tashjian briefly this morning. He expressly had me search for you, as he wants you to help him track her down. He said to relay her message to you: she's been kidnapped by three deities to help them with an active volcano. She doesn't have a lot of time. I'm afraid that's all we know; the call ended before she could tell him where she was."

If she was well enough, and in control enough, to be able to make even that brief call, then she couldn't be in serious danger. Or so he hoped. Arandur managed a smile, or perhaps a grimace, for the woman. "My thanks, Milly. Was she taken from Stillwater Dam?"

"I believe so, yes. Master said she looked like she'd been yanked out of bed."

That gave him a place to start. "Are you still in contact with him? Good, then tell him you've reached me. Tell him too that I'll go immediately to Stillwater Dam and see if I can pick up her trail there. His Caller is working?"

"I believe so. I can double check with him."

"Do that. It's vital we stay in communication while we search for her."

"You'll tell me when you find her, too?"

"Of course," he assured her gently. It might have seemed strange from the outside, but Milly and Sevana had grown to be rather good friends over the past three months. "I'm off—try to catch Tashjian before he leaves."

She gave him a firm, determined nod, then whisked away in an instant like only a spirit could.

Arandur sprinted out of the mountain as well, calling to Big as he moved, "I'll pass along news through Milly when I find her!"

Baby and Grydon should go with you, Big encouraged.

Shaking his head, Arandur leapt into his chellomi's saddle. "They won't be able to keep up. Guard the place, Big." With that, he set his heels and headed his chellomi toward the north. A chellomi was the wind itself when he moved at full speed. They did not tire, either, not like a normal horse would. If this was a normal trip, Arandur would take two days to get to Stillwater.

But this wasn't a normal trip, and he wasn't stopping until he had arrived.

As he rode, his mind turned in a whirl of confusion. Deities? Volcanoes? There was more than one place that could fit those two qualifications. Nanashi Isle, Kitra Isle, Lansky Isle, and Kesly Isles all had volcanoes, but he believed that Lansky didn't have any that were active. Still, he was hardly up to date on those areas of the world. If it involved the sea, Arandur didn't have much to do with it, and his information from there was sometimes years out of date. All of those locations had a variety of minor deities or mythical races posing as deities, so he wasn't sure which one was responsible for Sevana's disappearance. Worse, the isles were scattered in all four directions of Mander. It hardly gave him an idea of where to start.

When a chellomi moved at this pace, it was raucously loud, like rolling thunder. Arandur had a hard time thinking, never mind hearing something else as he rode. The noise became deafening after a few hours and it numbed his head to the point that he wanted to shut out all sound completely.

Not until he was within sight of the dam early the next morning did the question dawn on him: had she even had a chance to fix the dam before being kidnapped? One good look at the place in the dawn light sufficed in answer. Yes, she had. Or at least, it was patched enough that the dam had not failed. This was a relief by itself. Trying to track her through a flooded disaster would make things much worse.

Hopping free, he took three seconds to stretch out his legs, then he loosened the girth on his saddle and let his poor chellomi breathe better. "Apologies, Winnaur. I have ridden you hard this night."

The chellomi arched his head and gave him a soft wuff of understanding. "She is precious to you. I will help you find her."

"You are a good friend." Patting him on the neck, he asked, "Grain or grass?"

"Grain. But drop it here, I can fend for myself. You are nearly vibrating in place, you are so impatient."

He was at that, but he wasn't going to make his friend suffer when it would take two minutes to feed him breakfast. So he forced himself to slow down, be patient, to take a sack of grain from his saddlebags and open it up so Winnaur could eat. The saddle he left in place, as he wasn't sure if they would need to take off again immediately or not.

With Winnaur settled, only then did he turn for the town built around the top of the hill, near the dam, and stop the first person he saw. "Pardon, Master, but I'm looking for Artifactor Sevana Warren."

"We've been looking for her ourselves," the man responded, shifting the bag of carded wool on his shoulder. "Here, come with me, I'll take you the work shed. Everyone's gathered there, they can tell you more about her."

"My thanks, Master." He got many a curious glance as they went down the street and wound up to the top of the hill. Arandur was used to such. At first glance, he didn't look all that different from a human being. Then someone would take note of his pointed ears, and see that his clothes were not made by human hands, and then they would start wondering. Only the truly knowledgeable were able to recognize him as Fae, though. The rest just wondered and cast about odd theories.

The door to the work shed stood wide open, no doubt to accommodate the summer heat, and there were three people that stood inside, clustered around a table. His guide knocked on the door frame. "I've got a man here looking for the Artifactor."

The three stopped and looked up. Two men and a woman, they all had pencils in their hands or tucked behind an ear, and exhaustion tugged at them, suggesting they had not been resting well for days now. Then again, a dam threatening to break was not conducive to sleep.

"Thank you, Grahms," the oldest man said and stepped forward. "I'm Booker, head engineer of the dam. You are?"

"My name is Arandur."

A light went off in the man's eyes. "Aran. You're Aran."

Hearing him addressed so brought a smile to his face. "Yes. Sevana is my friend. I'm looking for her."

"We all are, sir. She disappeared sometime in the night. We thought she'd be back, as her flying device is still here, but we've not seen hide nor hair of her yet."

"Nor will you," Aran denied with a grim shake of the head. "We received word from her, briefly, that she had been kidnapped."

All three swore, in surprise and dismay. The woman stepped around Booker, a hand extended that didn't quite touch his arm. "She's alright? She wasn't able to tell you where she is?"

"No, something happened to disconnect her call a short way in. We know that she's near a volcano that is on the verge of exploding, that it was the deities of that region that took her, but nothing else. I hope to pick up her trail here, see if I can't follow it."

"Come with me," she urged. "I'll show you to the house she slept in. That should be a good starting place for you."

"My thanks, Mistress." He took no thought for the others as he followed her. Fortunately, she was a quick walker and he didn't have to shorten his stride in order to stay with her.

The house was empty, the occupants undoubtedly out on their own business, but his guide pushed through the main door and to the back as comfortably as if this was her own home. Perhaps they were relatives of hers? Arandur didn't ask, as it wasn't important, instead trying to pick up some clue from the air itself.

She stepped into what was apparently a guest bedroom, then stayed just inside the doorway, giving him room to enter. Arandur took it in from top to bottom, trying to notice every detail. A single bed shoved into a corner, with a chair next to it that had Sevana's clothes draped across it. The bed was unmade, obviously slept in, but there was nothing else of Sevana's within sight. The only other piece of furniture in the room was a wardrobe that had not been used. He didn't sense anything of her on the right side of the room. She'd spent all of her time on the left, where the bed was.

Squatting down onto his haunches, he stared hard at the area around the bed. "She slept here. There was something of hers that rested near the foot of the bed. It had a spell on it that activated."

"She had a bag with her, when I showed her here the other night," the woman offered.

Arandur looked over his shoulder to regard her. "Dark brown, bulky and square in shape, with only one strap?"

"That's it exactly."

"Ahh. Mystery solved, then. It was her traveling pack. She has an anti-theft charm on it, so that it can't get far from her without returning. It must have activated and gone with her when she was taken." This relieved him, as that meant she had at least some tools and things on hand. He moved onto the next spot that was near where the pack had been. That area was most definitely not Sevana's magic.

After being with her so many months, Arandur had learned how to read Sevana's magic. It wasn't just hers, it was tangled up with whatever elements she used to create the spell, but there was always a part of her mixed in. It glowed red to his eyes, a color entirely different from everything else he'd seen in the world. But this magic was different in color, purely one thing, and not a mix of things.

It wasn't like human magic, or Fae, or anything else he'd really seen. It was a green jade in color, strong even in its afterimage, with a peculiar scent to it that he could not put a name to. "Something else sat next to the bag. Something that was taken separately from Sevana herself and brought along."

"Perhaps her boots?" the woman offered tentatively.

Feeling like an idiot, Arandur huffed out a snort. "Of course. Why didn't I think of that? So they took her, the pack automatically came with her, but then for whatever reason they reached out again to take her boots." Knowing Sevana, she had demanded her boots before doing anything. "The magic here for the boots is more recent than the magic on the bed. She was taken first."

Standing, he fetched the clothes from the chair, draping them over an arm. "I'll return these to her. Where is *Jumping Clouds*?" When he got a blank look in response, he clarified, "Her flying device."

"Oh, that! Come this way." As she led him back out of the house, she said, "Sevana mentioned you a few times to us. Mostly how she wished you were here to help her fix the dam, as your magic would be suited to this sort of thing."

That brought a pang to his heart. How dearly he wished that he *had* been here. Maybe she wouldn't have been kidnapped if he had been. "Is that how you know of me?"

"Yes." She gave him a quick smile, there and gone again in a flash. "She said once that you are a Tracker?"

"I am." Arandur had never blessed his calling before as he did now.

"Then you can find her." The woman was not questioning his ability. It was a statement of fact to her mind. "When you do, tell her the solution she thought up worked. The dam's fine. We'll be able to fix the rest of it and she's not to worry about it."

This absolute faith in his abilities from a total stranger was somewhat flattering. "I will tell her."

They came around the bend in the road and there sat *Jumping Clouds*, still damp from the recent storms, but undamaged. It was a slimmer version of *Bouncing on Clouds*, her other device. That one was meant to hold a cargo of things or many passengers. *Jumping Clouds* was like its child, about the size of a large wagon. It could hold two passengers and a horse at a squeeze, but little more. Sevana used it when she felt like she would be traveling through weather and she only needed to transport herself. As Arandur stepped on board, he found another trace of that alien magic, in exactly one spot near the front dashboard. Something had been here, something that Sevana had needed, and her kidnappers had fetched it for her.

It was the most recent trail he had, and from it, he could see a faint glow in the air. It gave him a direction and he seized upon it. "Mistress...forgive me, I never got your name."

"Kira."

"Mistress Kira. I need to take this device. If anyone comes asking, inform them I have it. Did Sevana leave anything else behind?"

"Some of her climbing equipment. She had us use it to make repairs to the dam."

"Gather all of that up and bring it here. I will take it all with me."

Giving him a serious nod, she spun on her heels and took off at a fast jog. Arandur also started running at a much faster pace, going to where he had left Winnaur. The chellomi paused in eating and looked up, ears flickering back and forth.

"You found her?"

Arandur shook his head. "No, but I have a trail. It goes through the air. I won't be able to track it on the ground. Fortunately Sevana's flying device is still here. I'll use that to go to her."

Winnaur gave him a look of undisguised horror. "I'm not getting on that thing."

"It might be best you don't go with me," Arandur admitted. "I'm heading toward an island, I think. Due north. Can you return and report to Aranhil what I have learned? My Caller is becoming low on magic, I don't want to drain it in case I need it later."

Pawing at the ground, Winnaur ducked his head in agreement. "I'll go. Unsaddle me first."

Arandur promptly did so, removing all of the tack, although he left the bag of grain behind as he doubted Winnaur was finished with it yet. As he worked, he told his friend everything that Aranhil needed to know. Winnaur repeated it back to make sure he had it all straight.

"You've got it," Arandur assured him, giving him a gentle pat on the neck. "Thank you. Go. Tell Aranhil I'll call in later once I have her."

Winnaur gave him a sympathetic look. "She's fine, you know."

"She's making demands of her kidnappers to fetch her things, of course she's fine." It was the volcano that worried Arandur.

"Can't believe they yanked me here in the dead of night," Sevana groused to herself even as her hands flew, going through an inventory of what she had in her bag. "Don't even have a third of the tools I'll need, not that I have any idea of how to stop *an active volcano*. Really, what do they take me for?"

"A part-Fae with a bad temper," Cheng-Huang drawled, giving her an impressive look under his drooping eyebrows.

Sevana stabbed a finger in his direction without looking. "If you knew that, why didn't you summon a true Fae? Someone, you know, who can *talk to elements* and control minor hiccups like volcanoes and typhoons."

"One does not summon the Fae as we did you."

That stopped her dead in her tracks and she looked at him with mouth dropped open in mild astonishment. "Truly? Even the demi-gods of Nanashi Isle do not dare to jerk a Fae's chain?"

He cleared his throat and looked impassively elsewhere.

"Well now. I learn new things every day." She went back to searching through her bag. Curse the luck, but she didn't begin to have the ingredients she needed to make a new Caller. If there was anything in the world that she could have, it would be that. Or one already made up, of course. In the course of her life, Sevana had felt woefully out of her depth exactly once. This just became the second. It was one of the few occasions where she would freely admit that she wanted help and would call for reinforcements. So, of course, her luck said that she wouldn't be able to do so.

She must have been truly evil in the previous life to have such bad luck in this one. Maybe even a serial kitten killer or something equally atrocious.

Fed up, she threw her hands into the air and sank back onto her haunches. "Hopefully what little I managed to get out to Master will help them figure out where I am. I can't call them now. Alright." Blowing a strand of hair out of her eyes, she shoved everything back into her pack. "First, show me a place I can work. It should be a clear room with multiple tables."

Chi-Lin gave her an elaborate study, tail swirling in the air like living fire. "You just said that you can't do anything without your tools."

"I *said,*" she corrected testily, "that I only have about a third of the tools that I need. I am an Artifactor. I create tools, I do not depend on them. Now give me a workspace."

Cheng-Huang openly grinned at her. "A proper space to work in is important for any craftsman. Come with me."

Now that was an interesting reaction. Sevana fell readily into step with him and decided it would behoove her to ask some questions while she had the leisure to do so. "What are you?"

Understanding what she meant, he answered, "I am a builder, you can say. I govern over anything constructed, be that roads or bridges or government buildings."

Interesting. Sevana could see how he would be tapped into by the people that believed in him. If she had a volcano threatening to blow near her, she would certainly think of trying to build something to either stop it or protect her home from it. Turning, she glanced at the two following. "And you, Da-Yu?"

"I am a river god in this area."

A river god. It made sense, in a way. The only thing known to stop hot lava was water, because it had the cooling power necessary to slow lava down and turn it back into an inactive state. "And you, Chi-Lin? How did you get dragged into this problem?"

"The Qi-Lin are in charge of all animals, land and sea," he stated simply. "We are also known for bringing good luck."

At first glance, this gathering of gods for this particular problem seemed very random and thrown together. But all in all she could see why people would pray to them for help. They all had connections to the problem in their own ways. "I see. How well do your powers blend together?" She got quite a speaking look at this question. "Ah. I take it they don't."

"It's why we called you," Cheng-Huang explained.

Now she was getting the full picture. Minor deities didn't have the same overall reaching powers like a true god would. They were like advanced magicians with immortal bodies, really; they were only good at their chosen vocation. Anything outside of their area of expertise and they were quickly at a loss of what to do. Because of that, knowing how to blend their abilities in with the others would be extremely difficult for them. Not only were they very different, in terms of power type, but they had no experience working with the others.

Nanashi Isle was not flat. Far from it, as it was basically one hill stacked on top of another to form an overall mountain. It was also incredibly green with trees, climbing vines, bushes, flowers, and moss all competing for the same space. Visibility was ten feet at best in some areas and there was only a winding trail to follow. Without a guide, Sevana would have been terribly lost, and by the time she'd found the town, the volcano likely would have already erupted. She was sure of it.

"There are other duties we must attend to," Chi-Lin informed her as a sort of brusque farewell. Then he snapped off in a flash of light to…somewhere.

"I must go as well," Da-Yu stated in a sort of rhetoric fashion before he too disappeared, although not as flashily.

Cheng-Huang did not appear surprised or upset about their sudden disappearance. He kept walking down the path as if their behavior was only to be expected. It made Sevana think that these three might not really get along. There were many religions where the minor deities constantly scuffled with each other over one matter or another. Was Nanashi like that as well?

They rounded a bend in the trail and finally the first glimpses of the village came into view.

Unlike major cities or towns in Belen, there apparently were no real roads in Nanashi. The trail she followed went right into the village without growing any wider. It weaved its way between the one-story, sometimes two-story buildings, leading off who knew where. It was not particularly large—in fact smaller than Milby—and her initial estimate of the populace was less than a thousand people. Probably more like five hundred. Sevana's first impression of the place was 'rustic green,' as the buildings were made properly of stone but semi-covered in creeping vines. Even here, the plants seemed intent on taking over. The top of every building displayed potted plants, what looked like small box gardens, which made sense. The place didn't have the space to spread out, so why not use every available square inch? It also explained why the buildings were smack on top of each other, with barely any alleys in between. Sevana had never seen a more crowded village.

There was noise and bustle, people chattering to each other in a language she didn't speak. It had the air of a fishing village here, and the smell of one for that matter, but it was not an unpleasant place by any means. Sevana had been called into worse places to work her magic.

The first person to spy Cheng-Huang was a middle-aged man with a thinning hairline and short mustache. He carried two buckets of eels, but he dropped them immediately and went straight for the ground in a bow, like a crouching turtle. "Cheng-Huang-o!"

Everyone within hearing turned, caught sight of the god strolling in their midst, and immediately went to the ground in a bow as well.

Sevana had half-expected this reaction because no matter what she thought of him personally, he *was* still a god. Of course these people would revere him.

"Da-Chin!" Cheng-Huang called out.

From the sea of prostrated people one popped up, an elderly man stooped a little with age, white hair tied back, wearing simple clothes in dark grey with a white belt tied around the waist. He headed for them with a slight limp in his gait that didn't seem to hinder him in speed. "Cheng-Huang-o, you honor us," he greeted with a deep bow.

"Da-Chin, this is Artifactor Sevana Warren." Cheng-Huang paused a moment as everyone gasped in recognition. "She will be working here to deal with the volcano. You will provide her with the space, tools, and help she needs."

"Of course, Cheng-Huang-o," Da-Chin assured him with another deep bow.

Satisfied, Cheng-Huang turned to her and said, "Call our names if you need us." Then he, too, disappeared into thin air.

Sevana stared at the spot in irritation. Perhaps she had questions she needed answers to before he popped out like a soap bubble? Shaking that off, she turned to Da-Chin. "I need a workspace with tables, some tools that I'll list out in a moment, a guide, and answers."

Da-Chin nearly vibrated in place, tears in his eyes, probably from relief that they finally had obvious help with the volcano. In his place, Sevana would be just as overjoyed. "Of course, Artifactor. Ho-Han, Ji-Gang, find a place for her."

Two younger men that looked like younger versions of Da-Chin immediately popped up and went running down the street.

"Artifactor, I will act as your guide and answer all the questions I can," Da-Chin assured her with a respectful bow.

"Are you the village elder?" she hazarded a guess.

"I am."

Of course, that's why Cheng-Huang would call for him. Well, that saved her time, as this was the man that had authority to order people about. "Good. First, tell me more about the volcano. How long has it been active?"

"Since Feng-Huang was sealed there one year ago."

Sevana's next question stuttered to a stop. That was so far off from what she had expected to hear that she just stared at the man for a long moment. "Feng-Huang." And what in the world was a Feng-Huang? "You're telling me another minor deity is sealed inside that volcano?"

"That is correct, Artifactor."

She resisted the urge to swear. Or scream. Or call Cheng-Huang to beat sense into him. The last one was particularly hard to resist. "Elder. This might be a silly thing to ask," she felt rather stupid saying it, anyway, "but if you know that this minor deity is causing the volcano to be active, wouldn't it be better to just unseal him or her? Move them to a different location?"

"We cannot," Da-Chin reported sadly. "If she awakens, the volcano will blow."

"And it's not possible to move her while she's still sleeping and sealed?" Sevana had a feeling she knew the answer to that question before even asking it.

Da-Chin just shook his head, eyes trained on the ground.

Why a goddess was sealed inside a volcano…was insane, no matter how one looked at it, Sevana decided. She felt a little surreal being in this situation as it was. Instead, she went to the next most obvious question. "So, in summary, a goddess is sealed inside the volcano and every time she has a bad dream, it gets a little more volatile. Your gods here can't interfere with her because she's been sealed by a higher power—that's correct? I figured—but the volcano is causing problems. I was called in to find a magical solution to protect the island while somehow circumventing her. Do I have all of that correct?"

"Precisely so, Artifactor." Da-Chin gave her a hopeful smile. "This can be done?"

She had no idea. "First, a workspace. Then, tell me why a goddess is sealed in a mountain and who exactly she is."

Da-Chin gestured for her to follow him and spoke in a rasping voice as they walked. "Feng-Huang is the Phoenix, the Guardian of the West and a sacred beast that presides over our destinies."

Now why, Sevana couldn't help but wonder, would someone lock a deity in charge of destinies in a volcano? Wasn't that just asking for trouble?

"She is very alluring, very beautiful, almost fearsomely so. I fear that one night, during a grand banquet, she became a little too…"

"Drunk?" Sevana offered dryly.

"She was not quite herself," Da-Chin demurred, apparently afraid of saying something about Sexy Goddess that would get him in trouble. "She made some advances toward Lei-Gong, or so it is said."

"Keep in mind I know the bare bones of your mythology," Sevana stated with some exasperation. "Who?"

"Lei-Gong is the Thunder God Dragon."

A phoenix and a dragon? Sitting in a tree? Now didn't that mental image boggle the mind. "I take it he didn't like this?"

"It was his wife, Tian-Mu, that did not care for it. She is the Lightning Goddess."

Oh-ho, the plot thickened. "So did Tian-Mu put her in there?"

"No, no, Tian-Mu complained to the Jade Emperor. He sat in judgment over this and agreed Feng-Huang should be punished for her flirtations. He sentenced her to imprisonment for fifty years. It was the Jade Emperor that put her in the volcano."

Well, as a phoenix, the intense heat of the volcano wouldn't hurt the goddess. And it would keep people from accidentally tripping over her or trying to set her free again. Sevana supposed that she could see how this would all work out...except it hadn't. "Surely the three gods in question realize she's causing trouble where she is and they're willing to move her?"

"The Jade Emperor has returned to his Palace and cannot be reached at this time."

Now wasn't that just convenient. "Hence why I was called in. Got it."

Again, he asked hopefully, "You can solve this problem?"

Sevana blew out an aggravated breath. "Not the question, Da-Chin. Whether I can come up with a valid solution before the volcano blows. *That* is the question."

5

Sevana's very first task was creating the tools she needed. It was terribly inconvenient that the gods had yanked her here without a by-your-leave. If she'd had a few days to prep for this situation, then she wouldn't be scrambling like this in a foreign land.

Fortunately Da-Chin's grandsons had taken her to a place that was good to work in. It was someone's apothecary room—there were still plants hanging from the ceiling and shelves of neatly labeled jars filled with different medicines either mixed or in the process of being made. The three tables had been completely cleared so that she had space to work in, and there was a tall stool that let her sit if she wanted. The place had that peculiar smell of medicine and plants—not unpleasant, but it made her nose twitch.

In the course of her years, she had never been called upon to do something about a volcano, so Sevana chose to go at this problem the same way that she would any other. She would take measurements first, get an idea of what was happening, and then go from there. What was vital was to first figure out how badly the slope was changing. That would give her an idea of the stresses involved in the magma movements underground. She'd have to find a way to analyze the gas compositions too, although how to do that safely escaped her at the moment.

First, slope. Fortunately for her sake, she had things that would measure long distances; all she had to do was modify them a little and then link them to a journal so that it would update at a periodic time. Setting it up would be the hard part—monitoring it after that? Easy.

"Cheng-Huang!" she called to the empty air.

It took a few seconds, but the deity appeared next to her elbow as if he had been standing there all along. "What, Artifactor?"

"I need equipment and supplies."

He gave her a superior, amused look like a parent teasing a child. "I thought you said you can make whatever tools you need?"

She gave him a withering look. "Which would you rather have me do? Spend two weeks making all the tools I need or actually trying to solve the problem?"

Cheng-Huang cleared his throat and looked elsewhere for a moment. "What do you need?"

Ha, thought so. "I need six sets of magical far-see glasses, my box lens, two journals, measuring wands, the ingredients to make another Caller with, and my skimmer." The skimmer simply because she refused to do any more hiking up and down a volcano's sides more than she had to. "Two more changes of clothes, while you're at it, and how in the world do you know what to fetch?"

"I don't," he denied calmly, "but you do, and that is sufficient."

Was that supposed to be an explanation? What, he was picking the image of what she meant out of her head and then using that? The idea was a little scary. Was he a telepath then, or was it something divine-powered that had nothing to do with magical or humanoid abilities? "If you can fetch things, can you deliver them?"

"To specific places, yes."

Not to people, then. Curse the luck. Although it still might help in some cases. Not with Aran, obviously, she had no idea where he was in that moment. But she could send a letter to Master's workroom, and to Aranhil, and that would help.

What she requested appeared neatly on the table in front of her as if she had brought them here and unpacked them herself. Sevana decided to dig into her questions about deities secretly, as she doubted they would forthrightly answer any questions she had, and shelved the matter for now. "The skimmer?"

"Outside. There is no room in here."

Cheng-Huang shifted his weight from one foot to another,

obviously preparing to go, so she flung up a hand to stop him. "Wait. Let me write two letters. One to deliver to my Master, the other to Aranhil."

Even minor deities weren't in the habit of being ordered about, and Cheng-Huang's expression told her so, but she didn't let herself be deterred. Sevana ripped two pages out of her journal, set pencil to them, and scratched out quick notes to both men. To Aranhil, she gave a concise summary and a reassurance that she didn't need a rescue at this moment. To Master, a demand that he contact her through Milly, as they needed to trade information if at all possible. Folding them in half, she handed them to Cheng-Huang. "The top one to Master's workroom, middle table. The other to Aranhil's seat."

Both letters disappeared in a twinkling. Breathing a little easier, she went to the next question on the tip of her tongue. "I was told earlier that there is a goddess trapped inside that volcano. Why didn't you mention this before?"

He stared at her as if the answer was perfectly obvious. "She has no bearing on this. It is the volcano that must be stopped."

Sevana rolled her eyes to the ceiling and prayed for patience. And not from the god in front of her. "Cheng-Huang. You don't find it an amazing coincidence that the very year that you put a god inside a volcano, it starts acting up?"

Frowning, he denied, "She is sealed and in a deep sleep. This cannot be her doing."

"It's likely unwitting on her part," Sevana agreed with as much patience as she could muster. Which wasn't actually much. "But think for a minute. Fire from the Eternal Flame is an eight in power. And that's *captured* fire, not connected to its source anymore. If I threw that in there, it would spark a volcano for a day and make it active. We're talking a living, breathing, phoenix of deity level that's trapped deep inside of a volcano. It didn't occur to you idiots that putting her in there would make the volcano eventually blow?"

Cheng-Huang opened his mouth to retort, froze, and then subsided into a deep and troubled frown.

No, apparently it really hadn't occurred to him. Sevana resisted the urge to go find the nearest hard surface and start banging his head into it. "Now, the next question is, is it really impossible to break her out of there with your own power? Put her somewhere else?"

"We have neither the power nor authority," Cheng-Huang denied readily. This part, at least, he was clear on. "And the Jade Emperor is currently away and unreachable. We tried for many months before giving up and asking you."

There had been very little 'asking,' but whatever. "So we absolutely have to solve this on our own. Lovely. This is the most ridiculous situation I've ever encountered." And it was so typical at the same time, that the person who caused the problem to begin with had gone elsewhere so that he didn't bear the consequences of his actions. Why did that always seem to be the case?

Pointing to her tools, he demanded, "How do these help you?"

Going on the offensive, was he? "I have to measure something in order to come up with a counter to it, don't I? Alright, this is all I need for now, you can go back to what you were doing."

Cheng-Huang was not a person used to being dismissed. With a huff and glare, he disappeared in a snap.

Sevana spun on her stool and went immediately to work. As much as she would dearly love to get the Caller made first, other things took priority. She had to get measurements of that volcano first, otherwise it would delay matters severely. In essence, getting a level built for this wouldn't be very trying at all. After all, her far-see lenses already had a built-in telescope, and partnered with a measuring wand, it would instantly tell her the height differences on a set point. All she had to do was create a set point for the wand to recognize.

Part of the materials needed for a Caller went to a marker. The very base element of a Caller was a piece of ore from a fallen star. With a wand, she carefully carved out chunks of it, each piece long and thin so that it would be easy to stake it in the ground. That done, she snagged everything up, threw it into her bag, and then collected her skimmer outside. It hummed to life as she threw her leg over it.

Da-Chin scurried over before she could lift off, looking more than a little panicked. "Artifactor, you are leaving?"

"Just to the mountain," she assured him, feeling a pang of sympathy for this worried old man. She didn't want to scare him because at his age it would likely lead to heart failure. "I've got to get measurements of what's really going on up there before I can work on a solution. While I'm gone, find me a mirror and put it in that room—" she'd call Milly if she couldn't get the Caller to work "—as well as a meal. Those idiot deities of yours yanked me out of bed and then didn't feed me all day."

Relieved that she was working already, Da-Chin bobbed a bow at her. "Of course, of course, I will see to it."

"Be back in a bit." Sevana kicked off and into the air. She first angled her way toward the top of the volcano, where it was giving off visible gases. The skimmer was set to protect her from outside elements, but she honestly wasn't sure how effective it would be against volcanic gases. After all, she hadn't thought of this situation when she designed the settings. Hopefully it would at least partially protect her, as she absolutely had to get a direct sample of the gases.

The situation was tricky because the extreme heat of the gases being released was no joke. And getting close to the vents in order to get the sample was dangerous in its own right. Worse, she risked botching this on the first try by contaminating the sample with regular atmosphere. So she would have to hover inside the gas for a moment and stopper the bottle there before moving.

Sevana fully expected to feel like a broiled lobster after this.

Reconsidering, she angled a little downward instead. She'd get the gases last. Yes, that would be better; that way she wasn't trying to work while impersonating a lobster. Decided, she headed down to the top of the slope. It was far enough away from the vents to avoid any real danger, close enough to give her good readings. Up here it felt like a sauna and her armpits quickly soaked through and started sticking to her.

She really would need a quick bath by the time she got done up here. Thank heavens she could just set the system up and then go back and not have to make this trip again.

Landing carefully, she angled the skimmer so that it wouldn't automatically slide down the slope. It was a very steep angle up here. In fact, she had to crabwalk sideways to be able to move without tripping headfirst. She winced a little as she went down on her haunches. The slight ache in her muscles was worse than usual today. It made her feel twice her age. Grumbling under her breath, she shifted forward—she didn't dare kneel—she drew her pack around and dug out the first set of wand and far-see glasses.

This was a little tricky because the glasses had to be angled just so and the wand had to be on the same level—otherwise it couldn't measure either distance or angle correctly. Sevana cast about for a few minutes before finding a nice, sturdy rock. It wasn't the right height, but a quick slicing spell took off the top and after that it was perfect. Setting things up, she cast the spell carefully to link it to a particular fallen star shard. When it was set, she then linked it to the journal, which was also successful.

Sevana breathed out a sigh of relief. After what had happened with the Caller earlier, she was very afraid that her magic was just going to be wonky today, no matter how careful she was. But apparently it was going to behave for now. If it would just last until she had this done, the gases collected, and the new Caller made, she wouldn't complain.

Getting up, she hopped back on the skimmer and went to the next location, repeating her actions there. It was a large volcano, and just six levels wasn't really enough to do the job with, but it would give her an adequate enough idea. She would just have to make do for now.

Once the top part was set up, she went to the base of the volcano and carefully aligned her shards. It took a little finagling to get the angle right, but she knew the instant that she did, as the journal started giving her readouts. Satisfied, she hopped back on her skimmer and once again flew to the very top.

This time she had a better sense of just how hot it would be and braced herself for it. To her relief, though, the skimmer shielded her from the worst of the emissions, so she could at least breathe while hovering just on the edge of one of the vents. Her hair was soaked through with sweat at this point and the *smell*...ugh. As expected of a volcano, it smelled strongly of sulfur—or as she liked to think of it, rotten eggs. Carefully, she scooped up two vials of the gases before stoppering them and stowing them back in her pack.

Then she took out of there like a mouse with a cat on its tail.

She went lower in altitude almost immediately, escaping the volcano's plumes, and the air dropped in temperature by several degrees. By the time she reached her impromptu workroom again, it felt like it was at least twenty degrees cooler than it had been near the top.

Da-Chin hovered near the door, weight shifting from foot to foot. Sevana barely had the skimmer a foot from the ground when he leapt forward and demanded, "What news?"

"I don't know anything yet," she responded in exasperation. "I barely got my measuring system set up. We'll have to monitor things for today and see what changes. Then I can predict just how much time we have to work in."

That was not the answer the old man wanted. Fortunately, the woman beside him had more sense. Or at least more patience. She elbowed him out of the way and bowed. "Artifactor, I am Ling-Ling. I have prepared a meal for you inside."

Ling-Ling looked to be of an age close to Da-Chin, although she was not quite as stooped around the shoulders. From the way that he rubbed his ribs and glared at her, but didn't retort, she was either his wife or his sister. Only someone family could get by with that kind of casual abuse without a spoken protest.

"I am very ready for a meal," Sevana stated as she got off. "Is it possible to have a quick bath as well?"

"There is a spring nearby that is designated for the villagers. I will lead you there, if you wish."

Sevana weighed food versus a bath for a moment but the truth of the matter was, she stank so bad that she couldn't really face food at the moment, even though her stomach was rumbling at her. "Bath first."

This must have been the right thing to say as Ling-Ling gave her an approving nod. "I will lead you. You have clean clothing?"

"I do." Sevana strode through to the workroom, grabbed her

clothes, and gingerly held them away from her body to avoid getting them smelly. As she came back out, she found Da-Chin still looking very worried although he didn't say anything to her. "Oh cheer up, man. It's not going to blow today. Or even tomorrow."

Da-Chin's head lifted. "You can solve this?"

That she didn't know. "Even if I can't, I have Fae friends that can." One of them was likely coming after her even as she spoke. "Nanashi Isle will not fall victim to that volcano. One way or another, we'll keep the people safe."

Or so she hoped. In the end, it might come down to an emergency evacuation.

6

Sevana rethought her idea of leaving a note for Master in his workroom. It initially had sounded like the best plan, but she had not taken into account two things: First, nothing could be found easily in Master's workroom. Nothing. Even a pink elephant could hide in there. It might take years for him to find her letter. Second, with her missing like this, he likely wouldn't step foot into the place. He'd be off searching for her.

Delivered letters would likely not reach him. Worried, she decided to try making another Caller, so she could at least tell him her location.

Of course, Sevana had used up all of her luck while setting up the level system on the volcanic slopes. The minute that she sat down to craft a Caller, her magic flared up again and there was a strange hiccup in her spell, so that instead of materials, she was left with charcoal. Well, the piece of fallen star was more like twisted, burned metal, but essentially charcoal.

Disgusted, she threw it all in the nearest waste bin and went back to her backup plan: Milly.

Her hosts had brought in a vanity mirror, barely large enough to see her own face in, and propped it up on the table. Sevana gave a quick double tap with her index finger and called strongly, "Milly."

She didn't get an immediate response and she hadn't expected to. Even if Milly was somehow in this general area and heard her, it would take a while to get to this particular mirror. Sevana would likely have to call for the woman dozens of times before getting any results.

While waiting, she pulled out the two vials of gases and set them up on the table. Thanks to her box lens, she could analyze these without any real trouble. She was set to dig back into the problem when a strand of wet hair dangled along her cheek. Wet hair dripping along her exposed skin, or down her back, bugged the daylight right out of her. Huffing a breath, she scooped it all up and used a straight pencil to capture it on the top of her head in a messy knot. There, that would do.

Now, back to gases. Holding the lens up to her eye, she carefully activated it and gave the vial a good look. It looked like a combination of carbon, sulfur, and hydrogen gas. She wrote down the ratios in the journal and then sat back, lips pursed. Was this normal? Having never worked in or with a volcano before, Sevana had only the basic understanding of how they worked. She knew enough to know that bulging along the top was a very bad sign and that degassing was a good sign, as it meant some of the pressure was letting off before the volcano could just explode.

"Milly," she called absently, still thinking. So was the volcano going to explode imminently soon or not? The signs were very conflicting. Going by the bulge, they had bare days. But the degassing indicated that it might take weeks. Sevana really hoped for weeks, as she needed all the time that she could get for this problem.

"Milly," she repeated, even as she flipped a page in the journal, going to where her measurements for the slope were recorded. All six of her diagnostic wands/far-see glasses were working perfectly so that she had six sets of numbers to work off of. Sevana was very glad for the baseline. It would make it easier for her to tell when things were about to go drastically wrong. It was also a relief, as apparently whatever her magic was doing, it wouldn't mess with spells already in motion. Although seeing her incantations have hiccups in them twice in two days was unnerving to her. Just what new problem was developing with her magical core this time?

Shaking her head, she mentally focused back on the more immediate problem. Volcano aside, what was she supposed to do about the goddess trapped inside of it? No one seemed to be of the impression that she could be removed from that spot, that they literally did not have the power to overturn the seal, but Sevana wasn't convinced of this. Likely they hadn't even thought to try. Of course, she could hardly waltz inside an active volcano herself to take a look. Not even a Fae could pull that off. The question stood, could any of the minor deities that had called her here go inside without danger? Hmm. "Milly."

Knowing the full attributes of the goddess in question might be the best next step. All she had been given was a rather sketchy description and that wouldn't help much. She also needed an exact accounting of how many people were on this island, how long and deep it was, and what it would take to get everyone off in a hurry if it came down to an emergency evacuation. Although it did beg the question of where to evacuate *to*. The size of this volcano guaranteed that if it blew, the ash would be very far reaching. It would impact most of the mainland's coast. At least.

The more she thought of the consequences, the more an icy tendril curled around her spine. No, if they could, they absolutely had to stop it from blowing. Or at least find some way to contain it. The backlash of this was going to be far too erroneous otherwise. "Milly."

"Sevana!"

Her head snapped around, a smile unconsciously stretching across her face. "Milly. That was amazingly quick, I thought I'd have to try all evening."

"I was already looking in this general area, thanks to Arandur's hint," Milly explained. She nearly vibrated in place, she was so agitated. "He and Master Tashjian are simply beside themselves with worry."

Considering her rude kidnapping, Sevana could hardly blame them. "If Aran knew enough to point you in this direction…wait, how did he know? Master?"

"Yes, he called him first thing."

Now that figured. Somehow (Sevana wasn't sure by what means), Aran had become her keeper. If they couldn't find her on the first try, the next person they called was the Fae tracker. Sevana couldn't fault the system, as most of the time, Aran truly did know where she was. "So then are both of them on their way here?"

"I'm not sure. I know that Arandur is, he's following some sort of magical trail that is leading its way to you."

Magical trail? Sevana blinked at her. Was a divine's power close enough to magic that a Fae could see it? Now that was a fascinating little nugget of information. She would definitely have to ask more questions of Aran when he came. "Milly, my magic is acting up more than usual. I've now fried two Callers. I can't seem to contact Master on my own. Tell him I'm on Nanashi Isle and that I need him and every tool that he can think of that might stop or contain a volcano."

Milly's eyes flew wide. "Nanashi Isle?! How did they transport you over such a great distance overnight?"

"Divine magic apparently doesn't have the same limits." Sevana gave her a grim smile. "Believe me, I want to figure that out too, but later. My first priority is the volcano. The situation is desperate enough to make three minor deities kidnap me in the dead of night and drag me here, but I don't have the tools to do anything about this."

Milly looked at her closely. "Can you work magic at all right now?"

"Just diagnostic tools, as all I have to do with those is flick them on with a hint of power. Anything that requires a steady stream of magic being fed into it is completely impossible. I fry anything I try it with."

"Oh dear," Milly responded faintly.

Sevana was of the opinion that it needed stronger curse words than that, but let it pass with a flick of the fingers. "I need Master immediately. Call him for me, and tell him what he's heading in for."

"I will," Milly assured her before disappearing in a snap.

Hopefully the other woman had been keeping track of the men even while searching for Sevana and would be able to relay the message quickly.

Idly stroking a finger against the journal's blank page, she frowned down at it. Aran was already on his way, was he? How? He knew how to operate *Jumping Clouds*, so he could be flying toward her. If it came down to a race between her flying devices and a chellomi's top speed, they would be dead tied in speed. But a chellomi couldn't cross country like the crow flew, either. It would be faster in the long run to take *Jumping Clouds*. Is that what he'd decided too?

Even if he'd discovered her disappearance this very morning, and left for her last location, it would still take him the better part of the morning to reach Stillwater Dam. And from there, hopping on *Jumping Clouds*, it would still take him at least two days to reach Nanashi Isle. And that's if he flew through the night. It might be safer to say that he would be here in three days.

Master, on the other hand, could be anywhere in the world at this moment. He didn't stay at home for long stretches of time, especially not now when most of his students were grown up and out of the house. He could be very close to her or completely on the other side of Mander, for all she knew.

Would the help she needed even arrive before the volcano blew?

Sevana spent the next two days investigating. In those two days, she learned the basic structure of the island, the volcano, and more about the goddess sealed inside. She wrote it all down so that she could hand it over to Master when he arrived. He had poor oral retention and did better reading things. It would also save her from repeating it twice, if Aran arrived before Master did. She simply hated repeating herself.

Bright and early on the second day, coming in with the morning sun, was *Jumping Clouds*. Sevana heard it as it sailed in, the sound like giant fluttering wings and snapping sails in the sky. There was nothing else like it in the world. She left her breakfast cooling on her temporary work table and sprinted outside, lifting a hand to shield her eyes.

There it was! It was coming in hot and fast and only then did Sevana question: had she ever thought to teach Aran how to land? She remembered teaching him to fly…but landing?

In this crowded street, and with so many houses stacked almost on top of each other, there was no place to land. Sevana realized that in a split second, swore, and ran up the street and over, heading for a "clear" spot that she knew of. It was sandwiched between the fishing docks and the base of the volcano, a rocky area that people couldn't farm or build on. It was barely wide enough to give room for a landing, but it should still be doable. If Aran knew how to land, of course. Otherwise he'd miss it entirely and she'd be short a flying device.

He must have seen her from above, as he rotated the ship three times, slowing its speed down, and then dropping almost directly in the clear area. It made a grating sound that sent a shiver up her nerves. He hadn't punched a hole in her hull, had he?!

There was no time to think about it as Aran hopped off and ran for her. "Sevana!"

She put up two placating hands. "I'm alrigh—oomph!" Her words were literally knocked out of her as he grabbed her up in an embrace strong enough to cut off circulation. Gasping in air, she tried to struggle back a little. Just an inch.

Aran wasn't having it. Into her hair, he demanded hoarsely, "You're alright?"

"Of course I am." It felt a little awkward, but she had to try something to soothe him, so she pulled an arm free and stroked the back of his head. Strangely, the gesture worked almost instantly and half the tension racing through him drained out. She absolutely had to remember this trick. "Well, I have a volcano on my hands, but other than that I'm fine."

Slowly, reluctantly, he stepped back a few inches so he could look her properly in the eyes. "What happened, exactly?"

"There's a very long, involved story, but I have a feeling you didn't eat or rest while flying to me." She didn't need his confirmation to know she was right. It was impossible to make that kind of time without skipping all meals and sleep. Even without knowing the logistics, it was obvious from his general state. He looked like something the dog dragged in and then abandoned. "Come back with me, I've got breakfast waiting, and I'll tell you."

Shaking his head angrily, Aran tried to drag her toward the ship. "We're leaving."

Sevana dug in her heels, literally, and pulled him the other direction. "Of course we're not!"

"You don't help your own kidnappers," Aran snarled, his aura turning more vibrant and red.

Once, only once, had she seen angry Fae. Their aura had done something similar to this, only more intensely, and what had followed had not been pretty. To see Aran that enraged honestly scared her right down to her marrow. "Aran. They brought me here without asking, yes, but I was the one that chose to take on the job and stay."

The muscles in his face twitched with repressed anger. "You chose to stay."

"I did, yes. Because I can't ignore what's going on here. It has far-reaching consequences, far beyond this island. I need to stay and help them find a solution."

He closed his eyes, shuddering under the weight of his own emotions. "So you're telling me that I can't be angry with them?"

"You can be angry all you want," she responded honestly, "just don't level the place I'm trying to save."

For some reason that made him snort in laughter. Throwing his head back, he stood in place for several moments and breathed heavily. When he lowered his head again, he was calmer. Not calm, but not livid anymore either. "If you were going to stay, you should have called. Sellion."

Oh dear. Hearing that name out of his mouth was never a good thing. "Well, I tried, and fried two Callers in the attempt."

"Ah," Aran said in understanding. "We do need to do something about that."

"We do, yes, but the way you said my name there makes me worry. By any chance, did you report to Aranhil that I had been taken?"

"Of course I did."

Sevana felt a brewing headache start in the base of her neck. "Please tell me that his Caller and yours are still charged? So that we can prevent him from riding off to war on my account?"

"I believe we can contact him." Aran couldn't seem to help himself. He brought her in again, but this time the hug was gentle, and he swayed a little from side to side in a more relieved and happy manner. "If you were not alright, I would not have tried to stop him. I would be joining him."

"Pfft. What are you saying?" Sevana grinned into his shoulder. It was hard not to feel very loved right now. "You'd be leading the charge."

"I would," Aran admitted openly and without any remorse. "I suppose we should call him now."

"I'd prefer that, yes. Before things get truly heated up. Also, we might need his help in subduing this volcano."

Aran drew back and gave her a look that expressed extreme doubt and exasperation. "You expect him to help your kidnappers?"

"Arandur." Sevana tried to be patient as she knew that he was severely sleep deprived, but it was hard. "If we don't fix this, it will have a direct effect on the Fae living near here. Not to mention your cousins, the Unda."

"Oh."

"Oh is right. So help me call Aranhil. We need all the help that we can get on this one."

7

Sevana's King of the Fae was not at all happy that she chose to stay and help her kidnappers either, but once she explained what was going on, Aranhil did agree that the situation was too dangerous to ignore. He promised to contact the Fae living nearby and alert them to the problem so they could make preparations.

While speaking to him, Sevana carefully did not touch the Caller. Aran had devoured her breakfast while she spoke, but Sevana did not begrudge him the food. She wasn't all that hungry and the man had skipped two days' worth of meals getting to her. If he wasn't Fae, he likely would have been half-faint by now.

When the Caller was still, she commanded, "Call Master for me."

Aran obediently said, "Call Tashjian."

It took a moment for the Caller to come to life, then it shifted over into Master's form. He was sitting, dressed in some of his favorite traveling clothes of loose britches and a poet shirt, which meant he was en-route to somewhere. "*Arandur! You found her!*"

"He found me," Sevana drawled. "And before you ask, I'm fine. I have a volcano hanging over my head, but I'm fine."

Master slumped in on himself in abject relief. "*Thank all mercy for small favors. Well, sweetling, you've gotten yourself in over your head this time.*"

"I would like to take this moment and remind you that I did not volunteer for this. I was voluntold. There is a difference."

"*You're still in over your head,*" Master said with a pointed look.

He did have her there. "Why do you think I called for help?"

"It's wise of you. Although it does scare me that my usually fiercely independent girl is calling for help. It bodes ill."

"Love you too, Master."

Chuckling, he went on, *"So explain to me in detail what's going on."*

"I'm not sure we have enough magic in this Caller for that," she hedged, staring at said Caller in worry. "First tell me where you are and when you're expected to be here."

"You need to tell me where you are first, sweetling."

He didn't know? She looked to Aran for explanation, as she would have thought the two would've kept in contact while searching for her.

"I didn't dare use up the magic in the Caller until I found you," he explained. "And it's hard for me to gauge how much power is in this thing."

Good point. Although she did wonder why Milly hadn't reached him yet. Maybe he wasn't near anything reflective? "I'm at Nanashi Isle."

"That makes life a little easier. I just passed Sondack. I plan to pick up what I need and fly from home."

If he was past Sondack, then he was likely hours away from home. Good, that was actually perfect, as it would give her a chance to give him a list of things she needed. It was easier to pilfer his storerooms than try to make things up here with limited resources and tools.

Considering how little communication time they had, she gave him only the bare bones of the situation. "There is a phoenix, a minor deity of this pantheon, sealed away in the volcano up here. She's supposedly deep asleep, although I have doubts of this after watching the volcano for three days. Things shift and settle again without any real rhyme or reason."

"A sealed phoenix?" Master rolled his eyes. *"Have they lost their collective minds?"*

"Funny, that was my first thought. Anyway, the volcano is degassing, and judging from the collections I've done, it's changing from day to day. Sometimes it has more carbon, sometimes more hydrogen, or more sulfur, and then it will flux back to what it was the day before. I think she's not as sealed in there as everyone believes. Now, because of political reasons, no one is willing to talk about taking her out of there. Also, for power reasons, it doesn't seem quite possible. The Jade Emperor was the one that stuck her in there and no one here has the power to overrule what he has done. Or at least, if they do, they won't own up to it."

Master frowned deeply, heavily in thought. *"This does not sound good at all. What's the size of the volcano?"*

"It's a cinder cone, about 900 feet tall."

"So, not the largest of them. Well, considering the small size of Nanashi Isle, that shouldn't surprise me. You say it's degassing?"

"Regularly. Almost constantly. There's vents around the top, too. It's also showing signs of bulging around the top and the slope on the sides is expanding a little, but only an inch every few days. It gives me hope that we can solve this before it actually explodes."

"Those are good signs, yes, although it worries me that you're seeing obvious signs of bulging already. I'd say we have about two weeks, three at most, to solve this problem."

That was her estimate exactly, but what worried Sevana was that it was only an estimate. They could be wrong. They could be very, very wrong and a lot of people would die if they weren't right.

"What can we really do about this?" Aran asked the two of them. "If we can't move the phoenix out of there, then doesn't that mean the volcano really will blow?"

"Her presence is severely agitating matters. I think that volcano was meant to be dormant for a few centuries more. Without her presence in there, it would have been safe to ignore the area. We truly do need to do something about her. Sweetling, you can't convince them to move her?"

"I don't think this is something that I can argue with them about. It's not just a matter of protocol but power. They literally don't have the necessary power to overturn the decision. We'd have to get a more powerful deity in here to do the job, and I don't have the connections to pull that off."

"Then we have to find some way around it. The ash cloud alone from this volcanic eruption would destroy far too much territory. Alright, I'll think of possible solutions and bring anything that I think might be handy with me. For now, keep investigating. They might know something that will help and aren't thinking it important enough to share. Strangely, this occurs to me more often than not."

It often happened to her, too. Why was that? "We will. Master, bring any fallen pieces of star, as much as you can. I have a feeling that we're going to need it."

He pursed his lips off to one side. *"You have an idea already, don't you?"*

"A very, very vague idea. I'm not at all sure it will work and I can't do the experiments I need to verify it one way or another. Get up here quickly." Staring at the Caller itself, she realized in concern that it was running very low on magic. "Take a mirror with you. Milly can relay messages for us when the Caller—"

The white statue lost its shape of Master and reformed itself into the default setting of a somewhat shapeless humanoid figurine.

"—dies," she finished in aggravation. "Curses. I had a list of things I wanted him to bring."

"Milly will have to tell him."

Yes, she would. Fortunately, the woman now knew which mirror Sevana was near, so she should be able to deliver the message to Master fast enough for him to pack what she wanted. Tapping the mirror a little to make a knock-knock sound, she called, "Milly."

As she waited for the other woman to reply, she turned and really looked at Aran. As a tracker, the man was of course used to staying up all night if he needed to, but two days and two nights in a row was stretching things mightily. Now that his belly was full, it was all he could do to keep his eyes open. Frowning, she pointed to the futon folded up and resting in a corner. "Go sleep."

"I don't need—" He cut himself off as he yawned.

Sevana gave him a Look. "I promise to wake you if the volcano blows. For now, sleep. You're so tired you're actually swaying while sitting."

"It's a skill," he defended mildly.

"Ha."

His eyes crinkled up at her obvious disbelief and he capitulated silently with a shrug. There was enough space to lay out the futon against the back wall, which he did, then rolled into it. His eyes were closed before he could even cover himself with a blanket.

"What am I, your mother?" she asked him in amusement as she threw the blanket over him and moved his head properly on top of the pillow. His greasy head. "When you wake up, mister, I'm going to insist on you getting a bath."

For now, she supposed she should see what she had on *Jumping Clouds*. Maybe she'd get lucky and some of what she needed would be on there. Snagging the mirror, she skipped out the door, calling for Milly as she went.

Sevana's memory of what she had stored on *Jumping Clouds* was rather murky, but she had a notion that she had things on board that might help. If nothing else, more tools and another change of clothes would be welcome. While Aran slept, she skipped over to it and did a thorough raid on her own storage cabinets below the main deck. It turned out she had more in there than she'd thought.

Happy with her finds, she bundled it all up and headed back for her impromptu workshop. As she walked, a faint voice came from her pocket. Pulling it free, she looked into the small hand mirror. "Milly, did you talk to Master?"

"I did," the woman confirmed, shifting anxiously from side to side. It made it look like she was bobbing her head to some internal tune. "Master asks, he has dwarven mountain stone, fairy's kiss, and dragon's breath. Do you want them?"

"Yes," Sevana said promptly and secretly bounced on her toes in glee. Those were precisely some of the elements that she had hoped to have for this job. Not that she was sure she'd need all of them at this moment, but the possibility in her mind called for them. "Tell him to get all of the leprechaun gold he has as well."

"Anything else?" Milly's head turned as she went sideways, ready to take off in a moment's notice.

"No, go." Pocketing the mirror, she looked up, only to find Da-Chin hovering nearby, clearly waiting on her to stop speaking. "What is it, Da-Chin?"

"Artifactor, forgive my interruption, I wished to know if there is anything we can do to help you?"

Which was the polite way of demanding an update. Sevana didn't blame him for wanting one, it was just deuced difficult for her to say she didn't really have one. "My Fae brother, Arandur, arrived this morning."

Da-Chin's eyes grew very wide in his face. "He is Fae?"

"He is, yes." Sevana had a feeling that when Aran woke up, he was going to get quite the welcome from awed villagers. Better him than her. "I called my Master just now and he's gathering supplies before coming directly here. I expect him in about two days. Prepare lodgings for both men, will you?"

"Ha-ha," Da-Chin gave an immediate bow.

Their version of a 'yes?' Sevana judged so from his tone. "Da-Chin, I need to examine this phoenix sealed in the volcano more closely. She's the lynchpin to this whole problem. Is there any way to get closer to her?"

"The Jade Emperor created a tunnel through the mountain to place her inside. But he sealed it again immediately."

Of course he had. Sevana growled a choice word under her breath. Well, even if he hadn't, it wasn't like she could waltz through a tunnel while the volcano was active. Aran probably could have, though. It was him that she had been betting on.

Thinking hard, she tried to find some way around this. "Was there anyone that witnessed the phoenix being put in there?"

"Yes, of course. I witnessed it, the gods of this land witnessed it, and most of the village, for that matter."

"Who had the best view of it?"

"The gods, of course."

Of course. Then she knew who she needed to ask questions of.

8

"That's a very interesting bed head you have going on," Sevana observed. "Rather like a skunk. Or a drunk rooster."

Aran glared at her blearily, one eye still not completely open. "You let me sleep this long?"

"I have very little to do until Master arrives," she explained with a shrug. "He has most of the ingredients I need to work with."

He thought about that for several seconds (it likely took that long to process in his sleep-fogged mind) and then grunted understanding.

"Bath," Sevana ordered firmly, grabbing his hand and pulling him up to his feet. "Then I have an early dinner coming in for us. After that, it's story time."

Aran didn't have the best of balance, but he kept his feet, all while staring at her in a perplexed manner. "Story time?"

"Yup, yup. I want the full story as well as a detailed description of our phoenix in the volcano. The gods who brought me here are going to supply it. I also need a breakdown of what their power levels are, if I'm to make any plans. I don't want to put my ladder up against the wrong wall. Better to have facts to work off of rather than assumptions."

"Sev." Aran's head canted a little to the side. "You already know a way to solve this, don't you?"

"I do not. I do, however, have an idea of how to blend their powers together. And that might be the key to this whole debacle." Stopping the volcano was another matter entirely, however. She wasn't even guessing how to do that yet. She really hoped that Master had an idea that he could pull out of his sleeves. Sevana was currently running very low on inspiration.

Aran grabbed clothes from his pack, and Sevana showed him the way to the bathhouse, leaving him there. Now that he was awake, she wanted his help in setting up another measuring device. Until he had come and brought more of her tools, Sevana hadn't the necessary equipment to measure the active lava in the volcano. But now she had two different tools that she should be able to cobble together. Measuring how much lava—if there was any—would help her determine just how much time they had to work with. The degassing wasn't a scientific measurement at all.

The slope measurements weren't changing much, so surely—

A rumble like a distant earthquake rolled through the ground. Sevana nearly pitched forward as her balance was upset. Awkwardly, she twisted sharply about and stared up at the volcano in alarm. Was it trying to blow now?!

From the top of the volcano a plume of thick, dark ash puffed out and spread in every direction. She became immediately covered in a fine layer from head to toe. Spitting ash out of her mouth, Sevana tried to look through it, but all that did was make her eyes sting.

All she could do was wait, nerves taut, and see if there was any sign of lava coming from the top.

From every direction, people came running, screaming to each other, snatching up baggage or children as they ran. Several times they knocked into her, but didn't slow or even try to apologize, so intent they were in trying to escape.

Escape where, that was the question. They didn't have enough boats to get everyone off the island in one fell swoop, and as soon as the lava touched the water, it would turn it acidic and eat through the wooden hulls. There was no escape for these people unless through magical or divine intervention. And Sevana had to know for certain at what speed the lava would travel to know what help to offer.

So she waited, watching intently even though her eyes stung and teared up.

"SEVANA!"

She intended to only glance over when she heard Aran, but her attention was snared completely. His hair was wet and full of suds, pants on, boots barely on, a shirt clutched in his hands. It was the first time she'd seen him shirtless and, my-oh-my were all Fae built like that? Or was it being a tracker that gave him such excellent musculature?

"Sevana." Aran grabbed her by the shoulders and shook her once, gently.

Blinking, she forced her eyes up and focused on his face. "Muscles."

"What?" he asked in confusion.

Mentally, she kicked herself. What had just come out of her mouth? "Your eyes are better than mine, can you see lava coming out of the top of the volcano?"

Still with that odd look on his face, he obediently turned and peered ahead. A Fae's vision could put an eagle's to shame, almost better than her far-see glasses or box lens. He stared hard for several seconds before shaking his head. "No. No lava. In fact, I think the ash has stopped pouring out of it too."

"The ash stopped too?" Sevana raised a hand to protect her eyes and tried to study it. Even though her vision was better now, being Fae-enhanced, she still couldn't see what he was describing. "That is very, very strange."

"How strange?"

"When a volcano discharges ash clouds like this, it's generally a sign of eruption. And by generally, I mean about ninety-five percent of the time. It's even more odd because in the days I've been here, it's altered a little in chemistry and slope but nothing significant enough to indicate that it would do something like this."

Why, why, why? She had far too many questions and not enough answers.

Aran's eyes narrowed as he studied the volcano again. "It'll dissipate completely within the space of an hour. I think you're right, Sev. I don't think the phoenix in there is as deeply asleep and sealed as everyone assumes she is."

"You think she's responsible for this volcanic hiccup?"

"I'm almost certain of it. I wonder if the volcano reacts to her presence itself or if it's an indicator of her mood?"

Sevana growled a choice word under her breath. "So it's not just reacting to her physical motions, like if she turns over in her sleep? Lovely."

"Just a theory on my part."

"It's a theory we need to verify one way or another," Sevana said grimly. "Otherwise every time something like this happens, the whole village is going to panic, like it's doing now, and I'm going to have heart failure before this job is out."

"I have a notion or two on how to go about that, but..." he ran an illustrative hand through his hair, "I think I'll finish my bath first."

"Shame."

"What?" he asked her, perplexed.

"Ah, I mean, sure, go ahead. I'll deal with these panicking idiots while you do that." Sevana turned immediately on her heel and struck off blindly. For the sake of her dignity, Aran really could not appear shirtless around her ever again. The most absurd things came out of her mouth when he did.

Da-Chin. That was what she needed to think about. She needed to track the man down and settle the villagers so that she could have the peace and quiet she needed to think about the problem at hand.

"Artifactor Warren!" Chi-lin appeared with both Da-Yu and Cheng-Huang in flanking position. The flaming tail lashed from side to side, snapping in irritation. "What is the meaning of this? You told us that the volcano would not erupt in the next two weeks at least!"

"It's not erupting now, either," Sevana snapped. Her recent embarrassment with Aran lit her temper, as it was easier to be angry than to recall those stupid things she had said. "That is an ash cloud, nothing more. Calm your people down. I can't work if they're panicking and tripping over me."

Cheng-Huang asked uncertainly, "Just an ash cloud? Are you sure?"

"No lava, so yes, I'm sure." Sevana pointed an authoritative finger. "Go."

Perhaps because he had more experience with her than the rest, Cheng-Huang took her words at face value and immediately went, going to the nearest people and calming them down with softly spoken words.

Chi-lin was more in a fighting mood, as his tail was still lashing. "Doesn't the ash cloud signify that you were wrong in your calculations, Artifactor?"

"No, it signifies that what you told me is wrong," she growled. Squaring her shoulders, she faced off with him, nose to nose. "Let's get this straight, you fake unicorn. You're one of the idiots that thought it would be fine to stick a *phoenix on top of a dormant volcano*. Sealed or not, this is what's going to happen!"

Said fake unicorn bristled so that every horn stood up and his entire back lit in a hazy fire trail.

Before he could lose his temper completely, Da-Yu stepped smoothly in between them, forcing Chi-lin to step back several steps. "Artifactor, are you saying that Feng-Huang is directly responsible for this?"

"I can't be sure of that until I hear exactly how she was sealed in there, but that's my and my partner's guess. We think that the volcano is reacting to her—her moods, her movements, something."

"She's asleep," Chi-lin snarled, the flames becoming nearly white in anger.

Sevana could feel the intense heat from here and only pride kept her from backing up a step or two. "And you don't toss or turn in your sleep? Have bad dreams? You think she's just lying there like a breathing corpse?"

Da-Yu, at least, understood and made a silent 'ah' with his mouth. "Your point is well taken, Artifactor. It is not something we considered, but surely with the Jade Emperor's seal, such a thing—"

"You thought that the Jade Emperor's seal would keep her from having any influence on the volcano at all," Sevana cut through what he was about to say with a firm tone. "You are obviously wrong. I'm not going to make a single plan or theory until I find out from you exactly how's she sealed in there, what her power levels are, and what her physical makeup is. Every assumption you've made is in error. I need facts, gentlemen, and no more guesses."

Da-Yu spread his hands in a placating manner. "We will tell you the facts as we know them, I assure you."

He'd better. Sevana would start beating answers out of him soon otherwise. "Right now, I can't think with all of this noise. Get your people settled, get this ash out of here, then we'll sit and talk."

As there was not enough space for everyone in her temporary workroom, they located their meeting on the top of Da-Chin's home. Due to the flat roof architecture of Nanashi, everyone had little gardens and sitting places on their roofs. Everything was in pots and long trough planters, but it was green and growing.

At least for now. Any more ash plumes like that one, and the plants would choke on it and die off. For a fishing village this poor, that would mean a great deal of short term hardship.

Da-Chin and his wife were equally nervous about having a Fae, an Artifactor, and three gods convening on the top of their house. Aran, all charm, took them aside and explained what it was that they were going to discuss, and extended an invitation to sit next to them so that they could hear and contribute as necessary. With wide eyes, clutching tightly onto each other's hands, the couple settled tentatively on cushions next to him.

Sevana watched this play out and wondered to herself: was there anyone in this wide, green world that Aran couldn't charm? She was beginning to think that he'd gotten the job of Tracker not because of his woodland skills but because of that lethal charm of his. It wasn't the same as Kip's, who used his looks to smooth things out; instead it seemed more like he put himself on the same level as the person he spoke to. He tried to empathize with how they felt, which formed a connection between them, and then talked them around to what he wanted done. It was so simply executed that most people didn't realize that it wasn't their idea to begin with.

No, this wasn't surprising to her, to see him in action with the old couple. After all, Aran had charmed his way into her life, and that took considerable doing.

With people settled, Sevana focused on the deities. "Alright. You told me why she's in there. What I want to know is how she was put in that volcano."

"It's very simple," Da-Yu answered, his tone and expression indicating that she had just asked an obvious question. "The Jade Emperor opened a hole in the side of the mountain, sealed Feng-Huang with his own power, and placed her inside. Then he sealed the hole shut again to make sure she would remain undisturbed."

Sevana gave him a weary look. The problem with asking questions from someone outside of her chosen field was that they usually didn't know how to answer her and give the information she needed. They always seemed to think a basic summary would answer every question she had. "Let's try this again. The Jade Emperor's power. What type is it? Purely divine, elemental, mystical, what?"

All of them now looked at her as if she had just sprouted horns out of her head.

"He is the supreme sovereign," Cheng-Huang explained, slowly, as if to a child. "He is light and kindness itself."

Sevana resisted the urge to go and start knocking heads together.

Aran put a restraining hand on her wrist. "Wait, Sev. They don't understand what you're asking. Let me try, mmm?"

She waved him forward.

"All beings, all elements, all gods in this world have an energy level and type," Arandur explained, his patience as deep as a mountain's. "Even the Jade Emperor is not an exclusion to this. Artifactors do not see the world as purely this, or purely that. They calculate power in terms of its strength, its type, and how it can be blended with other powers. What she needs to know is what type the Jade Emperor's power is, how strong it is, so that she can calculate what's happening inside that mountain."

Cheng-Huang, builder that he was, grasped the concept first. "Ah.

Ah, yes, I see, I should have realized what she meant. Artifactor, the Jade Emperor's power is purely divine. He emitted pure light when he was born, such that it filled the whole kingdom in the Majestic Heavenly Lights."

Sevana latched onto this. "Light. Divine light. Alright, good, that answers part of my question. Now, compared to you, how powerful is he? Exponentially, just a little more?"

"Twice my strength," Chi-Lin answered promptly. "Perhaps a touch more, but I would guess twice my power."

Oh? Now that was interesting. Sevana hadn't measured them properly yet, but she had a guess as to what they were each like, power-wise. Taking her box lens from her pocket, she studied each of them in turn. "You're remarkably equal in terms of power. I would say about an eight each."

Aran let out a soft whistle in surprise. "That's very powerful."

For a mystic being, only the strongest came near that rating, and those were the dragons and the Fae. Minor deities like this were more powerful because of their divinity, but still, they were a little more than she had expected too. "And the Jade Emperor is twice this?" She let out a low whistle. "A sixteen, at least, huh. Heavens, he's more powerful than an anti-spell."

No one around her but Aran knew what she was referring to, but they liked her surprise and reaction, and beamed at her. It made them more open to her, which Sevana took full advantage of. "Now, your phoenix, Feng-Huang. How powerful is she?"

"A touch more powerful than we are." Chi-Lin pondered for a moment before adding, "If you say that I am an eight? I would think she would be somewhere around a ten."

Oh. "That would explain it," she breathed to herself.

Aran's eyes cut to her. "What?"

She blew out a breath, leaning back and looking toward the sky, her eyes blind to it as her mind whirled with numbers and science. "When you seal something, it's not just a matter of power. Say I was trying to bottle a spark from the eternal flame. I wouldn't use fire, or light, or any mystical power that related to them to do it. Even though they might be more powerful, it wouldn't work long-term. The powers would be too alike, so they would be attracted to each other and start to blend, which would eventually lead to sparks going off. Given enough time, the shield would fail on its own."

Cheng-Huang scooted up on his cushion, leaning toward her, eyes intense. "But the Jade Emperor is more powerful than she is."

"That's actually detrimental in this case, not helpful. Because of his power, it made the situation that much worse, as it magnified hers. If he really wanted to seal her long-term, then he should have had a powerful river god do it, like you, Da-Yu. Because your power is the complete opposite of hers, it would have lasted." Well, that was neither here nor there, she wasn't interested in keeping the phoenix sealed. It was better to break the seal and get her out, actually, although Sevana wasn't sure if that was possible.

"You think we should have me re-seal her?" Da-Yu asked doubtfully.

"No, we're far past that point. The volcano is too volatile; sealing her inside it all over again would just delay the inevitable, especially since you don't have the overwhelming power difference you need to properly seal her." Sevana twisted her head from side to side, trying to work out some of the kinks in her neck. She could feel the tension building in her shoulders. "What we need right now is to think of a way to buy time until I can figure out a proper solution to this mess. We can't have the volcano threatening to blow every time she fidgets."

"As to that," Aran pointed toward his own nose, "I do have an idea."

9

Sevana twisted to face him. "I'm all ears."

"I think our best option is to explain to the phoenix what is happening when she moves and ask her to be very still. Also, to perhaps ask if she can do anything about limiting her own power so that she doesn't affect the volcano as much." Aran looked straight at her as he said this, his words calm and unhurried.

"She's asleep!" Chi-Lin objected.

"Dragons can talk to anyone in their dreams." Aran's mouth stretched into a small grin.

Sevana grinned right back at him. "Are you volunteering?"

"I am. There's a clan of them not far from here. I can probably go and come back within the day, if you let me borrow your skimmer."

"Done and done." Seeing that everyone else was only half-following, she explained, "He's going to go and barter for a dragon's help. The Fae are the only ones that the dragons actually listen to, so he's the best one to go."

"They listen to you too," Aran objected, grin widening.

"Yes, sure they do, when I'm covered from head to toe with gold," she shot back, voice dripping with sarcasm. "Speaking of, the price of getting their help is on you lot," she pointed to the three deities, "so think of something suitable before he leaves. Aran, I need you to go sooner rather than later."

"If I leave now, I won't be back until tomorrow at noon, latest. The skimmer isn't equipped for night travel, you know that."

She did indeed. The skimmer was meant for quick trips and so didn't have more than a compass on board. It didn't have the complex navigational system on it needed for nightly navigation, not like *Jumping Clouds*. "Do you dare take the other one instead?"

"During a dragon's hatching season?" he objected in true horror. "They'd slap me down before even questioning who I am."

"That's what I thought." The skimmer was marginally safer as it didn't shield him from sight and the dragons could clearly see who was coming. Even then, Aran would have to be careful in his approach and even more careful with his landing. "You're sure you can arrive before nightfall?"

"If I leave within the next hour, yes."

"Then it's an overnight trip for you."

Aran grimaced agreement. "Da-Chin, a portable breakfast and dinner for the trip would be very welcome."

"We'll prepare it for you," the old man assured him and scrambled to his feet, his wife right behind him.

Sevana knew that Aran hadn't meant right this second but she sensed that the couple was glad for an excuse to leave. Casually sitting with three gods had probably strained their elderly nerves to the breaking point.

"Speaking with Feng-Huang is only a temporary measure," Cheng-Huang started, eyes narrowed in suspicion. "What do you propose for a permanent solution?"

She had been afraid that someone would ask her this question once she had everyone gathered. Her answer would start an argument, she just knew it, but there was no way to put off the inevitable forever. "I'll say this first: there's no way to stop the volcano."

All three deities erupted at her. They yelled, they cursed, their words overlapping so that she couldn't make heads or tails of them. Sevana wasn't one to shy away from an argument, but she didn't believe in trying to communicate at the top of her voice, either. Nothing good ever came from that. So she folded her arms over her chest and waited them out.

When she sat there, like a river stone, they started shaking fingers and fists at her.

Aran's aura sparked and flared, heat rolling off of him in a visible wave. It was intense enough that Sevana, sitting next to him, felt scorched by it even though it did no damage to her. It shocked the deities into silence and they stared at him in agitation, worried that he would leap at them.

"Be still," he commanded them in a quiet, firm tone. "Act like gods and not children."

Sevana blew out a covert breath and eyed her friend sideways. Sometimes she forgot just how scary Aran could be when he had a mad-on. "Ahem. As I was saying before I was rudely interrupted, with the collective power that we have here, there is no possible way to stop the volcano. I do, however, have other ideas."

"We are listening, Artifactor," Da-Yu assured her, keeping a weather eye on Aran.

"I think it's possible to contain it. I would like to explore the option, at least, of building a device that would blend your three powers and create a magical barrier to keep the volcano's ash and lava from pouring out any further than this immediate area. We can't stop it from exploding, but we can mitigate its effects."

"Is that possible?" Da-Yu stared over her head toward the volcano. "When a volcano erupts, ash spreads for many miles in all directions. The lava is too hot to touch, and it turns water into acid, killing everything near it. Containing it will surely be the harder path to take."

Sevana started shaking her head before he could get the full sentence out. "No, it's easier. The problem that we're facing is that the volcano is under a great deal of pressure. It's almost unmeasurable. Trying to cap it off at the top will do no good whatsoever, and aside from drilling into the sides to try and drain it, there's no way to relieve the pressure. Who wants the job of drilling into an active volcano and coaxing all of the magma out?"

The gods looked uneasily between each other but not one volunteered.

"See? No good solution on trying to stop it."

"Perhaps your Fae brother can do so?" Da-Yu suggested with a sideways look at Aran.

"Perhaps, but I'm not convinced I can," Aran responded with a troubled frown. "Speaking to the rock and tunneling through is one thing. It is the extreme heat of the magma that will cause me difficulties."

And that was a problem that Sevana had not thought of a solution to. She would love it if Aran really could pull that off, but doing so would be extremely dangerous, and until she thought of a method that would lessen that danger, she wasn't trying it. "It's a possibility, but one fraught with problems. I'd rather find a different solution that doesn't put him directly in harm's way. What worries me is that this is a cinder cone type of volcano, and because of that, there's a possibility that it won't be limited to a single eruption if we leave it to its own devices."

All of the color just drained out of Chi-Lin's expression, making him look like a white ghost. "This is no time for jests, Artifactor."

"Do I look like I'm joking? There's a volcanic chain in the far south that has a cinder cone volcano about the size of this one. It's been erupting for the past ten years and it's not showing any signs of slowing. Some of the volcanoes are monogenetic, with just one big eruption, but not all of them. Once this thing starts, it might carry on for several years without stopping."

Cheng-Huang had his face buried in his hands and was muttering something that might have been curses under his breath. He was not speaking in a language Sevana recognized, and that was a shame, because she was suddenly very curious on this point. Men cursed the gods, but who did the gods take in vain? With one eye on him, she continued, "Now, with a little magic and divine help, I think we can make sure that this volcanic eruption is a single instance that will only last a few days, not years. That's why I want to talk to your phoenix so badly. She's the one that started up that volcano prematurely. I think she should take partial responsibility and make sure that it empties out in one go so we don't have to go through this again."

Da-Yu gave a firm nod. "I am in agreement with this. What are your other thoughts?"

"I'm not quite sure how, I need more numbers and measurements to make sure, but I'd like to use that lava. Perhaps we can control it so that it stays next to the isle? It will take time, perhaps decades, but eventually it will become livable land. This place is crowded; gaining more girth or length to the isle will only benefit you later."

At this, Cheng-Huang unburied his face. "Use the volcano to build onto the isle. Now that is a splendid idea. It should have occurred to me earlier; after all, that was how this isle was originally created."

That was usually the case with islands of any sort, actually, that they were the result of volcanic activity. Either that or the mainland lost a piece that started floating away into the sea.

"I think if we coordinate this right, getting all of the people, animals, sea creatures, the Unda and so forth to evacuate, then we can make this volcano work to our benefit."

"That is something that I would like to discuss in more depth." Chi-Lin turned his head to include all of them in this question, "How do we propose to evacuate the people? We have a little over five hundred souls here, too many to put on the fishing boats and ferry to the mainland. Not to mention the animals."

"We can't use the ships anyway," Da-Yu stated thoughtfully. "The water will be too acidic; it will eat straight through the hulls."

"We need something like *Jumping Clouds*," Sevana stated in aggravation, "but of course, mine can only hold six at a squeeze. It doesn't have the right size for the task."

"But surely we can build something on the same principle that would be large enough?" Cheng-Huang's tone was not really a question, more like he was thinking aloud. "Is there a limit to how large it can be?"

Sevana nearly opened her mouth to say of course, but then bit it back as a thought struck. "Everything has limitations. If I created it, certainly, I wouldn't be able to make one big enough. But if you, a deity, were to make it...." She trailed off suggestively.

"I am very inclined to do so," Cheng-Huang answered, staring off into the distance with a calculating gleam in his eye. "Artifactor, after this, sit and speak with me. Tell me your design, and let us see if we can adapt it to my power to make this feasible."

"I think it feasible already, I'm just not sure if we can make one giant ship to do the trick, or if we'll have to split it into two." Sevana felt relieved at this suggestion, as it hadn't occurred to her, although it should have. Cheng-Huang was the builder after all. Of course he could create something like this. "But you're right, that's a problem to hash out between the two of us. We'll talk about it more after this."

"Let's assume that the two of you can manage evacuation." Aran cocked his head at her. "What then?"

Sevana picked up the thread of the conversation again. "The trick will be getting everything in place before this thing actually erupts. But gentlemen, mark me on this: I do not say we can do this without damage. There will be damage. I can't do anything about that. How much damage, that is the question."

Chi-Lin stared at her hard, an argument broiling in his eyes. "How much damage can you limit this to?"

"I need numbers to crunch," she reiterated succinctly.

"That's her way of saying she doesn't know yet," Aran translated helpfully.

Sevana stoutly ignored him. "There's no way of knowing how much I can contain the ash until we can put together a working model. It might be limited to just around the volcano. It might be that we can't do it that tightly, that it will spread to the entire isle, or just past it."

"We called you here to prevent that," Chi-Lin almost snarled out.

"You kidnapped a sleeping woman in the dead of night without thinking it through," she snapped back. "And you did it at the twelfth hour! If you had summoned for me before this, giving me a few months instead of a few days to work with, I might have been able to give you a better option! As it stands, you're going to have to make do with whatever plan I can throw together in the heat of the moment."

"You blasphemous—!" Chi-Lin lunged for her, horns shining in a particularly menacing way.

Sevana tucked and rolled to the side in pure instinct, as she didn't want her body anywhere near those horns. Her movements were almost superfluous. Aran reacted in the same moment she did, with greater speed, only he went forward instead of back. Dodging the horns, he grabbed Chi-Lin around the snout, just below the eyes, with an iron grip. When the unicorn tried to jerk free, his head didn't budge an inch.

Aran stood like a mountain, impassive, unmovable, keeping his opponent firmly locked in place. He stayed like that for several seconds, proving his point, before asking calmly, "Have you regained your temper?"

Chi-Lin couldn't speak or nod but his eyes conveyed a mulish agreement.

"Good. It is not wise to shoot the messenger. Especially when the messenger is a daughter of the Fae, yes?"

The tableau froze. Sevana, deeming it safe enough to resume her seat, did so and studied their faintly horrified expressions that were mixed with disbelief and a sort of trepidation, as if they had stuck their hands into a hole expecting treasure only to encounter a den of vipers instead.

"D-daughter?" Da-Yu repeated, voice climbing.

Aran regarded them for a moment and she could just see it, when it clicked that they had not known until this moment her true connection to the Fae. Then an unholy, evil grin lit up his face although his tone remained innocent. "Yes, daughter. Sellion, as we call her. You knew this."

Cheng-Huang, if he had anyone to pray to, would have been on his knees in that moment. His words sounded strangled. "We did not."

"Is that so? We wondered at your actions. Aranhil was especially distraught to find her missing, and was ready to order the Fae nation to search for her, when I found her."

The gods understood that 'distraught' meant 'infuriated' and the mental images that accompanied the idea of an enraged Fae King made Da-Yu look faint.

Aran continued, still in that calm, unhurried tone as if he were discussing nothing of specific importance. "I have of course informed him that she is safe. He is currently standing by until he hears from her."

It was hard to keep a straight face while laughing maniacally on the inside, but Sevana managed it beautifully. The way that Aran phrased all of this was perfectly executed. It looked reassuring on the outside, but the three of them heard it as a threat, and they were clear that if they upset her too much, she could tattle on them. What the consequences would be, they didn't know. Aran was smart to not detail it in any way.

What a person imagined was always so much worse than reality.

Clearing her throat, Sevana gave them a cheerful smile. "Well, now that everyone's caught up, we need to get into motion. Aran, go talk to a dragon for me. As for you, gentlemen, go find him some nice gold to pay the dragon. After that, find me. I have tests that I need to run."

People scattered in their various directions, all but Cheng-Huang who moved in closer to her. "The ship?"

"Yes, let's get you started on that first. I can't give you the scale of the volcano model yet until Master arrives anyway. He has part of the information I need to predict with." Sevana grabbed a pencil and notebook from her bag and laid it out on the floor between them. In quick strokes, she sketched out the design. "Here, this is the basic structure. I based it on barges, as they are very stout and sound, hard to tip over. You can change the design if you wish—"

Cheng-Huang shook his head. "We don't have time for me to come up with a different design and experiment with it until it's correct. I'll use your template for this."

"We're going to be doing a little experimenting anyway," Sevana warned him, although she took his point well. "I don't know how we're going to adapt the power and navigation systems over so that they'll work with your power, and I don't have the elements here that I used for *Jumping Clouds.*"

"I understand and expected as much."

At least she had one god that seemed to be logical and levelheaded about such matters. Sevana blew out a secret breath and went back to sketching things out. "I know that you don't know about how human magic works, but I'll write all of this out anyway. Between the two of us, we can figure out how to adapt it. Let's start with the basic structure first. If we're to transport both humans and animals, how big does it need to be?"

"The size of a junk ship, I would think," Cheng-Huang offered slowly.

Sevana had some experience with this type of ship. Junk ships varied in size, and they were employed for cargo as much as for passengers, but it gave her a good idea of what he was envisioning. "In that case...." She fell to scratching out calculations off to the side of her drawings, figuring out dimensions and such. Cheng-Huang tilted his head to be able to read what she was writing, either making humming noises as he followed along, or broaching ideas as he thought of them.

Within a few hours, they had a working idea of what needed to happen, and Cheng-Huang nodded in satisfaction. "I'll start building this immediately. It will likely take me a few days, however. When I start on the power and navigation systems, I'll need you to supervise. I don't wish to take up needless time tinkering."

An opinion she agreed with wholeheartedly. "Tell me when you're ready for me. In the meantime, I'll work with Da-Chin to devise a quick evacuation plan for the village as a whole. The new ship will be useless if we can't get them there quickly enough."

"I quite agree. I leave that to you, Artifactor."

10

Master arrived like a storm blowing in. His land carriage could not traverse the sea channel, so he'd been forced to hire a boat to get him across. But he did so with such dramatic and magical flare that his normal mode of transportation still seemed fantastical to the villagers. One of the faster runners, a boy of about ten, came to fetch Sevana as she checked all of her readings near the volcano's base. He was so frantic she only understood that Master had arrived but everything else was garbled as his words ran into each other.

Since she only had one more thing to check, she did so, which made the boy nearly dance in place with impatience. Only with her numbers recorded did she finally turn and head back into the village. Not at a dead run like her escort wanted, but at a steady lope. Sevana made it almost to the first row of houses when Master spotted her. For an old man, he moved like lightning, catching her up in a bear hug that threatened the soundness of her ribs.

Sevana put up with the hug, and only to herself admitted that she was relieved he had finally arrived. With him here, the chances of them saving the isle from complete destruction just increased by thirty percent. "Master. I need to breathe."

He put her down like Aran had, only a few inches away, and he kept his hands on her shoulders. "Sweetling. This disappearing act of yours is bad for an old man's heart. Kindly stop doing it."

"You think I enjoy being kidnapped? Tell those three idiots that."

Master looked this way and that. "Where are they?"

"Hiding, probably. Aran already scared them last night." Sevana waved a hand, setting this problem aside. "Master, I have everything written down for you. Why don't you read my notes, catch up on the situation, and let me unload what you brought with you. We don't have time."

"You have a workspace set up?"

"Of course, this way." She took him by the elbow and drew him in the right direction. "I haven't had a chance to notify anyone on the mainland, but that needs to be done—"

Master held up a hand, forestalling her. "I did that on the trip up here. Everyone knows what's happening and is preparing for the worst, just in case."

Relieved, she nodded, and because it was inevitable, gave him the highlights of the situation as they walked. He didn't have the patience to just read her notes—Master had questions he wanted immediate answers to. On the way, she signaled the village matron that had taken charge of her to bring food, as she knew good and well that Master had skipped meals to get here as fast as he had. No one thought well on an empty stomach and Sevana needed Master to think, and think well right now.

Once she had him settled in the workspace, she doubled back to the village entrance for the traveling carriage and brought it down the streets. The narrow, switchback streets. Seriously, even with space as a premium on this isle, did the people have to cram everything together? The docks were half the size of the village and they only had six! Cramming everything to be right on top of the other made for ridiculously tight quarters and, in Sevana's opinion, there was no need for it. They could afford to make the streets two feet wider without hurting anything.

There wasn't much room to park it in front of her building, but she managed to squeeze it along the side, and from there unload it. Master had brought far more than she had requested, and some of what she saw made her scratch her head in confusion. Still, he was the one that had experience with volcanoes, not her. Maybe he knew something she didn't.

With the last of it stacked along the wall, Sevana joined Master at the table. He was on the last page, where her most recent measurements were recorded. He glanced up at her and tapped a finger against the pages. "I'm not seeing a factor that would explain these flare-ups. If they were natural causes, I would expect all the numbers to rise instead of returning to normal."

"I didn't actually note this down, but our theory is that the phoenix trapped inside the volcano is setting it off every time she tosses or turns in her sleep."

"Ahhh. Yes. Yes, that is very possible. I'm not sure what we can do about that from here."

"Aran left earlier for dragon lands. He's going to barter for their help, have one of them talk to her in dreams and see if we can get her to lie perfectly still."

Master pursed his lips together in a silent whistle. "With him asking, he'll likely get at least one dragon to agree. That was good thinking, sweetling. Now, your notes are good, it gives me a foundation of what the situation is, but it doesn't tell me much about our possible solution. You've thought of one?"

Sevana grimaced. "I'm not sure how viable it is. This is my first volcano after all."

"Well, the first volcano is always the hardest," Master drawled.

She glared at him sideways. "Was that an attempt to be funny?"

"Heaven forbid." Master chuckled at his own joke. Not having her laugh didn't faze him. "I can't proclaim myself an expert, but I do believe this is the third one I've faced. With the others, we had plenty of warning, and were able to evacuate until it was over. Then, of course, I helped with the cleanup of the area so we could move them all back in. It took several months. In this case…" he trailed off with a frown. "I don't think there'd be anything left of the isle if we let it run its course. Even with magical help, it might take decades before this place is habitable again."

"Which is their fear. There's no way to keep it from blowing, though, that's not possible. Trying to cap it or drain it will be futile at best." Sevana felt grateful she was speaking with someone who understood the forces involved and didn't have to go into the details of why. Again. Repeating that tedious explanation twice would have made her patience snap. "I think our best bet is to let it explode, but manage it so that the effects are mitigated. My thought was this: we have three deities, a Fae, and two Artifactors here. Can't we somehow combine all of our powers and use them as a joint force?"

Master sat back in his chair, staring blindly up at the ceiling. "Use all powers involved as a joint force. Mitigate the damage by containing it. You're talking of creating a shield large enough to cover the volcano, to keep the ash from spreading."

"I know," she said patiently.

"And you're also talking about another shield, one that will keep the lava from covering the isle."

"I know."

"And still another shield that will keep it from spreading throughout the sea. If it turns this entire area into acidic water, it will destroy all life, and it will defeat the purpose of preserving the isle. These people are fishermen. Without the sea life, they'll starve. Not to mention you have to protect the Unda clan that is right next door."

"I know." Sevana was tired of repeating those words.

Master's eyes came down to meet hers. "That's a tall order, sweetling."

"We have three deities, two Artifactors, and a Fae," she reminded him.

"And if we didn't have at least that much magical and divine power, I'd say it was impossible to do what you're suggesting." Master frowned up at the ceiling again, thoughts whirling. Sevana recognized the signs of when he was calculating things at high speeds. "I don't know whether we'll want to divide this into three separate shields or if it might be better to try to make one big one."

Not sure if this would complicate or help, Sevana offered, "Cheng-Huang likes the idea of using the lava to help expand the isle. He hoped that we could create a channel for the lava to direct its flow to form a cap around the edge of the coastline."

"Oh? It's not a bad thought. It certainly helps to have an area to direct it to. That might complicate our shield, though." Master tapped his finger against her notes again. "I think the deciding factor will be if we can blend powers or not. That might be our restriction. Let's work on that problem first."

It was a sensible suggestion and one that she could get behind. "Flip the page, that's their power ratings and types."

Master's eyes scanned through the page. "They're remarkably similar in power ratings. All 8's, eh? Although they're different in type. Water, life, stone?"

"Cheng-Huang is a building type of god," she explained. "My box lens quantified his power as 'stone' as a sort of default. I don't have the right tools to dig into a more accurate assessment. 'Life' I think was also a default for Chi-Lin. He's over all of the wildlife of both land and sea."

"It's a very interesting mix." Master put the notebook aside on the table to tick points off on his fingers. "So between all three gods, we have a 24 power level. Add us two Artifactors in the mix, it's another 12."

Sevana perked up at this. Actually, an Artifactor's power was more like a 3, but given the right magnification, they could stretch it up to a 6. She had not factored that in because of course she didn't have the right tool. "You brought something to magnify power with?"

"I always do. It's a precaution."

While that sounded good, she had her doubts. Uncertainly, she asked, "What if—" A cough took her by surprise, feeling like it was digging a well into her lungs. She covered her mouth, hacking and wheezing, tears springing to her eyes.

Springing into action, Master dug into a pack, rooted around for a moment, and then pulled a glass vial free. Unstopping it, he waved it in front of her nose.

Sevana took in a deep breath, knowing well what was in that vial, and grateful he had some on him. Fine Mist Salts were the perfect remedy for coughing fits. The salts did the trick and she was able to drag in a full breath without hacking it back out again. "I'm glad you have some of that."

"How often is this happening?" he asked her quietly, eyes

troubled.

"First coughing fit since I came here," Sevana admitted sourly. "Every time I think my body's adapted, I get another coughing fit to prove me wrong." And having one now, of all times, proved that her doubts were right on the money. She dragged the words into the open. "Are you sure you should factor me in?"

Master studied her levelly, his expression giving nothing away except perhaps a hint of concern. "Your magic still giving you trouble?"

"It's still flaring out. And I've also had this weird development in the past several days where sometimes when I say an incantation, the magic hiccups for a second."

"We'll focus on helping you after this," Master promised her, voice somber. "This needs to be a priority."

Truly. If they didn't figure her out soon, then she would be basically out of business. Sevana had managed so far just by using her wits and making others do the majority of the work for her, but she couldn't survive like that forever. Jobs like this one would come up—they always did—and she wouldn't be able to handle them. Rain and drought, but she didn't even have the ability to call for help if she needed it!

They had given her time, given her body a chance to adapt to her new magic to see if it would work itself out. Apparently that wasn't going to happen.

Master cleared his throat and moved on. "I'm assuming that Arandur will lend his power to this?"

"He's already said as much."

"You're probably the only human alive that likely knows this answer...how powerful is a Fae by himself?"

"A seven," she responded promptly, almost gleefully. "The best part? They can alter their magical properties to fit the situation. Straight Fae magic is just that. Magical energy and nothing more. But if we need fire, or water, or whatever, then Aran can channel his magic along those elemental lines and give us what we need."

Master's eyes lit up like a child that had been given five birthdays, all tied up in a bow at his feet. "You've seen him do this?"

"Seen? I've had him do this for me twice now. Who do you think has been magically covering for me on the job for the past few months when you're not available?"

"That…is extremely handy, given this situation."

"It's extremely handy given any situation." And one of the reasons why Sevana had been so relieved when Aran had shown up. She desperately needed him.

Master went back to ticking things off on his fingers. "So if we assume deities, Fae, and me, then our combined power is 37. That's quite impressive."

"Impressive enough to contain the explosion of a volcano?"

"That's the question." Master gave a sage nod.

Not at all fooled by that expression, she drawled, "And how large of an explosion are we going to have, anyway? I've been trying to calculate that for days, but not having any prior experience or ways to research past explosions, all I've been able to do is guess."

"Oh? Let me see your calculations." Master lifted the notebook he'd been handed, looking for another.

Sevana knew a diversion when she saw one. In other words, he didn't know either.

Lovely. Just…lovely.

11

Sevana and Master were debating numbers over dinner when another earthquake rumbled under their feet. As earthquakes went, this one was a tad more severe than the one that Sevana had experienced previously. She had to brace herself against the table and put a foot against the ground to avoid being dumped out of her chair.

Master rode through the short quake with eyebrows raised. "This is the second quake?"

"That I've felt since my arrival, yes."

"How would you compare the two? Force wise?"

"Well—" she started, only to be cut off by the abrupt appearance of Cheng-Huang in the only clear space left in their workroom.

The god looked undeniably nervous, although he didn't jump down their throats demanding an immediate fix. That much, at least, he realized wasn't possible. "Artifactors."

"Cheng-Huang, my master, Tashjian Joles," Sevana introduced, waving a hand between the two. "Master, Cheng-Huang, the Building God."

"Pleasure, Cheng-Huang." Master threw up a staying hand. "And please, relax. I realize the earthquakes are unnerving, but it doesn't mean the volcano is imminently going to explode. In my younger days, I saw an area experience earthquakes for nearly four months before the volcano actually blew. All they mean is that a great deal of magma is being shunted about under the crust of the earth and it's making things shift from side to side. Unsettling, but not dangerous."

As long as they stayed at this minor level, that was correct. Sevana wasn't so sure that they wouldn't escalate, though. She took one look at Cheng-Huang's face and decided not to say that out loud.

"Months?" Cheng-Huang repeated doubtfully. "Even though we've had two of them within the space of two days?"

"I don't think it'll be months in this case because the presence of the phoenix is speeding matters unnaturally along," Master stated calmly. "But I don't expect the volcano to go tomorrow either. It's not exhibiting the right signs for that. I think we have at least another two weeks to sort this out."

That was a generous estimate. Sevana would bet they actually had less time than that. Again, not something she was going to say out loud. She did not need panicking gods hovering.

"I'm glad you're here," Master continued, gesturing the god to take a seat. "Sevana tells me that you're willing to build us a to-scale model of the volcano to experiment with? Excellent. We're not quite ready for that yet. There's a small experiment that I would like to run first."

Cheng-Huang promptly sat, his attention centered on Master. "What type?"

Master put his chopsticks aside and fell into lecturing mode. "You are familiar with the human smelting process of metals? Good, good. You've seen how metals blend and sometimes become stronger because of it? Like steel."

"I have, of course."

"That makes this easier to explain. Magical properties are similar to blending metals in order to form a stronger whole. Unlike what one would think, however, doing an equal amount of each does not mean that that it will blend well. I cannot, say, put in fifty percent of my magical power in with fifty percent of yours and expect it to magically be in perfect harmony. The balance is usually off. Do you follow?"

"I do, Artifactor, and have seen many occasions where that is the case."

"Excellent, it saves tedious explanations on my part. Now, I have never worked with divine power individually like this. It's a complete first for me and Sevana. I would like to try different blends with just us two, to give me something of a baseline, so that I can start running simulations and calculations. Once I have an idea of what might work best, we'll start adding in the others' magical power."

Cheng-Huang nodded agreeably. "How do you wish to proceed?"

"Since what we truly need to build are different types of magical barriers, let's focus on that spell first. I assume that you have divine barriers you can erect?"

"Of course, it is a basic for us."

"Good, good." Master cast about, finally picking up a peach from the table, and set it on his open palm between them. "Cast your spell at seventy-five percent strength and then hold it open."

Cheng-Huang obediently cast a circular barrier that encased the peach on all sides. Sevana snatched her box lens up and held it to her eye so that she could properly read power levels as they did this. In the magnifying glass of the lens, the power that wrapped around the peach was jade green, the consistency of it like a fine mist that had yet to form into a proper fog.

Then Master's power flowed into it, blood-red human magic in its pure form. Sevana expected a collision of magic, but instead the human magic seemed to adhere to the divine. Oh? Interesting reaction, and one that she noted carefully, as that was vital information to know.

"We'll close the barrier on the count of three," Master ordered. "One, two, three."

In near unison, they both cemented the spell and the barrier snapped into place.

Master lifted it closer to his eye, then without looking held his hand out to Sevana, snapping his fingers in silent command. She knew what he wanted and handed over her box lens without a fuss. Putting it to his eye, Master took a closer look at it and gave a dissatisfied hum. "No. It's slightly unstable. I think the ratio if off."

Sevana plucked the peach out of his hand, put it on the ground, and reached for the heaviest tool she had at hand. It turned out to be a wrench and she swung it at the peach without hesitation. The barrier cracked under the force of it before disintegrating completely.

Cheng-Huang winced. "I think that ratio is not correct."

"You could say that," Master agreed mildly. He reached down to pick up the peach and examined it. "Although it did protect the peach, so arguably, the barrier did its job. Alright, let's try this again. Sixty percent divine this time."

They repeated the process, this time with Master adding in more of his power than before. Sevana could tell seconds after the barrier was complete that this had not been the right direction to go. This barrier was weaker than the previous version and she could see visible arcs as the power fluctuated in the barrier. "No."

This time Cheng-Huang did the honors by flicking it hard with a finger, breaking the barrier like one would fragile glass.

"Less human," Master declared. "Cheng-Huang, eight-five percent, please."

The god complied with a shrug, Master adding in the other fifteen percent. Sevana took back her box lens to take a look. This time it looked stronger, more stable, less like glass and more opaque like a barrier should. "It looks much better. I hesitate to say this, but I think it's still not quite right."

Master borrowed the lens to take a look for himself. "You're correct, not quite right. Very close, though. I think if we did a ratio of eighty-six and fourteen, we'd be right on the money."

That ratio sounded familiar to her for some reason. When it clicked where she knew it from, Sevana snorted. "What are we making here, magical pykrete?"

Cheng-Huang sat up a little, interest perking. "What is that?"

"Pykrete is a strange building substance that humans invented," Master explained, still staring at the barrier through the lens. "It's eighty-six percent wood pulp and fourteen percent frozen water. Strangely tough when solidified. Of course, you can't use it outside of a cold country, but it's so thick and impenetrable that an arrow can barely scratch it. I knew one fool that actually built a boat out of it. It lasted him through a good section of the winter months, as long as he took short trips in it."

"It's great for buildings, though, and walls," Sevana opined. "As long as you don't have a source for heat anywhere nearby, it lasts a long time. The ratio you two are proposing is what reminded me of it."

"I think that's exactly the ratio we need to use, too." Master finally set the box lens aside and handed the peach to Sevana. "Try hitting it again."

She promptly did so. Destruction was fun sometimes and she had quite a few frustrations to burn off. It felt inherently satisfying, swinging at it. This time the wrench did not destroy the barrier in one go, and in fact, it barely created a hairline fracture in it. Not dismayed by this, she grinned and hit it again, harder. The crack grew a little more pronounced, but it held firm. "I don't think a wrench is going to break this."

"I don't think it will either. And I think an adjustment to our ratio will prevent even that small crack from forming." Master sat back, satisfied. "I'll have to do a more conclusive test later, but that gives me the information I need. Thank you for the cooperation, Cheng-Huang."

"Not at all, Artifactor. I am relieved to see progress, no matter how small." Cheng-Huang openly hesitated, studying Sevana from the corner of his eye before daring to ask, "You said that you wish to form 'barriers.' I take that to mean that you have a plan in place, then?"

"We have a theory in place," Sevana corrected. "I told you part of it, did I not? We've since tried to define the parameters. We believe that cordoning off the island with a barrier and forcing the lava to flow toward the outer edge is feasible."

"Lava in and of itself doesn't have much force, you see," Master put in as an aside, picking up the peach to stare thoughtfully at it once more. "What makes it dangerous is the extreme heat that it carries. Granted, once it starts moving, it can flow very quickly. We have a record of a volcano emptying out within an hour once it erupted."

"This is actually to our benefit," Sevana observed. "It means that we don't have to keep a barrier around it for very long. Once the lava is settled into place, we can leave it there for a few hours to make sure that it cools, then release it. It will lessen the magical burden we're carrying." And they needed all of the help they could get in that quarter. Even with five of them actively pouring magic in, there was too much demand.

"Aside from the lava, we will also place a barrier around the volcano itself, to enclose the ash that will spill out of the top." Master poked at the peach, mouth pursing into a frown. "That is the part that I am uncertain of, to be frank, as most of the explosive force we'll face will be from the top. A great deal of gases and force will come from there, so it will be the hardest to contain, and arguably the most dangerous. I wish there was a way to test this in small scale before we commit one way or another."

Sevana opened her mouth, paused, then closed it thoughtfully. "Surely we can. We have three deities and a Fae, after all."

"I can replicate the island and volcano," Cheng-Huang offered. "The effects of the volcano might be a little challenging to replicate."

"Aran can do it, I think, if you need help." Sevana had seen him do things that were similar, at least. "It should be close enough for us to gauge things with."

"Then we'll wait for him to come back before trying it. In the meantime, Cheng-Huang, if you can start work on the volcano itself? That way we'll have it ready to go when Arandur returns." Master rubbed at his chin. "I have a terrible suspicion that we won't have the power necessary to contain both ash and lava at the same time."

Sevana had initially believed they could, but after discussing numbers with Master, she was harboring some of the same doubts. "But the only other option we have is drilling in the side of the volcano and draining the lava out so that it can't explode. And how are we going to manage that?"

"I'm not saying we have to do go that route, sweetling, I'm just saying that the plan we have right now might not work. Let's not close off our minds to other possibilities." To Cheng-Huang, Master offered a relaxed smile. "Not to worry. We often go through at least one or two plans before we hit the magic one that actually solves the problem."

That was true, most of the time. It was part of why Sevana enjoyed her job—she could never predict how things were going to work out.

But really, if they couldn't contain the ash cloud then what alternative did that really leave them?

Cheng-Huang seemed satisfied by that answer, so he bid them a simple, "I will take my leave, then. Call me again if you require assistance."

"We will." Master kept up the benign smile until he was gone before turning to Sevana. "Sweetling. I've lost count, all things considered. What plan are we on now?"

"Plan S," she sighed, "for Screwed."

12

'Ash' wasn't just smoke from the liquid hot rock trapped inside of a volcano. It was actually coarse particles made from tiny fragments of rock, minerals, and volcanic glass. It looked like grains of sand—very fine particles that were powdery in nature. If the wind got hold of it, because of its light nature, it could be carried hundreds of miles out in all directions. Near the volcano it would collect in thick deposits, making life difficult in more ways than one. Never mind the cleanup effort it would take to get all of that ash out again, but it posed serious health concerns to any living creature on the isle as well.

That of course didn't take into account the force necessary for ash to be propelled out of the volcano to begin with. The eruptions were normally so severe that it would shatter the solid rock magma chamber and a good portion of the volcanic mountain itself. Doing that would send massive chunks of rock in every conceivable direction. On an isle as small as this? It would consume the majority of it and make the isle completely uninhabitable for decades.

Sevana sat cross-legged on the floor, charts and logs and numbers spread about her, absently chewing on the edge of her pencil in frustration. The numbers did not look promising. Now that she had reference books (thanks to Master) to confer with, she realized that she had underestimated the force behind volcanic explosions. At first she thought that the problem was not in having enough power, but in being able to blend the three gods' powers well enough. Now she realized the true problem was having enough magic to do the job. The lava they could contain. Sevana was absolutely positive on that.

The ash cloud and explosion? Not likely.

From outside sounded a general exclamation from several voices overlapping, some screaming, and not a few curses. Then it sounded like a herd of elephants panicking and running in every direction. What in the world?! Sevana scrambled up to her feet and bolted for the door. Wrenching it open, she got a foot outside when she caught sight of the shadow stretched out over the ground, there and gone in a second. There was no mistaking that very distinctive shape, and a smile lit her face.

Their dragon had arrived.

Knowing that Aran must be nearby as well, she headed at a trot for the unofficial landing area. Or tried to. There were so many panicking people that got in her way that Sevana found herself tripping every three steps. Fighting her way through them annoyed her, but not enough to dim her relief that Aran had safely returned. Even for a Fae, entering dragon territory during hatching season was dangerous.

Her skimmer was already on the ground, Aran heading her direction. When he caught sight of her, he waved an arm over his head in greeting, a smug smile on his face.

As well he should. She waved back and called out, "Good job! How hard was it?"

"Harder than I hoped, easier than I expected?" he offered, coming to a stop in front of her. "They were all interested in the bribe the gods sent along with me, but none of them were keen on the idea of trying to talk to an upset phoenix in her sleep. Apparently that breaks all sorts of godly protocols."

Sevana bet it did. "But you convinced one of them."

"It took some convincing, but yes. He's a younger fledgling, hoping to make a reputation for himself, or so I gathered. His name is Kenelm. I told him to land at the base of the mountain."

"It's the only clear space for him," Sevana agreed. As they talked, her eyes roamed over him, taking stock. He looked tired, as expected, and perhaps more strung out than he wanted her to see. Aran had this strange tendency to want to always appear strong in front of her, which was silly—no one could be strong all of the time. She'd rag him for that except she had the same tendency. "I think you need a hot meal and sleep."

"After we get a phoenix settled."

That wasn't an argument from him, but an agreement. Satisfied, she struck off toward the mountain and caught him up to speed as they walked. "Master arrived shortly after you left. He was able to bring the references that I need so we have better data and numbers to crunch."

"How does it look now? Will your plan work?"

"Part of it will. Part of it…it doesn't look very viable."

Aran frowned down at her. "So do we have a backup plan?"

"We do, although how we'll pull it off is beyond me." She eyed Aran sideways, a stray thought entering her mind. The Fae were masters at the different elements, so didn't it follow that he might be able to do their backup plan safely? Aran stated earlier that he had doubts on whether he could do it or not, but if fortified with human magic, it might be more possible.

Just how fireproof was a Fae?

They rounded the last bend of the road and found the dragon sitting there, waiting for them. He was indeed a fledgling, half the size of a full grown adult. Which meant he was the size of a small cabin. His skin still retained the paleness of a child, so that he was a sky blue, gold eyes alight with curiosity and perhaps a touch of nervousness. Around his neck he proudly wore his 'bribe,' a thick gold chain long enough to become more of a collar for his adult body, when he eventually grew into it. Considering his youth, this might be the first piece of his gold collection.

Sevana greeted him with politeness, as any sane person would do in the presence of a dragon.

"Kenelm," Aran greeted, "this is Sellion, of the Fae."

Kenelm extended his neck out to get a closer whiff of her. "You smell human and Fae."

"I'm human by birth, Fae by blood," Sevana explained. "It's a little complicated."

Drawing back, Kenelm gave a low hum that signaled…

thoughtfulness, perhaps?

If he wasn't curious enough to ask questions, Sevana had no intention of volunteering the story. She pressed on. "Arandur explained to you that we need you to enter Dreamscape and speak to the phoenix in the volcano. Did he tell you what we need conveyed to her?"

"He did not," Kenelm denied. "What words must I speak?"

Dragons as a whole tended to be a little arrogant in talking with humans. To converse with one so polite was very odd. Was this because of his age and trying to make sure he earned the right to keep that gold necklace? Or was it because he was in the presence of a Fae and a quasi-Fae? Either way, Sevana decided not to question it. "First, express our concern for her. Assure her that we wish to bring her out of the volcano."

Aran gave her a look of mild surprise. She knew why. That wasn't what the other three gods wanted at all, but what they wanted was unrealistic. They couldn't keep the phoenix confined inside of the volcano with no repercussions. To make the situation permanently safe, the first step was drawing her out of there.

"Tell her that in order to give us time to find the right method to release her without blowing the volcano sky-high, she needs to be perfectly still. Limit her own power as much as possible. Every time she even thinks of twitching, the volcano reacts, and that impacts how much time we have until it explodes." Seeing how intently the dragon watched her, and a little worried she might have given him too much to say at once, she added, "You don't have to repeat my words exactly. Tell her the important things."

"You wish to bring her out of volcano, she needs to be still, limit her power, give you time to find solution," Kenelm summarized concisely.

Relieved he could recite that so casually, she smiled at him. "Precisely."

"I will tell her." The dragon looked around, and not seeing a flatter spot than the one he sat in, he curled up with his nose resting on top of his tail and closed his eyes with a fixed determination. Kenelm drew in a deep breath, blew it out in a scorchingly hot gust of wind, and settled.

Sevana blinked at him in astonishment. "He can fall asleep that fast?" she whispered to Aran.

"Entering Dreamscape and sleeping is different for dragons," Aran explained softly.

"Is this one of those things that you would explain to me, but attempting to would frustrate me and make my head explode?" she ventured.

Aran shrugged, a little amused, which she took as agreement. It wasn't the first time they'd run into situations like this. Resigned, she let it lie.

In three seconds flat, the dragon's eyes opened again. "She will not speak with me."

Sevana stared at him with open-mouthed dismay. "Whyever not?!"

Was it her imagination, or was the young dragon pouting? "She claims I have no authority. She will only speak to the one in charge."

Well that was all fine and dandy of her to say so, but even a quasi-Fae couldn't enter Dreamscape. Or could she? Sevana turned to Aran, the only one of them remotely an authority on this. "Can I enter it?"

He rubbed at the back of his neck, looking thoughtful. "You can, and you can't. It's a little complicated."

"Un-complicate it," she ordered.

Aran gave her that look, the one that said she was amusing him on some level. "A dragon can bring you into Dreamscape so that your presence is there, but you can't communicate with anyone but him. He can hear you, you can hear him, but to anyone else you are just a figure standing there."

How would that make any difference, then? "Does the phoenix know this?"

"She does," Kenelm assured her.

"I think it's more she needs to see with her own eyes who's negotiating with her," Aran posited. "Either way, Kenelm is our ambassador, there's no way around that."

Kenelm's chest puffed up at the word 'ambassador.' Sevana eyed that reaction and wondered if Aran had used that term specifically to soothe the young dragon's figurative feathers. He likely had; he was nice that way. "Alright, well, I'm game to go in. But how do we manage that?"

"You must be dragon touched." Kenelm took in a slight breath and deliberately blew it over her.

Even though he had carefully controlled the heat in his breath, she still felt like she had entered a steam bath, or a hot spring, as that breath gusted over her.

"Now, lay down next to him," Aran instructed as he took her shoulders and guided her to lean against the dragon's side. "I'll guard both of you while you're in Dreamscape."

Sevana didn't think anyone would dare to mess with her while she was unconscious, but it was true that the volcano was still unpredictable, so she felt better that Aran was watching her back. She deliberately closed her eyes and tried to keep herself mentally open to the dragon.

Before she could think to ask if there was anything she needed to do, between one heartbeat and the next, she was in a very alien landscape.

Turning slowly, she took stock. She was no longer on an isle, but a flat expanse of earth that stretched out past sight. The land curved around the edges so that it led into small hills and farther on, mountains. Seemingly touching the ground was a planet, dominating the night sky, with smaller moons in orbit around it. The planet was streaked in creams and oranges and tans, looking rather uninhabitable.

This was Dreamscape?

There was an eerie tone to this landscape, a sense of wrongness that Sevana could feel, but not define. It felt uncomfortable, not painful, but as if she were in exactly the wrong place at the wrong time. She felt as much out of place as a fish in a desert, and the feeling grew the longer she stood there.

Kenelm sat upright next to her, looking very comfortable in this space, but also taut with nervous tension. Then again, the phoenix had kicked him out of here once already; he had every right to be worried she'd do it again.

From the distance, in between two of the smaller hills, a figure appeared and glided effortlessly toward them. Sevana had had a notion or two of what a phoenix looked like, and this culture's idea of a phoenix was very different, apparently. It had the head of a pheasant, the body of a mandarin duck, the tail of a peacock, the legs of a crane, and the wings of a swallow. Such a mismatch of birds should have looked very odd, but somehow it looked right, rather elegant. She glowed red and gold in the night sky and came to rest several feet away, head cocked in query.

Her mouth did not move, but Sevana gained the distinct impression that she was speaking, and so did not try to interrupt.

Kenelm turned his head slightly to address her. "She wishes to know who you are."

"Relate these words exactly," Sevana requested. "I am Sellion, daughter of the Fae. I am human, Artifactor Sevana Warren. I speak for both races."

Kenelm did not open his mouth and yet he faced the phoenix as if speaking. Sevana began to understand why Aran had said that she would not be able to hear or speak with anyone other than Kenelm. Dreamscape communications happened on a completely different level, one that she couldn't even perceive.

"She is Feng-Huang," Kenelm related to her. "She hears you."

Meaning, they could finally start negotiating? Sevana phrased her words carefully. "You are aware that the volcano you lie in has become active?"

Kenelm dutifully repeated this before responding, "She is aware."

"You are aware that if you twitch in your sleep, or let your power flow, the volcano reacts to this?"

"She was not aware of this. Only that it was becoming more reactive."

"Your presence in the volcano is what is making it awaken prematurely," Sevana explained.

Kenelm's head rose a notch in interest. "Feng-Huang says that she cannot do anything about this. In her sleeping state, she has very limited control over her own power or body."

"We are aware of this," Sevana assured them both. "What we wish of you is that you keep as still as possible, limit your power as much as you can, until we can draw you out of the volcano."

Feng-Huang finally gave a noticeable reaction. The moment Kenelm had repeated those words, she flung her wings out, head rising in excitement.

"She demands to know if you are sincere, if you truly wish to free her."

"It's not a matter of wishing," Sevana denied. "We *have* to free her. If we leave her where she is, the volcano will blow for sure, and then we'll all be in a world of trouble."

The phoenix was very happy to hear this. So happy, in fact, that she lifted into the air and flew in a small, tight circle.

The sight made Sevana smile a little, although she couldn't blame the goddess for her excitement. In her shoes, Sevana would be just as ecstatic. "All we request of her is to be as still as possible, to limit her presence as much as she can, for a week or so. I promise we'll get her out as soon as we can figure out how."

"She promises to do all that she can," Kenelm relayed. "Also, she requests that I stay and keep her updated on a daily basis so that she knows what is happening. Her perceptions of the outside world are cut off."

It struck Sevana that actually, she needed Kenelm to stay in more ways than one. When it did come time to free the phoenix, they would need to coordinate with her, so that things didn't spiral out of control. "I too request that you stay, Kenelm. At least until this problem is sorted."

Kenelm was a merchant at heart, or at least a greedy teenager, as he eyed both females shrewdly. "And what will you pay me for this?"

Sevana had no idea, as she didn't have the gold on hand to pay him anything. Fortunately, Feng-Huang responded before she could. Whatever price she named made Kenelm's eyes light up and a rumbling purr, like a contented cat, rumbled out of his chest.

"I take it she'll pay you handsomely for your help," Sevana

drawled.

"We have reached a bargain," Kenelm agreed, tail flicking in a happy rhythm.

Well, the phoenix was a goddess, and one reportedly over wealth and good luck. It would make sense she'd have the goods to pay for a dragon's services. Sevana was perfectly willing to let her pay for some of the expenses. "Then, have we all reached an understanding?"

"We have," Kenelm assured her.

"Then tell Feng-Huang I will relay progress through you."

Without a by-your-leave, Kenelm brought them both abruptly back into the real world. Sevana opened her eyes to find that she was still leaning against the dragon's leathery side, with Aran leaning over her.

"Nice trip?" he asked her with a knowing smile on his face.

"That is the oddest thing I have ever done," Sevana stated, head still spinning a little. "I don't think I care to repeat it, either."

Aran offered her a hand up and she took it, regaining her feet. It was truly strange, but after being in Dreamscape, the real world looked a little different to her. Greener, more inviting, but also odd in some undefinable way.

"Did the phoenix agree?" he asked in concern.

"She did," Sevana responded. Taking in a breath, she tried to settle back into reality by giving herself a shake. It didn't quite work, but she forged on regardless. "Now the real work begins."

13

Sevana and Aran came back to find Master had taken her spot, sitting cross-legged on the floor, surrounded by books and her notes. He was not studying any of them, however, but was quickly sketching something out in one of his own notebooks, muttering numbers and elements to himself as he did so.

Quite used to this sight, and knowing better than to interrupt, Sevana skirted around to his side and leaned over a shoulder to get a look at what he was doing. The design was similar to something she had seen before—not in real life, but in another drawing of Master's. It looked like a pedestal, one designed for water to flow freely through its base, with smaller versions of it that magically connected. The top of the pedestal had three clear markers, defined by magic circles, and it was those designs that Master was refining in great detail. Aside from the spell invocation, the design was a perfect match for something that Master had built before.

"Appleby's flood ten years ago."

"Oh?" Master blinked up at her and gave her a quick grin. "You remember that story? Good, saves explanation."

Aran pointed to his own chest, head cocked in query. "I wasn't there, so I can't remember anything. What's this about?"

"I recognize the design," Sevana explained. "He's used something similar to this before to hold back the flood waters from destroying a city. It was something he'd barely had a day to concoct, so it wasn't as refined looking as this is."

"And it's not actually the same design," Master confirmed, still steadily drawing. "I had to tweak it quite a bit to incorporate different inputs of magic, and to make it strong enough to withstand extreme heat. The original design didn't have to do anything like that."

Even with the modifications she was seeing, there was one glaring hole in his design that Sevana saw. "Now where are you going to get the Dwarven stone in order to build this thing? We don't have anything like that up here."

"Now why would I need Dwarven stone when I have a deity that builds things?" Master outright smirked at her.

"Cheng-Huang?" Sevana pursed her lips together, saw what he was thinking, and let out an admiring whistle. "Neat way to solve that problem."

"Isn't it? I admire my own cleverness."

Aran lifted a hand with a resigned sigh. "Still out of the loop, here."

"Sorry," Master apologized with a chuckle. "You're around so often these days, and have picked up so much from listening to us, that I forget sometimes you can't understand everything we're saying. The problem that we've faced from day one is how to incorporate the magic and divine power from everyone. It's all radically different, after all, but we can't leave one person out just because his magic power doesn't jive with the others'. We don't have that kind of luxury. Cheng-Huang's power, out of all of them, was the most challenging to incorporate. His ability is more in building things, after all; his divine power doesn't flow out smoothly."

At that point Aran caught on. "You're going to have him build these pedestals?"

"Precisely so. That way his magic is active and incorporated as we use them, flowing freely with everyone else's power."

Aran gave him a judicious nod. "That is clever."

"Why thank you, Arandur, kind of you to say so." Master gave another chuckle that was more like a cackle. "Now, how this works is, aside from Cheng-Huang's stone, we'll have the sea run through the pedestals and power some of them. These smaller pedestals? They work as boosters all the way around the shields, so that they feed and strengthen each other. Individually, they'd fall, but because they'll be connected together, they'll stand much firmer. The only downside to this is that I can't include Arandur's power. I'm having trouble just blending the three gods together; putting Fae magic in that mix will not help matters."

With that problem solved, Sevana did the math again in her head and frowned when she realized it didn't quite cover the distance. "But still, the force of the explosion...."

"It will not contain that, most likely." Master lost his joviality and stared off into the distance. "Of course, it's also very hard to calculate how much force we're going to have to contain. There's no way to really know how strong of an explosion we're facing. All we can do is guess based upon other volcanoes."

"But we'll make a batch of small versions of this to try on our scaled volcano?" Sevana verified. "Just to see how it will play out?"

"I think that prudent, don't you? Too many times the numbers make perfect sense on paper only to work out completely different in real life. We cannot afford any mishaps here. I should have enough to-scale pedestals ready to go by the morning, enough to run a quick test on, and then we can adjust from there."

"Seems like a viable plan to me," Aran admitted. "But are you sure you don't need my magic?"

"There's a reason why I'm not fretting much on somehow working your magic in. I might need it for a backup plan, or in a separate shield, to help cover the distance."

"Ah, I see. Then just tell me where you need my help."

"I will," Master assured him. Shaking his head, he shelved that problem for a moment and asked, "How did the talk with our phoenix go?"

"Well," Aran responded, dropping a tad too heavily into a chair. He was more exhausted than he was letting on, and Sevana gave him an hour before he finally admitted that and settled for a nap somewhere. "Our dragon ambassador had to bring Sevana into Dreamscape with him—"

Master's eyebrows shot into his hairline. "Really, sweetling? I've done that before. It's subtly unnerving."

"That's exactly what it is," she agreed sourly. "I'm not doing it again, either."

"Funny, I said exactly the same thing after my first experience. So far it has remained my last, and I'm quite glad of that. But the phoenix has agreed to cooperate, then? Good, good. I'm relieved to hear it."

"I'm not sure how much good her cooperation is going to do," Sevana sighed, "as her simple presence in there is causing all sorts of problems, but at least this way we're not living in fear that having her turn over in her sleep will set the volcano off. Now, what to do next? Speak with Cheng-Huang?"

"Precisely," Master agreed, already returning to his drawings. "Now that we have rough estimates of what the volcano's force will be, we need him to set up a version for us. I think a 1:100 ratio would be best."

He wanted an eight foot miniature volcano to work off of, eh? Sevana thought about it and realized that was likely the best way to scale down. Any smaller than that, and the magical scaling became hideously complex. "I'll inform him. And find a safe place to conduct the test. There's not a lot of free land here."

"I did notice that on the way in. Go and report back, these won't take me too long to make."

They likely wouldn't. In fact, he'd probably be done by dinner. With that estimate in mind, she turned smartly about and headed out the door. Aran, of course, was on her heels, but she had a different task for him. "Check in with Da-Chin, would you? Make sure that the evacuation plans for the village is going smoothly. I haven't had time to follow up with him about it."

"Why don't you?" Aran asked, a trifle reluctantly.

"Because the man's a little scared of me and likely won't tell me the truth if there are problems," she responded promptly and with a good dose of exasperation. Aran's normal level of protectiveness had reached an all new high since her kidnapping. If she didn't kick him out of this mood of his soon, she was likely to murder him herself. "Go on."

He didn't like it, but apparently realized that staying meant his execution, as he took himself off toward the village proper.

Sevana heaved out a breath. With the proper amount of thumbscrews and a judicious amount of lye, she would admit that she was fond of her Fae friend. But that didn't mean she could stand being constantly shadowed by him like this. Sevana was not a people person; she needed time alone for at least a portion of the day. Aran usually understood that and gave her space, but this place set him on edge.

Shaking her head, she set him aside and went for the docks. There she found Cheng-Huang, laboring over the flying ship that they had designed. Sevana was pleased to see that the physical body of it was complete, if a little rough around the corners. There wasn't even a trace of stain or paint to be found, just roughhewn wood. Cheng-Huang stood in the prow of the ship, and if tone was anything to go by, cursing the ship's ancestry soundly. "Trouble?"

He looked up and for the first time in a long while seemed happy to see her. "Artifactor. Excellent timing, I was thinking I needed to call you. The ship meets the specifications well enough, but I can't seem to get it airborne. At all."

Sevana frowned. "Help me on."

Cheng-Huang extended a hand and helped balance her as she clambered on board. Sevana promptly bent over the navigational display, but of course the top didn't tell her much. All of the instruments that she had drawn out were beautifully captured in crystal, hardwood, and copper. He had duplicated everything exactly and was sensible enough to not add any embellishment. Satisfied with his workmanship, Sevana ducked and twisted so that she was underneath where she could see the spell insignias.

The problem was obvious at a glance.

"Your levitation spell's not activating," she announced with some perplexity. Tracing the insignia, she found that she couldn't follow it fully, as parts of it were written in his native tongue. Sevana had so far been fortunate that everyone knew trader's tongue and so could speak to her in that language. But this was beyond her. "I can't read what you've done here. Break this down for me, what did you put into the spell?"

"My own power, of course."

Sevana waited for him to elaborate. When he didn't, she twisted so that she could meet his eyes all while keeping her back on the deck. "Is that it?"

"That is all that is needed, surely," he protested, perplexed and frustrated.

Obviously not. "Cheng-Huang, as a deity, you automatically can fly?"

"Of course."

"So you think that because you can fly, anything you make and imbue with your power can as well?"

"Of course," he repeated, patience snapping.

"Then your bridges and buildings must be hazardous to walk on," she quipped dryly. "Seeing as they like to randomly fly about."

He opened his mouth on a hot retort, froze when her meaning penetrated, and growled wordlessly.

"I do not think your power or spells are as sentient as you believe them to be," she continued, returning to her original position so she could study the spells better. "They don't have the ability to realize what you intend, just what they are designed to do."

"I copied what you told me to do," he said in a near whine.

"Yes, but I didn't tell you what to do with your power. I didn't think that just building power was the only one you had, so I expected to see a different type mixed in here." Struck by a thought, she twisted to see out again. "How is it that you can fly, anyway, if it's not tied into your power?"

"It is a special prerogative given to us when we ascend immortality."

"So it's tied into your physical makeup, not something linked to your power."

"That is correct." When he said it, Cheng-Huang growled again, sounding like a wounded bear. "I should have realized. Of course it wouldn't work."

The nice thing about Cheng-Huang was that unlike the other gods, he was quick on the uptake. At least with him, Sevana was saved from tedious explanations. "In my design, I have the main levitation spell powered by dragon's breath."

Cheng-Huang's attention snapped to her. "Is that so."

Knowing very well what he was plotting, Sevana suggested, "Bring lots of gold, something he can wear. Young dragons are very bribable, and this one will be more inclined to barter because he's stuck here waiting anyway."

"I'll go speak with him today," Cheng-Huang swore. "Is dragon's breath all you use?"

"Heavens no, I have two other magicks in the mix as well. Captured sunlight and of course my own human power plays a small part. But in this case, the ship is much too large, captured sunlight will not be enough to make it move. I think it's going to be your power that will propel it forward. But obviously you don't have the right type of magic for levitation, so we'll have to play with ratios of dragon's breath, captured sunlight, and your own power to find that magical happy spot."

Cheng-Huang extended a hand, which she took, regaining her feet. "Before you go, we'd like to run that scaled experiment. Can you find a spot somewhere to build our miniature volcano with? We're doing a 1:100 ratio."

"I already have an area in mind," Cheng-Huang admitted to her absently. "Just there."

Sevana followed his pointing finger and gave an approving nod. It was on the rockiest part of the beach, far away from both docks and village, so that if something went wrong, the damage would be minimal. "That looks fine. I'll notify Master and we'll meet you back here after dinner. It'll take that long before we have all of the pieces ready to test with."

"After dinner is fine," Cheng-Huang assured her. "I'll work on the ship until then."

Satisfied that things were well enough in motion, Sevana hopped back out of the ship and onto the dock, returning to her workroom. If she was very, very careful then she might be able to help make those miniature markers.

No, on second thought, maybe not.

When she returned to the workroom, Master already had twelve of the twenty-four miniature boosters crafted out of stone, with a main pedestal that was the size of his clenched fist. He greeted her with, "Where's the vial of Arandur's captured magic?"

So she was to play assistant and gopher to him. Sevana felt like she had returned to her student days, but even she had to admit that was the safest way for her to help right now. They didn't have the time to do things over. With a long, resigned sigh, she fetched what was needed, handling elements with care and prepping them so that Master could apply them. They were a good team after working with each other for over a decade, and so the task went smoothly.

Raising her head, she worked her head back and forth on her shoulders, getting some of the kinks out and found Aran leaning inside the door frame. "How long have you been there?"

"A while. The two of you were so close to finishing I didn't want to bother you." He knelt and picked up one of the boosters. "They almost look like toys."

Master wasn't at all offended by this observation and laughed. "They're about the right size for that, aren't they?"

Peering at it closely, Aran studied it from top to bottom, flipping it in every direction. "How are you doing this? Scaling the magic down to match, I mean."

"That's the trickiest part," Sevana said as she stretched her arms over her head. "Hence why we've been talking numbers most of the day. Some of the power we're using in the design, like yours, we have to specially filter before using. Others we can only use a trace of it, just a fraction of the available power, to make it the right balance." Sevana's mouth screwed up to the side. "At least I hope it's right."

"It's right, it's right," Master assured her with a casual wave of the hand. "Don't worry so much, sweetling. What we need to worry about is whether the volcano's power is scaled correctly and if our test will work."

"I believe the volcano is correct," Aran informed them. "I came to tell you that Cheng-Huang is ready when you are."

"Really? Then let's gather all of this up and go." So saying, Master grabbed a handful of boosters and the pedestal, leaving the rest of them up to Sevana and Aran.

She could only grab three in each hand, but between them, they managed to grab everything they needed and headed for the rocky area of the beach. Cheng-Huang was not there waiting for them, but tinkering on his ship. There were no insults being hurled at the ship's ancestors, which Sevana took for a good sign. The god noticed their approach and left the ship readily enough, a smile on his face.

"It's working better?" Sevana asked.

"It will at least levitate now," Cheng-Huang informed her with a relieved nod of acknowledgement. "Although the navigational systems are fighting me."

"I'll help you after this," she promised. "Assuming this goes well." Turning, she regarded the volcano and found that she had no complaints about how it looked, at least. It was an exact replica of the cinder cone standing behind her. Taking her box lens out of a pocket, she lifted it to her eye and studied it more closely. The power ratings seemed more or less on par as well, scaled down as they were. "An excellent model, Cheng-Huang."

The god beamed at her. "I did my best. I'm not sure how accurate this will be, however, as no one is able to accurately determine how powerful the volcano truly is."

That was the burning question.

"Still," Master said as he sat his markers down, "I think you did a close enough job for this test to tell us what we need to know. And that's all I can ask for. Sweetling, I'll put the pedestal here, you space the markers out to the left, I'll go right. Arandur, give me yours."

Knowing what he wanted done, Sevana placed the boosters evenly out so that they formed a giant ring around the volcanic base, each marker in line of sight with its neighbor. Stepping back, she eyeballed it, then came back to make a few minor adjustments. "Are we connected, Master?"

Stepping back to the pedestal, Master touched a finger to it, putting just enough human magic in to make it power up. "We are. Cheng-Huang, if you will touch the pedestal with just a trace of power? The barest amount you can put in, please. Yes, that's perfect, thank you."

A shimmering barrier lit up and covered the volcano like a dome. Sevana reached over and gave an experimental tap to it with her fist, and it rang hollowly but held firm. "Well, it's not fragile enough to shatter under light pressure. Maybe we got the ratios right."

"I told you we did," Master said with some exasperation. "Don't you trust my math?"

"Master, I can't read that chicken scratch you call handwriting well enough to figure out if they're even supposed to be numbers," she retorted.

That made Aran laugh, as he had the same problem.

Master gave them both the stink eye and straightened his jacket with a jerk, along with his dignity.

Cheng-Huang came to his rescue and inquired, "Shall I let the volcano explode now?"

"Yes, please do," Master responded, and gave Sevana another sniff before properly turning his attention to the experiment.

To Sevana's magical eye, she couldn't quite follow everything that Cheng-Hunag was doing power-wise, but she was able to get the gist of it. He was combining rock and a mortar-like steam in a compact version that contained the same sort of pressure as a volcano. From the top of the mini-volcano, there was a rumbling sound, a great cloud of ash and steam, and then hot rocks glowing red spewed upwards like fireworks. It was actually rather pretty to watch. As a builder, Cheng-Huang naturally could do forging as well, and the sparks were reminiscent of a forge at work. Sevana was tempted to just enjoy the show but it was her job to make sure the shield was holding, so she watched it with an eagle's eye.

At first nothing looked out of place. The ash and lava were well contained by the barrier, although it got difficult to see anything after a minute, as the ash obscured everything. It became this dense fog of grey that was impossible to see through. Perhaps because of that,

Sevana missed the first hairline fracture that developed in the shield until it split open with a sharp, cracking noise.

"Shut it down!" she ordered sharply.

Cheng-Huang promptly did so but it was a little too late by that point. The pressure was enough to make the shield crack like an egg, and it exploded into a fine shimmer of dust motes that quickly dissipated.

Swearing, Sevana skipped back several steps to avoid getting a face full of ash or lava all over her boots. While this might be a mockup, the elements of it were real enough, and she didn't want to be near even a mini-volcano. It was just as well she did, as the lava was quick to pour out, heading for the water's edge where she had been standing.

"I think," Master said faintly, "we'll need to make some adjustments."

14

They tweaked and adjusted and modified through most of the night, but the answer came down to this: they just didn't have the power. They could contain part of the volcanic explosion, but not all of it, and there was little getting around that.

In the pre-dawn hours, Master threw his journal down and glared at it, as if it were entirely the fault of magic itself for not cooperating as he wanted it to. "We're going to have to devise some way of either draining the volcano before it can explode, or we'll have to make two separate shields. One for the ash, one for the lava itself."

"We're going to have to bring others in if we're making a separate barrier for the ash." Sevana lay flat on her back, wishing she had a cold cloth for her eyes, or that she could just sleep for a few hours. Actually, sleep was preferable. "I think our young dragon friend would be willing to help. He's been remarkably amiable about helping, actually."

"We'd have to devise a completely different shield to incorporate dragon's breath—" Master started out, sounding grumpy and tired.

"No, not really, I have used it before in a barrier. I'd have to modify my design a little to make it more powerful, but the basics of it are already designed."

"Oh? But it will take more than just a dragon."

"That's the problem," Sevana agreed sourly. "Aran, I might need to call in favors. Not now, obviously, but we might need to do that."

"I think considering how far-reaching the effects are, you'll have plenty of people willing to come to your aid," Aran assured them both.

"I think most are waiting to hear if you wish for their help."

"It's who to call, that's the question." Sevana paused and slowly sat up as a thought occurred. "No, before that, let's try something. Master, most volcanoes have underwater vents as well, correct?"

"They do." Master was a little slow to cotton onto her meaning. Likely because he'd been awake and thinking for nearly twenty-four hours. "Underwater would be cooler."

"Automatically so," she agreed.

Aran got that expression on his face that suggested he was trying to be patient. "What are you two scheming now?"

"We talked earlier, about possibly venting the volcano from the outside, draining it before it could explode," Sevana explained rapidly, words nearly tripping over each other. "But I dismissed it because even a Fae can't approach a volcano carelessly, it's just too hot once you get anywhere near the magma. But if you can do it from the ocean floor, it might be cool enough for you."

Aran looked at her steadily. "The Fae ability to speak to elements will let me tunnel through rock, true, but I'm not sure if I can do what you're suggesting."

"I'm not either," Sevana admitted with a shrug. "But can you try? It'll help us tremendously if you can manage it."

He stared thoughtfully at the ground for a long moment. "I can try. At least, I'll contact the Unda and have them show me around, see if this is possible."

"That's all we ask," Master assured him.

With a hand on his knee, Aran pushed himself up to his feet. "I'll be back in a few hours, then, and tell you the verdict."

"Wait, rest first," Master protested. "You've been up as long as we have."

Aran shook his head in gentle disagreement. "The Unda are nocturnal. I have a better chance of getting someone's attention right now, before they retire."

Oh, right, they were. Sevana had forgotten that.

"Sleep," Aran urged as he slid his feet back into his boots, getting ready to head out. "I won't be back anytime soon."

That was likely true. Sevana pulled a pillow and blanket to her, from where they had been folded up in the corner, and snuggled into them. She was barely under the blanket when she was fast asleep.

***

Sevana was up, breakfast (lunch?) consumed, bathed and dressed, and there was still no sign of Aran. Depending on the answer he brought back, the next step would radically change, so Sevana wasn't sure what to work on. It left her with nothing but the flying ship puzzle to sort out, and she couldn't do that until Cheng-Huang returned from wherever he had disappeared to.

Bored and twitchy, she sat at the table and sketched out a miniature shield that could be attached to the ship. Just in case the ash caught up, she wanted it protected. It was a simple design, so it wouldn't take more than an hour to install it. The navigational system, that was going to be the real challenge to work out.

Just after noon, Aran returned. "Good news," Aran informed them as he ducked into the workroom. "I found the vent you told me to look for. Or I should say the Unda already knew where it was and showed me."

Sevana perked up, excited to hear this, until she saw the look on his face. "You say good news but your face says bad news."

He gave her a sour smile that was mostly a grimace. "The bad news is there's no way for me to really approach it. Even underwater, the area is scorching hot. It nearly stripped the skin right off of me."

"That would be problematic," Master agreed drolly. "No way for you to create a lava tube underground, then."

Aran shook his head remorsefully. "I can talk to the stones next to me, of course, and start a tube, but I can't get deep enough in to continue it all the way to the center of the volcano. It's just too hot. Even for a Fae, it's too hot. We have some control of heat, of course, but that much heat? From every angle, at that intensity? I can't shield myself against it for long."

"That plan's a bust, then." Master didn't sound surprised by this, which meant he had been half-expecting this answer.

"Wait, the Unda helped? I assumed they were some distance away. Are they nearby?"

"Quite so. They are, say, about an hour's walk from here if one could walk along the top of the water."

An hour's walk? That was about twice the distance it would take for her to get to Milby, if she were leaving from Big. Hardly any distance at all. No wonder he had made sure to contact them! "I hadn't realized they were that close."

"Neither had I. That's good to know." Master's brows wrinkled into a frown. "I had a thought this morning as I woke up. I have a colleague that worked with me on a similar problem, on a chain of volcanoes in Sa Kao. He's more of an expert on this situation than I am, or at least more experienced."

"Then he'd be the person to call, wouldn't he?" Aran asked as he more or less collapsed into a sitting position on the ground.

"The problem is he's notoriously difficult to get ahold of. It'll likely take me a day or two before I can reach him. I think we have the time for that, or least I hope we do, as he's likely the person to have an answer to our riddle." Master nodded to himself, decided. "I'll try contacting him through the day. In the meantime, I feel that creating our barrier for the lava should still be done. At the very least, we can protect the village and the sea from being destroyed by lava, if it does explode. The ash is hazardous, but we can deal with it separately. Protecting this area from lava is the first priority."

Sevana could agree with that. "In that case…markers?"

"Markers," Master agreed equably. This time he explained to Aran without a prompt, "Someone needs to go out and mark where all of the pedestals and boosters need to be placed. It'll take quite a bit of calculation and experimentation to get the optimum placement figured out, best it's done in advance."

"I'll do that, if you want to start on the build," Sevana offered. It was a task that didn't require much in the way of magic, if any, which was best for her at the moment. They *really* had to sort through a solution to her magic imbalance soon. "Although, really, should we be doing this before we figure out a solution to the ash?"

"Probably not." Master's mouth screwed up to the side in aggravation. "But no good solution comes to mind right off-hand."

Unfortunately. Sevana didn't have a good idea on how to circumvent the problem either.

"Let's focus on protecting everything we can first," Master encouraged, "have that in place, so that if an emergency crops up we can at least mitigate the damage."

It was logical and Sevana could find no fault with it. "I'll try to put the main pedestal within close reach of the village, so we're not frantically running if something does happen."

"Wise of you," Master agreed drolly. "And my aging knees appreciate it."

Sevana normally would have immediately set to it, but one look at Aran told her that he was set on going with her, and he didn't have the energy for that. "I'll need time to gather up all of the tools and things I'll need to set markers. Aran, take a nap while I do that."

He opened his mouth on an automatic protest.

Flinging up a hand to stop him, she said, "It'll take me at least an hour to gather everything I need, it's not something you can help with, and you're dead on your feet. Catch some sleep so that you have the energy to actually be useful later."

"Hard to argue with that," he responded with a shrug. "Alright, fine."

●

Sevana might have taken longer than an hour to gather up what she needed. It was because Master's tools and hers were so disorganized in this tight space, was all. Things were harder to find. And she might have taken a half hour to design something that was more non-magical in nature to mark the land with. Also, they would be out for several hours, right? They might skip dinner altogether. So she packed snacks, just in case. So, all told, it was more like two hours before she was ready to go.

She let Aran sleep until the last possible moment, and he was still a little groggy as they walked out of the village, rubbing the sleep from his eyes. Bad nap, eh? Aran normally sprang awake as if he had been pretending to sleep and was ready to open his eyes at a moment's notice. But even he was not immune to the grogginess that followed after a bad nap. Still, she knew better than to suggest he stay and get more sleep. He wouldn't hear of it. Prior experience had taught her that. Also, she had a feeling that she'd need him. Part of these boosters would need to be placed on the sea floor itself. Sevana didn't have a single device that would let her walk about under the water that didn't require a constant draw on her magical core. Which meant at the moment, she couldn't use any of them.

Not to mention she didn't have any of them here to begin with.

In the time that she'd known him, Sevana had never seen Aran really interact around a large body of water, so she wasn't sure what he'd be able to do. But she was fully confident that he would be able to do something. The man was nothing if not resourceful.

Starting at the base of the volcano, she worked her way steadily around. After making multiple trips around this thing, she knew more or less where the boosters should be placed, so it wasn't like she had to go back and forth willy-nilly. Fortunately, for her calves' sake. All of this hiking about had already given her sore muscles.

It went smoothly enough until she hit the coast. "So, Aran."

"Yes?" He looked at her with a pleasantly blank smile.

"About this barrier. It rather needs to be placed under the water, along the sea floor."

"I would imagine so," Aran agreed easily. "It won't be a very effective barrier otherwise."

"Precisely. Now, as I do not possess gills, I'm going to need some assistance in getting them marked and placed. What trick do you have up your sleeve to get me down there?"

Aran beamed at her. "Not a one."

Blinking, she stared at him, a little slack-jawed. "Seriously?"

"I'm Fae," he reminded her patiently. "While water is part of us, it is not something we have great control over. I certainly can't walk through it like it is air."

"I learn something new every day," she muttered to herself. "Well, this is a fine pickle. I need to get down there. Not just once, but twice."

"Then we must contact the Unda."

That would be the sensible approach, yes, assuming, "They're willing to help?"

"They assured me they would as long as we're not asking for unreasonable things." Aran went directly to where the waves gently lapped up against the rocky beach and knelt on one knee before leaning forward to stick his hand into the water.

To Sevana's magical senses, it was like he extended a ribbon of air and water forward, letting it flow along the top of the sea. It formed no message that she could discern, but then, it hardly needed to. Seeing that power flow out was like a smoke signal—obviously someone wanted to talk.

Knowing that it might take a while for someone to notice and respond, Sevana found a nice, flat rock and sat as well. "Aran, Master and I vote that after this situation is settled, we not take any jobs for a while. We need to focus on getting my magical core back in balance."

He glanced over his shoulder at her, eyes unreadable. "I agree. It is handicapping you severely."

That was an understatement, in her opinion. "Ailana mentioned to me that she would send letters to the other Mothers, try to get their opinions. Do you know of anyone else that might be able to help?"

"Not near us, no. But I know of one or two people that are experts in matters like these, or at least, in power malfunctions. I think we should see them." He gave her a wry shrug and smile. "I would have taken you to them before, but truly, I'm not sure if even they can help. No one living has seen a case like yours before. And both people are on opposite sides of Mander. It won't be an easy trip to see either of them."

Hence why he'd put it off, hoping that time would heal everything. Sevana couldn't blame him—it wasn't like she hadn't done the same thing, and it was her problem. "After this, we'll go see them. I can't keep ignoring it."

"I understand." Aran opened his mouth, closed it, and then seemingly forced the words out into the open. "Do you regret the choice I made?"

"I'm alive and breathing," she pointed out sarcastically. "Your choices were me dead, or me with screwed up magic. I prefer the choice you made."

"I know, but sometimes you get so frustrated...."

"Of course I am. Things that should be easy for me got ridiculously complicated. And I'm having to rebuild so many tools because I carelessly melt them in moments of flare-ups. Who wouldn't find that frustrating? But I'm alive to feel the frustration, and that's the important part."

Her answer relieved him, as his face softened into a smile. "I'm glad. Sometimes your master gives me the stink eye so I wondered."

"It's not just that, you know," she said, looking out sightlessly over the water. "Master realized early on that because of my Fae blood, my lifespan would no longer be that of a human's."

Aran gave her a quizzical look. "That follows, yes."

"No, think about this," she chided. "The last time we saw an Artifactor that lengthened his life unnaturally, he was a madman. Making humans live more than a hundred years doesn't always turn out well. In fact, it usually doesn't. Our minds aren't equipped for it, I guess. Or maybe our hearts fail us first, to lose everyone we know and love without any hope of having companionship that lasts us through most of our lives. Master worries about what will happen to me fifty years from now, when I no longer have any human relations still living."

The quizzical look on Aran's face deepened. "What a nonsensical thing to worry about. Of course once you are at that point, you will no longer be living with humans."

Sevana blinked at him. He couldn't possibly mean...? "I'll be living with the Fae?"

"Of course. You realize, I trust, that Aranhil is not entirely happy that you're living apart from us. He finds it dangerous in many senses. That's why one of us is constantly sent out with you, or to check up on you. It's unnatural, to have you live outside."

Her jaw dropped soundlessly, eyes growing huge. Aranhil had referred to her as both 'sister' and 'daughter' of the Fae several times, but Sevana had always thought of it as more of an adopted friend than anything else. An honorary term for the help she'd given them, the friendship they had, and her new status as quasi-Fae. Had she jumped to conclusions she should not have? The expression on Aran's face made her think so.

"Aran. Correct me if I'm misunderstanding something here. But does Aranhil want me to become true Fae?"

"Of course," he repeated, exasperated. "We all do. But we respect your human ties. You have a great deal invested in the human world, and you do us many services because of it. We will not push you to come home sooner than necessary. We will wait until you are ready."

Sevana's head reeled. She propped it in her hand and tried to stop her whirling thoughts. Become Fae? "Ailana suggested I could do that, but wouldn't becoming full Fae be too problematic for me? I'm a full grown adult, a magician, after all."

"The way that your body adapted to my Fae blood tells us that this is not so. Aranhil observed your progress for several days, and conferred with the Mothers, before coming to the conclusion that you would not be in any way harmed if you chose to complete the change." Eyes sparkling, Aran added softly, "We all hope that you will choose to do this in the near future."

"Stop, stop," Sevana pleaded with both hands in the air. "You've thrown too much at me. I need to mentally digest this."

"As you will." He turned to look back over the sea. "Just know that we agree with your master. Your time with humanity is limited. In time, you will likely become Fae, or at least live with us."

Sevana had a hunch that he might be right, but he truly had given her too much to think about. It was not the right time to tell her any of this, either, as she had enough on her plate as it was.

"The Unda have noticed me and someone is coming," Aran announced before standing. "All things considered, let me introduce you before speaking. It is the polite thing to do."

Considering the reputation of the Unda, Sevana was all for politeness. They were not exactly known to be nicer or more tolerant than the Fae. Triggering a war between Fae and Unda over a breach of manners was the very last thing she ever wanted to do.

From the water came out a large seal, who flapped onto land without a care. He paused there, dark eyes looking them over, nose busy taking in their scents. A selkie, eh? This lasted for a moment, until he was satisfied, and then his skin melted and sloughed away, slowly revealing a human form, like that of a Fae. As with all of their people, he was fair of skin, but instead of blond, his hair was dark as midnight, eyes a penetrating blue. He wore a loose robe of seafoam green that looked more like water mist than actual clothing. His eyes took Sevana in with great curiosity but he inclined his torso in an elegant bow to Aran first.

"I am Risdon of First Moon. I greet you."

"I am Arandur of South Woods. I greet you, Risdon, and thank you for coming so promptly." Aran turned and gestured toward her. Obeying that silent summons, Sevana came to stand at his elbow. "This is Sellion, daughter of the Fae and my sister."

Being a polite Unda, Risdon didn't ask why she looked so peculiar, or why someone with human and Fae blood was referred to as both 'daughter' and 'sister.' Instead he gave her a bow as well. "We meet, Sellion."

"Well met, Risdon," she responded and hoped that was appropriate. "I am sorry to call you out like this so suddenly. You are aware of the volcano that is threatening to explode?"

"I am, thanks to Arandur's visit in our lands. We were grateful for his warning."

Oh? That sounded quite positive. "I am in charge of trying to contain the volcano so that it does as little damage as possible, but I was called to this task with no time to prepare. I am sadly lacking some of the tools that I need. I hoped to borrow your help? Also, I will likely need your guidance, as you of course know this place much better than I do."

"If it means protecting our lands, we are of course willing to aid you. What do you require?"

Sevana smiled. She had a cooperative Unda at her beck and call. How lovely.

15

In deference to Sevana and Aran's inability to breathe underwater, Risdon created air bubbles that conformed to their bodies like a full-on cloak would. It was a very unique experience, being able to walk around like this on the ocean floor without anything obstructing her view. It was amazingly beautiful and serene. This far below the sunlight, it grew increasingly darker and more cold as she walked, sending a shiver dancing along her skin. What she could see of her surroundings were made up of coral, schools of fish swimming lazily by, and some larger predators such as sharks and whales that eyed them sideways. Perhaps because of her escort, no one dared venture too close.

Sevana was very afraid that she would lose her bearings down here, having no line of sight with the mainland to help guide her, so she kept a strict eye on her compass to make sure she didn't veer off course. She set the first marker in place, and was glad when Risdon helped modify her markers so that they would shoot a beam of light straight up, to where they were visible even from the shoreline.

"How many need to be placed?" their guide inquired.

"I think a dozen along the sea floor," she answered, "perhaps less, depending on how the floor is laid out. Each booster has to have line of sight with its neighbor, you see, in order to function."

"Ah, is that so?" Risdon turned a half step in each direction, judging the situation. "How far from the isle do you wish to go?"

"We need to stay as close as possible," Sevana answered. "The farther out we go from the volcano, the more area we have to protect, and the more it strains us. That said, we're trying to give some space so that the lava has a place to flow to. We hope to extend the isle's landmass with the lava."

Risdon's eyebrows rose an nth degree. "We were not informed of this."

"I'm not sure if that was decided when I spoke with you," Aran offered slowly. "I think it was only mentioned as a possibility."

"Yes, I think it was," Sevana concurred. "Regardless, we've set on this course now, if it's feasible, which I think it is. And it's only logical. The lava has to go *somewhere,* after all."

"This is true," Risdon allowed. "I will still need to report this properly."

He likely would as it would affect their territory. If they were in Nopper's Woods, and Sevana was altering the landscape, she would certainly report to Aranhil first before doing anything. "I will of course report fully to your ruler if you need me to. I understand that this is something that will impact your people as well as those on land. We made a snap decision just because we didn't know what else to do with the lava and we're not sure if we have the time to figure out another solution."

Risdon unbent enough to assure her, "Our queen will likely agree. I will inform her and call upon you, if needed."

Well enough. "Then let's get back to it."

They did so and Risdon quickly proved to be invaluable as a guide. Sevana, despite all of her best efforts, did lose her bearings a few times. It was hard not to do so down here. The sea floor was like an alien landscape in many ways, and the nature of it fought against her equilibrium in spite of her air bubble. The ground pitched and rolled down here like a drunk monkey, so much so that keeping the pedestal boosters in line with each other was more of an art form than a science.

It took far longer than she expected to setup the ocean floor, and by the time they had worked their way around the isle and back onto the shore again, it was nearly pitch dark. Sevana rolled her head around on her shoulders, trying to ease the strain of the past several hours, and took in a deep breath. Air bubbles became stagnant after a while and this fresh sea air was very welcome.

Sevana knew almost instantly that it was a mistake to do that, as it set off a coughing fit, although milder than her previous one, thankfully.

Aran immediately put a hand to her back, soothing a circle over it, his magic coming into play to ease her lungs. As he did so, she reached into a pocket and retrieved the vial that Master had given her, unstopping it and inhaling a lungful of the Fine Mists Salts. Ahh, much better.

There was a tightness on Aran's face that she noted but ignored, trying not to show any more weakness in front of their Unda guide. Instead, she turned back to the job at hand.

Because of the darkness, the lit markers were an open beacon against the ocean. She could see them easily. From her vantage point, Sevana could see almost all of the way around, only the first two markers not visible. Studying them with narrowed eyes, she tried to envision what it would look like if this whole section become part of the isle. "What do you think, gentlemen? Will this work?"

Risdon came to stand at her side and stared out in silence for a long moment. "I cannot confirm that for you, Sellion. But I will speak with my queen and notify you if this meets her approval."

A wise answer and one that Sevana had no problem with. "Please do so quickly, Risdon. We literally have no control over the volcano at this point. I will be putting in the barrier the day after tomorrow, at the latest, and we have to have a firm answer at that point. This is to protect your people as well as the humans on the isle."

"I quite understand," Risdon assured her, "and I will inform my queen immediately. She has been most anxious about this situation and is not one to dawdle when matters are urgent."

Good to hear. "Then I will wait for your word."

Risdon gave her a slight inclination of the head, a more friendly gesture this time instead of the formal one he'd initially greeted her with, and then returned to his seal form before splashing into the ocean.

Sevana turned to Aran and said frankly, "I'm worn out. And I can't see well enough in the dark to place markers, even with my new enhanced vision. Let's call it a night and get up early in the morning to finish them off."

"I won't complain." Aran put an arm around her waist, not so subtly supporting her as he led off to the village, taking the shorter route that skirted around the volcano's base.

Before her near death experience, Sevana would have taken umbrage at this handsy touchy-feeliness of his. But now was a different story from back then. Now, she felt aches all along her body that seemed to go straight down to the bone. She was so tired that, left to her own devices, she would be tripping over her own feet. Giving up on making it to the village under her own power and sleeping right here on the trail would have happened.

"I'm ready for my human blood to adapt to your Fae blood. Any day now would be just fine by me."

Aran smiled at her sarcasm, taking her grumpiness in stride. "We'll figure out how to do so, Sevana. Don't worry."

"Humans are supposed to be the most adaptable species. That's all I'm saying. I should have adapted by now instead of feeling like I have a constant cold or something. And don't remind me that it could be worse. I know that it could be worse, but it could also be better, and I want better."

"Of course you do," he soothed, bodily maneuvering her around a copse of trees. "I'm rather surprised at how much help Risdon was. Usually the Unda are much more touchy about someone else being in their territory. Perhaps the situation has worried them that much?"

Changing the subject, huh? Well, she'd let him. Sevana hadn't found the Unda's cooperation that surprising. She gave Aran a puzzled frown. The man might be missing some information. "Aran. Do you know what happens when lava touches water?"

"Ah, of course, it would become acidic. I had forgotten that for a moment."

Ha, that's what she thought. She drawled, "I'm not sure how effective Unda magic will be against massive amounts of acidic, boiling water. Still surprised at their willing attitude?"

Aran shook his head. "Not at all."

"Master and I have both been determined to protect them for a reason. It's not just for the Unda's sake, either, but also for Nanashi's inhabitants as a whole. Really, it's just as high of a priority as the people's immediate safety. If we physically save them now, but fail to protect their environment, we'll fail them in the end. They'll starve in a matter of weeks if they aren't able to fish."

"Yes, that's very clear to me now."

They walked in silence for several minutes. Sevana felt her exhaustion settle in a little more with every step, and it took serious willpower to stay in motion. Truthfully, she was so tired that even staying awake long enough to eat wasn't that tempting.

"I assume that you want to get up at daybreak?"

Just the thought of doing so made her want to groan. But Sevana nodded affirmation. "We'll need to. The barrier has to be in place as quickly as we can manage it, as a safeguard. The way the barrier will be formed, it will shoot up like a straight wall, as we don't have the power to make it into a dome. But still, it will protect the isle and the sea from the lava and somewhat shield it from the explosion if it goes."

"And having that safeguard in place will give you the breathing room you need to think about how to solve everything else," Aran stated knowingly.

Sevana sighed agreement. "That too. I just hope and pray there is a solution. Because right now I'm not seeing one."

Master had not been idle while she was placing the markers. He had the main pedestal built with the spells inscribed into the stone, ready to place. Three boosters were formed, although the spells were not drawn on yet, and Cheng-Huang was busy producing more stone so that Master had the materials he needed to keep producing booster pedestals.

Greeting her absently, Master pointed to the side table near the door. "There's dinner there."

Her nose had informed her of such and Sevana snagged a rice bowl of fish and vegetables, wolfing it down even as she asked, "How goes it?"

"Well. Cheng-Huang is invaluable during this part of the process. He can make the stones in exactly the shape I need, which speeds things along. We're having strange issues in the inscriptions, though." Master frowned as the line of power he was drawing with fizzled out with a small pop. "Like that."

Attention riveted, she took a step in closer, staring hard at the point of his wand. "How very strange. That's been happening to me as well."

Master's brows arched. "Since when?"

She was so tired it was hard to think. "Since my arrival here? No, it did happen once before I came as well. I thought it was just me, and my magic being more of a pain than usual, but…"

"That can't be the case, not if it's affecting my magic as well." Master sat back and looked around him with a slow pan of the head, eyebrows drawn together in thought. "I wonder. Here we have natural energy being disrupted, godly energy being thrown about, and human magical energy in the mix. The magical fabric of the world must be in an eddy of confusion."

Perhaps that was the case. It might even explain why she had seen the same thing happen at Stillwater. With that much running water, coursing freely, it would have an impact on her spells and equipment. Magic wasn't a stagnant thing—it flowed and reformed depending on its environment. It could be recycled as well, depending on what was going on in that immediate area.

Master's explanation was certainly plausible, but Sevana wasn't sold on it. If that was the case, shouldn't she have seen problems before, on other jobs? This wasn't her first time mixing human magic into an area chock full of other energies. She'd never had a problem before, so why now?

No one had the time to sit around debating magical theory so

Master shrugged it off, gave his wand a shake, and re-ignited the spell. This time it functioned properly and he was able to pick up where he had left off.

"Were you able to reach your friend?" she asked in between bites.

"Not as yet, but I'll keep trying. I didn't expect to reach him today anyway."

Hopefully he would succeed tomorrow. Sevana ate quickly and then tried to join in. She was extremely cautious about drawing out a spell insignia on the pedestals, which was just as well, as her first attempt melted the stone. Cheng-Huang had to fix it for her, which he was not pleased to do. After that, Sevana kept her hands off the creation process. She turned in early, woke up with the morning sun, and focused on doing something else to support them.

Several boosters had been created while she slept, so Sevana instead grabbed each one as it was completed and immediately put it into place. That she could do without magic.

Starting with the land markers first, she placed each one and then took a break and ate a late lunch, giving the crafters time to finish more boosters. Since she would have to borrow help from the Unda again to place the boosters, it would behoove her to take more than one in a trip. Although, truthfully, she couldn't manage more than two, as each booster was three feet tall and, even with lightening spells, heavy. As heavy as a full bag of soil would be. If not for Aran's help, Sevana would not have been able to lug these things around quite so easily.

Two were done by the time she finished eating, so Sevana grabbed them and headed for the shoreline. To her lack of surprise, a selkie lounged there, waiting on her. It looked just like Risdon, but Sevana had limited experience with seals and wasn't sure if that was a safe assumption to make. So she settled for a more neutral greeting. "Hello. Waiting on us?"

The seal skin melted away and revealed a woman that could have been Risdon's twin. Same long dark hair, pale skin, penetrating blue eyes set in a heart shaped face. She was not at all petite, having a long and willowy frame and a high nose.

"I am Sosha. You are Sellion and Arandur from South Woods?"

"We are," Aran confirmed with a slight bow. "Well met, Sosha."

"Well met," she returned with a warm smile. "My queen, Nia Reign, sends greetings and salutations to you both."

Greetings and salutations sounded good. Sevana gave her a relieved smile. "I thank her for them. She has been informed of our full plans?"

"She has, and has no issue with them. She offers Her aide as you need it."

Whoa! That was not an offer Sevana had expected. While help would be wonderful, she wasn't entirely sure what to do with it, either. "Your help today in placing these boosters will be very beneficial."

Aran cleared his throat slightly. "Perhaps, Sellion, they could help us with the other problem we've been pondering?"

Other problem? There were so many that Sevana couldn't begin to figure out what he was referring to.

"There are two we face," Aran continued when she didn't respond. "Sosha, we are concerned for all of the creatures that live near the isle. Even with the barrier in place, the water will get very hot here. Perhaps your queen can influence them to move further away until it safe again to return?"

"She has already sent out word to do so," Sosha assured him. The request had been very well received, judging by that beaming smile on her face. "We thank you for your kindness and worry for them."

"Our other concern is that we might lack the power we need to contain the volcano," Aran continued. "We are trying to consult with those who are experts in these matters, but they are proving hard to reach. If needed, may we call upon the Unda?"

Sosha blinked as if taken by surprise that he was even asking. "Of course you may. Nia Reign expects you to do so. We are protecting our home after all."

Sevana let out a breath, feeling like two different weights had fallen off her shoulders. Bless Aran for thinking of this. She hadn't dared, as encroaching Unda territory on a regular basis was scary enough. "Sosha, we are very glad to hear this. Know that as soon as we have an idea of how to solve the problem, we will inform Nia

Reign. We will be very glad for her help."

Sosha ducked her head, accepting this. "We will wait. For now, I will guide you," Sosha promised. "Let's place your…boosters? That is the word?"

"Boosters," Aran confirmed. "We will work our way around the vents, placing the boosters in a circular pattern around the volcano."

"Then let us begin."

16

Sevana worked well into the night to get all of the boosters in place. Sosha charmed a school of glowing fish into swimming around them, lighting up their path so they could continue to work even after the light had failed. Only for that reason was Sevana able to finish that day.

After heartfelt thanks for all of the help—she seriously would have been lost without it—Sevana dragged herself back into the village and rolled into the bed. Her head didn't even hit the pillow before she was out like a light.

She was scared into wakefulness by a rolling of power so strong that it felt like the earth shook under her. It was akin to an earthquake, but on a magical level that left her nerves singing and a fine shiver along the skin. Sevana was up and moving before her eyes were even all the way open. What was going on? Even birds weren't awake at this hour! She ran out of the house without even pausing to put her boots on, looking around frantically in all directions for the source of the disturbance.

Standing on the shoreline were Cheng-Huang, Chi-Lin, and Da-Yu, all arguing vehemently with a brightly glowing woman, sparks of power all around her. In her hands she held a pair of mirrors, both clutched tightly at her side. She was unmistakably a deity of this pantheon with the silk dress she wore and her dark hair elaborately done up on top of her head. She was pretty, like all the gods were, with her oval-shaped face and dark slanted eyes, skin pale and delicate. She'd look like a doll if not for the way that she was throwing power around.

Sevana swore, dove back into the house long enough to yank on clothes, then ran outside again. She had a feeling this argument would only escalate, leading to more work for her, and she'd be running around like a madwoman the rest of the day. She refused to do all of that in pajamas.

Master came running down the street from his guest quarters as she exited, demanding wildly, "What? What's going on?"

"We have an upset visitor," Sevana responded curtly even as she ran toward them. She was halfway there when Aran caught up, easily keeping pace with her, and looking unfairly awake.

For the first time ever, Da-Yu appeared glad to see her and he stopped mid-sentence to greet them. "Artifactors. Arandur. Please, come and speak with us."

The woman turned, pale skin flushed with an angry blush, literally crackling with energy that felt like miniature lightning bolts going off. "Who is this?"

"Artifactor Sevana Warren," she responded promptly before gesturing toward the other men. "My master, Tashjian Joles, and my brother Fae, Arandur. Who are you?"

"I am Tian-Mu."

That did and didn't answer the question.

Da-Yu sidled up closer to them and whispered behind his hand, "She is the wife of Lei-Gong, the one that Feng-Huang flirted with."

Ohhh. Oh this was so not going to be good.

"You!" Tian-Mu stabbed an outraged finger in her direction. "You are the one that says that woman must be removed from the mountain?"

Sevana prayed for patience. "I am."

"This will not happen," Tian-Mu snarled, slashing her hand through the air in a downward arc.

"She's either removed or the people that worship you, this whole isle, is destroyed in one fell swoop," Sevana growled back. Nope, when this rudely awakened at the break of dawn, she had no patience. Praying for it had not helped. "Not to mention you severely damage the sea around this area and create mortal enemies with the Unda for your carelessness. They *are* aware of who is responsible for this whole debacle, you know."

That made all four deities blanch, as well it should, as no one sane messed with the Unda.

"You told them?" Cheng-Huang demanded in a strangled whisper.

Sevana gave him a look of considerable asperity. "Now how do you think I'm able to traipse around under the water so easily? Hmmm? Not to mention, making changes in their territory without their permission would be akin to suicide. Of course I talked to them first."

No one had a good response to that. Sevana decided to forge on. "Tian-Mu, this is not a matter of 'that woman needs to be punished' and we'll leave her there. Her presence is causing considerable danger. We need to take her out."

"Her punishment has not been met!" Tian-Mu argued, the air around her charging even hotter, the mirrors glowing white.

"Then figure out how to lock her up somewhere else," Master suggested, tone and manner soothing. "We're not suggesting you permanently free her, we're just saying that we can't leave her sealed in *there*. The volcano is the issue. We'll remove her, then hand her over to you, and you can revisit her punishment."

"If she is released now, then the Jade Emperor's seal will be broken, and she'll flee!" Tian-Mu became increasingly more agitated as she spoke, the power around her flaring whiter and hotter so that it felt similar to standing next to a lightning bolt.

Sevana's survival instincts screamed at her to back away, that she would get burned if she didn't. She shifted a half foot back, skin feeling tight and scorched even though she knew that she had not actually been touched. She almost leapt out of her skin when she felt a hand settle at the small of her back. Head snapping around, she realized that Aran had put himself squarely within her personal space and was using his proximity to shield her from the worst of the divine magic flaring out.

Her heart warmed that even in this tense atmosphere, he had

realized what was going on and silently moved to help her. Really, what had she done to deserve this man?

Because of her preoccupation, she missed the first part of Master's response. "—keep her here until someone can reach the Jade Emperor?"

"NO ONE HAS THE POWER OR AUTHORITY TO KEEP HER IMPRISONED HERE!" Tian-Mu screamed. There was outrage, venom, and pain in her voice as her power exploded out of control.

Sevana swore, automatically ducking, trying to avoid the worst of it by hitting the ground. Aran caught her before she went more than a foot and turned both of them so that it was his body in between both women, shielding Sevana completely. Her own magic, already out of control, reverberated under the magical out-lash and she swore again as she fought to keep it from breaking free. If not for Aran's quick actions, she likely would have been burned and adding to the magical fury surrounding them.

There was a great deal of screaming back and forth, mostly cries of alarms, and then the conflagration was abruptly gone.

She didn't need to turn her head to see. Anyone with even a thimble of magical ability would be able to feel such an intense burning of power with their eyes closed.

Tian-Mu was heading straight for the volcano.

Sevana nearly wrenched her spine out of place, she turned that fast. Still half in Aran's arms, she whispered, "Please tell me she's not going to do what I think she's going to do."

"I'm afraid she is," Aran groaned. "None of us are fast enough to stop her."

"But it's not necessary, is it?" Da-Yu asked, although his eyes belied his doubt. "Tian-Mu is not more powerful than we are, so—"

Shaking her head roughly, Sevana corrected, "It's not a matter of power levels at this point. Tian-Mu's power is fire-based, like everything else around Feng-Huang. More fire added into the mix will be like adding fire to an open flame. The situation over there is already unbalanced—add any more power into the mix, the seal will easily break." Even as she spoke, Sevana frantically tried to think.

Could no one catch up with her, stop her? In a flash she remembered that there was one person that might be able to get to her fast enough. "Chi-Lin! What are you waiting for, chase her!"

The unicorn picked himself off the ground, gave himself a shake, and then he was off in a thundering cacophony of hooves as he tore the ground up, moving as fast as physically possible. At some point his power engaged and he took to the air, his speed not dropping.

Even as he ran, Sevana's mind rationally knew that Chi-Lin wouldn't be able to catch her, not fast enough to prevent the disaster looming in front of them. Her mind whirled, settled on a course of action, and she spun again. "Master!"

Master hadn't waited on her or any other person to give direction. He was already running, as fast as he could, snapping out orders over his shoulder as he moved. "I need everyone at the main pedestal, NOW!"

The barrier. They had to get the barrier up. That was the only prayer of keeping the village intact, the isle from being utterly destroyed, the sea in this area from becoming a boiling cauldron of acid. Sevana would be of no use to them at the pedestal—her power wasn't part of it anyway—and she grabbed Aran's arms urgently. "The Unda. Notify the Unda!"

He spun like a dancer and was off like a shot, sprinting the short distance to the shoreline. Aran slid to a stop on his knees, thrusting his arm into the water, and even from here it was obvious that the power he radiated was like an urgent beacon.

Sevana danced in place behind him, impatient and not knowing what else to do. No, wait, there was something else she could do. Turning, she frantically looked toward the village. People had been hiding in their homes and who was to blame them? Four deities having an explosive argument on the shore would make any mere mortal tremble and look for a bolt hole. But now there were a few brave souls sticking their heads out of windows or doors, wondering what was going on and if it was safe to come out.

They'd lose everyone here if they didn't act quickly. "Da-Chin!" she called as she raced up the narrow, steep path. "DA-CHIN!"

The elderly village leader stepped out timidly from his house. "Artifactor, is it sa—"

"It's not safe, it's going to be very dangerous in a moment, get everyone moving," she rattled out, words nearly tripping over each other. "I need them on the flying ship NOW."

Alarmed but understanding, Da-Chin started doling out orders, and the word spread from him. Sevana hoped that it spread correctly; things that were repeated often changed from one listener to the next, but all she could do was pray and correct them as she moved.

Darting into her temporary workspace, she grabbed up some of the smaller, portable shields they had been experimenting with. There wouldn't be enough, so she grabbed her wand and a few elements as well, said a quick prayer that her magic would behave today, at least for the next hour, and then ran outside again.

Two steps outside the door and the ground rolled and pitched under her feet. The volcano gave a loud groan and crack as if something had impacted it hard and was trying to tear it in half. Likely the case—an angry goddess was intent on getting to the center of it.

Sevana swore aloud but regained her balance and kept moving. She had only as much time as it took for Tian-Mu to get that phoenix out of the mountain and no more. As soon as the phoenix's seal was breached, the volcano would lose its semi-dormant status and become active and volatile.

People rushed past her in a frantic stream, nearly tripping over each other, and it took serious concentration for her to stay ahead of them. She had barely reached Cheng-Huang's ship when Aran caught up to her, a little short of breath. "The Unda are notified and they'll do everything they can on their end to protect the sea," he reported. "What are you doing?"

"This ship isn't fully protected," Sevana nearly wailed.

"What are we protecting them from? The ash?"

"And the gases, they're nearly as deadly."

"We can't just fly it out of this area?"

Sevana shook her head roughly. "It levitates but I didn't have time to figure out the navigational system. It's still buggy."

Aran thought hard for a full second before nodding to himself. "I can do something about the shield at least. Focus on getting people aboard, I'll set the shield up on the ship."

How many people were there in the village exactly? It was a vital question, but she hadn't remembered to get a count and so had no way of knowing the answer at this point. Cheng-Huang had said a little over five hundred souls, but there wasn't even a way for her to count them as they streamed on board. She could only pray that she and Aran could work fast enough to protect everyone and then do her best to fulfill her own wish.

Time blurred, along with any sense of direction, as Sevana kept an eye on the steady stream of people rushing into the ship. They came aboard in threes, sometimes fours as parents carried in children. They packed into the interior like living cargo, but not one person voiced complaint, just commands to each other to come in closer, make more room. Sevana's ears were hyper-sensitive to any sound coming from the volcano and every time she heard a groan, or the hiss of gases escaping, her nerves jumped. It felt like hours but it was mere minutes since Tian-Mu's mad scramble for the volcano. The ship was mostly full at this point, so Sevana had to hope that most of the village was here already.

She saw it before she heard it, as a plume of ash escaped straight up, like a dark thundercloud rising in a column into the sky. In that moment, she knew. Chi-Lin had either not been able to catch Tian-Mu or hadn't been able to stop her.

The phoenix's seal was broken.

Like a physical wave of thunder, a shockwave rushed over her, the sound loud enough that Sevana nearly leapt out of her own skin. The top of the volcano disappeared from her sight completely as smoke rolled out along the sides in every direction. It was likely the heat of the lava pouring out that was making it smoke like that.

Wrenching her attention back to the shields, she stepped out onto the gangplank, pulling people up and pushing them in, trying to hurry the stragglers along. There were still twenty or so people, mostly elderly, that were trying to get on board. They couldn't raise a shield until everyone was in, as the barrier wouldn't recognize anyone not already inside of it. Her eyes anxiously darted over her shoulder toward the volcano, and the ash cloud quickly heading their direction. Would they make it?

A hand caught her arm and whirled her around. Sevana spun, balance upset enough that she automatically grabbed onto the person reaching for her. She knew even as she moved who it was, and didn't try to lash out as Aran brought her in close. He slammed the door closed behind her just as the ash plume started pelting the side of the ship.

Sevana looked up into his face and saw every emotion she felt reflected back at her. The anger, worry, frustration, helplessness. "Did we get them all?"

"I don't know," he responded grimly over the roar of the volcano.

There was no time to sink into despair yet. She pushed away from him, heading for the navigation systems. There were people barring her way, of course, and she had to shove and elbow them aside to force her way to the prow. "Da-Chin!" she called as she rammed her way forward. "DA-CHIN!"

"Here, Artifactor!" a thin voice called from somewhere at the back of the ship.

"Get me a head count!" she commanded. He would know better than she how many people they had. And how many they had lost.

Finally, she reached the navigation, then paused when the realization hit that even if she knew how to operate it, it wasn't safe for her to touch it. Especially now, with her emotions all over the map and her magical core feeling twitchy. She turned, found Aran at her back, and requested, "Get us airborne. We can't risk the acid eating through the hull."

Aran leaned over her shoulder, hands grazing the dials. "This is the same as your design?"

"It is my design. It operates the same, we just can't move it from this spot."

He nodded understanding, touched the right button, and his magic flared for a moment as the ship responded to his command and lifted into the air.

Whatever happened next, at least the people were safe. Relieved, she sank her head to rest against his chest and for a moment, a long moment, just breathed.

All of this destruction, insanity, this fear and hurt that could have been avoided. And now she stood in the middle of it all, untouched only because of one man's solid protection of her. Without him, she and most of this village would have been completely destroyed, dead before they could even try to get off the isle.

Surely one woman's jealousy was not worth this much heartbreak.

17

It took two hours for the volcano to empty.

Sevana had blessed the fact that this wasn't a particularly large volcano several times, but never as much as now, after it had erupted. Because it was a little on the smaller side, it didn't take as long for the lava to flow out, for the ash and gases to escape. So they didn't have to stay trapped inside their hovering ship for days, waiting. That was just as well, as they had no provisions on board the ship, and it couldn't sail to somewhere else, so it would have meant a slow death to all of those on board.

Once the air had cleared enough to see, she almost wished that it hadn't. A thick layer of ash coated everything—mainland and sea—so much so that it looked like a macabre version of a winter's day. Not a single patch of land remained uncovered.

With her sight unimpeded, she could see straight toward the volcano. The tall cinder cone was no more. The top of it was completely gone, melted away, and there were traces of red hot trails all around its top. They were cooling fast, but it was clear evidence that the lava had flown out in all directions. Fortunately for her frayed nerves, Sevana could also see that their barrier had held up even under that extreme pressure. There were a few visible cracks, but it was still there, protecting the village from being buried under an avalanche of melted stone.

With the majority of the threat gone, Sevana went looking for Da-Chin. The elderly man looked beyond haggard and sagged with anger and depression.

"How many?" she asked him quietly.

"There are seven people missing," he responded just as quietly.

Seven. She closed her eyes and felt like screaming. Maybe she was, on some internal level. "We will look for them properly, but stay here for now. I need to go and make sure that the barrier held up. It seems to have, but at the same time, I'm not sure if the water under us is safe or not. Stay here. Aran and I will check out the situation and then come back."

The elder inclined his head, either in agreement or despair, she wasn't sure.

Sevana had no idea how to offer comfort in this situation and wasn't about to try. She wasn't in the best of moods herself. Instead, she moved off, going to the gangplank that was still attached by ropes to the dock. With Aran's help, she managed to slide down it safely enough to the docks.

The first thing she checked was the water. It looked choppy, and it smelled off, as if touched with sulfur. That wasn't a good sign. Sevana wasn't sure if it was dangerous enough to offer damage to the ship, but she wasn't willing to risk it just by eyeballing the situation. "Aran, can you tell if the water is acidic?"

He stared hard at it for a moment before stating decisively, "It is not. It does have traces of lava in it, but it's from further away. We can land the ship safely here. Should I do so?"

"Not just yet. I want to see how well the barrier held up before letting anyone off."

Aran didn't say a word to her, just stayed close to her side as they silently forged a path toward the main pedestal. The ash was thick here, like snow or sand, difficult to wade through. A little of it got into her shoes, underneath her socks, and became an irritant. The annoyance didn't penetrate through her fog of disbelief. She couldn't even recognize the place anymore. What had been a green, thriving area now looked like a ghost town that had been abandoned for centuries. Sevana was deathly afraid that most of the animals on the isle had not made it, as they hadn't had time to evacuate any of them, but if there were corpses nearby she couldn't see them under all of the ash. It was just too thick and pervasive. There were also signs that the barrier had not been high enough to contain the rocks thrown free of the volcano. Sevana counted four buildings that had chunks missing from the roofline, where high velocity projectiles had impacted them. It was infinitely better than losing the entire village, of course; the barrier had protected it for the most part. But that didn't mean there wasn't damage to contend with.

This was a nightmare. Only it was worse than a nightmare because there was no possibility that Sevana could wake up from the dream.

The main pedestal was just out of sight of the village and it took her agonizingly long minutes to reach it. The pedestal itself had not been under any protective barrier—they hadn't even had a chance to design a shield for it. She wondered if they'd had power to divert to create something.

When they rounded the bend, to her surprise, the pedestal was not within sight. Instead there was a simple rock box in its place, standing long and wide enough for a group of people to stand upright inside of it. "Cheng-Huang's work?"

"It must be." Aran sounded relieved. He strode straight forward and rapped on the side of the stone. "It's safe to come out!" he called.

The stone glowed briefly with power and then sloughed off, retreating to the earth so that it formed a perfect square free of ash. As it did so, it revealed the three deities and Master, all of them still with their hands on the pedestal, channeling in their energy. After giving his surroundings a long look, a tight expression came over Master's face. "And we were trying so hard to avoid this."

Sevana also felt just as frustrated, just as dismayed that this was their outcome after working so hard to avoid it. "Master, the barrier? Did it hold all the way around?"

"I don't think it did," Master denied sadly. "About twenty minutes in, we all felt a jolt; after that the barrier has been acting very strange. I think we have a hole somewhere. It doesn't appear to be toward the village, though, which is cause for thanks."

"The hole is not," Aran confirmed. "We managed to get the people on board Cheng-Huang's ship, so they are fine for now. But this concerns me. Is the hole at some other point of the isle, or facing the sea?"

They all shrugged their ignorance. Considering what they were doing, none of them could really leave and take a look. Right now it wasn't safe to venture far from this area anyway, so Sevana only saw one option. "Aran, did you see *Jumping Clouds* on the way in? I was looking but under all of this ash...."

"I know where we left it, I'll see if it's still flyable." Aran patted her shoulder in reassurance before moving off.

Sevana blew out an aggravated breath. "We're going to be in disaster relief for weeks at least. Master, do you have a Caller on you?"

"I do."

"If you'll activate it, I'll send the word out. I think we need reinforcements."

Master did not disagree and immediately fished out the Caller from his pocket and set it flat in his hand.

Sevana spent the next hour calling Sarsen, Jacen, Pierpoint, and anyone else she could think of. Sarsen, knowing her trouble, immediately offered to send out word to his own contacts and save her the aggravation of trying to do it all on her own. She received several promises that in the next twenty-four hours, people would be coming with as much equipment and food as they could haul with them. Considering the people that she was speaking to, that was a significant amount of help; Sevana knew that at the very least, the place would not be a disaster zone for long.

From what she could see, the barrier had done part of its job, and the lava was cooling around the edge of the isle. In time, it would be an extension of the land here and give people more room to spread out on. Right now, it was a very narrow silver lining in an extremely dark cloud, but it did give some hope for the future.

Emotions in a turbulent whirl of failure and growing anger, Sevana turned to walk back to the village. It was time to let people out of the ship. They had a lot of work ahead of them.

Any luck that Sevana might have had was not to be found today. Possibly because of her emotions, partly because of her exhaustion, her magic was wild and refused to cooperate in any way. Even doing simple things, like powering on a device, were dangerous for her to do. As she found out the hard way.

That meant that she was down to doing manual labor, as she didn't dare go anywhere near her tools for fear of melting them, and Sevana hated manual labor with a passion. It was drudgery, nothing more, and it didn't activate her mind at all. She found it more boring than sleep, and that was saying something. But on the other hand, she couldn't sit idly by while there was so much work to be done. They didn't have enough hands as it was. So no matter how reluctant she was, Sevana forced herself to keep going and to apply her back and hands to whatever task lay in front of her.

Doing something she hated doing, no matter how good of a service, made her already dark mood go pitch black.

Just then, Nia Reign, Queen of the Unda, came out from the ash-covered waves. She stood on the shore, radiating power in angry pulses, the like that no one had felt before. Even Tian-Mu's angry tantrum from before paled in comparison. In a voice like that of a mother storm, she boomed out, "SELLION OF SOUTH WOODS! I WILL HAVE WORDS WITH YOU!"

In a saner, calmer state of mind, this summons would have worried Sevana. As it stood, she was angry enough that she threw down the shovel in her hands and marched right for the upset Unda without a second's thought.

The whole isle heard her, of course, and Master as well as Aran were running for both women at top speed. But Sevana was closer and she beat them there by several hundred feet. Feet planted, arms akimbo, she faced Nia Reign head on and snapped out, "What?"

Nia Reign's power flared as her anger spiked. She was already glowing like shiranui, only a more volatile shade of blue with hot-white arcs strewn throughout. Her dark hair was filled with so much static electricity that it literally stood on end, looking like she had a dark halo backlighting her. With her rage so intense, this normally beautiful woman looked like every child's mental image of a sea witch. "You dare address me so?"

"You dare interrupt me while I'm trying to clean up this mess?" Sevana growled back. Flinging out a hand to indicate the area behind her, she continued heatedly, "I've already had one angry goddess today throw a tantrum and destroy this place just because her little feelings were hurt," this last part dripped in sarcasm, "and now you're standing here looking about as calm as she was. What are you going to do for an encore? Sink the isle completely?"

At that point Aran caught up with her and tried to wedge himself in between both women. "Apologies, Nia Reign, we are all very distraught by the destruction wrought today. Sellion worked long and hard to avoid this end, and—"

Nia Reign threw up a hand, silencing him, her eyes never leaving Sevana's. "What do you mean, a goddess caused this?"

Sevana wasn't in the mood for explanations and so spat, "Tian-Mu."

That seemed to be explanation enough. Nia Reign's eyes closed in a fatalistic manner and her anger flared again before abruptly abating. "I was told only that the volcano had blown, and that the barrier had failed to completely contain it. I assumed it to be the fault of those working on the problem."

"Apologies," Aran said again, quietly now. "I was rushed in giving you the message, I did not try to fully explain. Tian-Mu came this morning after learning that we were going to release Feng-Huang here, and she had a conniption when we refused to do things her way. We had no way of stopping her."

Nia Reign held up a hand again, this time in reassurance. "Peace, Son of Aranhil, I know you. I thought you careless, not destructive. No matter the reason, destruction like this is evil, I think. Tian-Mu was a gentle woman that was gifted immortality and power by the gods. Her jealousy has undone her good character."

Sevana didn't care if her husband had openly cheated on her. It didn't excuse Tian-Mu from this.

Master puffed up, finally joining them, a little winded from his mad sprint to the shoreline. Sevana spared him a glance but nothing more. She still had an upset Unda queen demanding her attention.

Eyes narrowed into dark slits, Nia Reign hissed, "I must think of how to deal with her."

"You won't get the chance," Sevana swore vehemently. "Not if I get to her first."

Regarding her thoughtfully, Nia Reign stated, "A mortal cannot harm a god."

Staring her down, Sevana replied flatly, "I'm half-Fae. I'll manage."

Aran shifted uneasily beside her but even he wasn't quite sure how to interrupt without having two women hand his head back to him.

After a long, tense moment, Nia Reign unbent enough to give her a cool smile. "I somehow believe you, Sellion. It is a shame that you are of the Fae. I would have welcomed you among the Unda otherwise."

Thereby suggesting she was ruthless enough to please even this woman? Sevana smirked back. "I'm flattered, Nia Reign."

"As you should be. I do not like many mortals, half-Fae or not. I now understand why Aranhil likes you." Clapping her hands, she dismissed the subject. "I am doing what I can to clean up the area under and around the shoreline, but there is damage there that will take many seasons to heal."

"I know." Sevana felt that Nia Reign was leading up to something and so left it at that.

"Do not concern yourself with anything other than the isle and the mainland. We will take care of our own territory."

Sevana's eyebrows rose in surprise. That was a lot of ground... sea?...to cover.

Master deferentially cleared his throat before offering, "Nia Reign, we do have other magicians and Artifactors on their way. I expect one of them tomorrow. We can offer you help as you need it."

The Unda Queen shook her head, the manner gentler than before. "I think you have enough to do, and working in the sea will be difficult for you. We can manage. I request only that I have updates on your progress here, and of course I want to be informed when you notify the Jade Emperor. He and I will…discuss…Tian-Mu."

Sevana had absolutely no intention of missing out on that conversation. She and the Jade Emperor were going to have a discussion of their own. "We haven't been able to reach him. In fact, he's been unreachable for months."

"Oh?" Nia Reign's head tilted in consideration. "I see. Hence this debacle."

"Exactly so," Aran replied. "If we'd been able to reach him, I think all of this could have been avoided."

"I have my own ways of communicating with him. I will try from my end." Nia Reign half-turned, ready to leave, only to pause and look back. "Sellion, did you see where Tian-Mu went?"

That was the thing that burned the most for Sevana. "No. The ash was too thick for us to see anything. Da-Yu is under the impression that she went directly north, but that's only a feeling on his part."

"So we have no way of knowing where she went, or what she has done with Feng-Huang." Nia Reign didn't like this one bit and the frown she wore conveyed that clearly. "I see. Continue to try contacting the Jade Emperor. Inform me if you succeed."

"I will. Do the same."

Nia Reign's mouth curved in a wicked, fleeting smile of agreement before she disappeared back into the sea.

Sevana watched her go into the ocean and had every intention of keeping that promise. There were some petty gods here that needed a comeuppance and if she had an Unda Queen willing to help her kick some arse, so much the better.

18

Ash was a highly irritating substance for a human to come into contact with. Not only was it dangerous to inhale, as it could cause respiratory problems, but even skin contact was not recommended. It would cause severe skin irritations with any kind of exposure. The eyes had to be protected as well, of course, as they were the most sensitive of all.

Because ash was so light and easily stirred up, any movement created problems, and it was hard to contain the ash with it constantly up in the air. Master created numerous breathing filters, to fit over nose and mouth. Cheng-Huang used his building ability to craft goggles for everyone, and for the most part, this protected them. Everyone wore long layers and gloves, and wrapped scarves around their heads to keep the ash off as much as possible. It made the already grey landscape look like some ghostly survival camp.

The only truly helpful thing was that Da-Yu, with his power, was able to guarantee clean water to drink. Without him, they would have been very shortly in dire straits.

The shield protected the town from the lava, of course, but that was all the buildings had been protected from. The ash had run free and because of that, they had a large quantity collected on their roofs. Some of the buildings were damaged because of the rocks that flew over the barrier. That part she didn't need to worry about at all, as Cheng-Huang had made it clear he would fix the damaged buildings. To avoid increasing his workload, Sevana focused on the ash first. Ash was very heavy when in great quantities like this, and if left alone for too long, it would cause the building to collapse.

Sevana drafted Ho-Han and Ji-Gang, the village elder's grandsons, to come up and work with her. As they scaled the ladder to the top of the first roof, she cautioned, "Be careful up here. Ash can be very slippery to work on and if you fall from here, I will not be able to catch you. We do not need injuries."

"Of course, Artifactor," Ho-Han assured her. The elder of the two, he was scrawnier than his brother, but she had watched them both work and knew they were about equal in strength. "What do we do with it?"

"Master gave you two pails, didn't he? Those are Vanishing Buckets. Whatever ash we put in those, it will be disposed of. Start on the outside and work your way in, let's avoid putting additional body weight on the center of the building just yet." The walls gave more support to the roof, it would be the safer place to stand and work for now.

Sevana had her own Vanishing Bucket but she ignored the small spade and handheld broom on her belt for now, using the bucket to scoop up the ash directly. It was a good three feet thick, so it wasn't like she needed another tool just yet. Because they weren't transferring ash into the buckets by hand, the area was cleaned up faster than she expected it to be and they moved on to the next roof.

She had to stop regularly to rest and inhale some Fine Mists Salts. Despite the breathing mask on her face, some of the ash still snuck in, and it set off a coughing fit every time. Her joints ached because of the physical labor as well, a culmination of it from the day she had arrived, and she literally didn't have the energy or strength to push hard. The boys, fortunately, seemed to realize she had some sort of sickness so they stayed well behaved and didn't ask any annoying questions.

They came down only twice, to eat and drink plenty of water, before going back up. Sevana's was not the only team working on the roofs, there were two others, and with nine dedicated adults working they were able to clear the rest of the roofs from the worst of the ash before nightfall. They were not completely clear, but at least the worst was removed, and the threat of collapse was gone.

Everyone retired early, beyond exhausted with the work, and were up again with the dawn to do it all again.

Sevana's mind was not quiet as she scooped up ash. It buzzed with plans of revenge. The problem lay in that she was reliant on others to find the Jade Emperor and Tian-Mu for her, as she had no means of doing it herself, and she couldn't move until then. It burned, this sense of having to wait, and her plans became more creative as time dragged slowly on.

It was probably just as well that Jacen appeared that afternoon in one of the flying barges that she had built for him. He landed on the sea and then drew it in to park at the docks like it really was a water vessel. Seeing him come in, she dropped her bucket and half-jogged down to greet him, waving an arm as she went. "Jacen!"

Jacen waved back, already putting on a filter over his nose and mouth. "Sevana. Thanks for the call. I wanted to help but wasn't sure where to start."

Many were not quite sure how to interact with Jacen, because of his splintered mind, but Sevana had discovered that if he were given a task like this then he usually did just fine. It was stimuli that set off his condition. Relief work wouldn't be enough to do it. Although she planned to keep him close to either herself or Master just in case. "We can use all hands so I'm glad you came. How bad is the mainland?"

"Bad, but…" he took a long look around before giving a low whistle, "not as bad as this. This is pretty bad, Sevana."

"I know it," she growled, vexed all over again. "But how bad is the mainland?"

"Lot of ash, of course, and it's making it a little difficult to breathe over there. Cleanup has already started and all of the local magicians, sorcerers and Artifactors are basically in charge of their hometowns and working there. I don't think we have to worry about them, they have plenty of help. Give them a few weeks, you'll never know this happened."

This relieved her and Sevana's prickly mood lightened just a hair. "What did you bring?"

"Anything I thought would come in handy. I have goggles, respirators, water filters, as much food as I could stuff in here, Vanishing Buckets, and portable tents that act as giant filters. I also have some ready medi-bandages for injuries. It will only work for cuts, sprains, and the like, though."

"Well done," Master praised as he came up to them. "That's exactly what we need. You did think it through. First, let's set up some of those tents so we have a clear space to prepare food in. That's our major struggle at the moment. I'll get some hands over here to help you." Clapping a hand on Jacen's shoulder, Master said softly, "Very glad you came."

Jacen ducked his head and blushed a little. "You know I will if you're calling me, sir."

"I know, I know." With a final clap, Master let go. "Your priority is getting some space clear, getting those tents up, and getting the food and bandages into the right hands. After that, come see me, I'll tell you what needs to be done."

"I will." Jacen paused and really looked at Sevana. "I almost hate to ask this, but...ah, how are you doing?"

Knowing what he was really asking, she resisted the urge to start cursing. "I can't use my magic at all at the moment, I melt things."

"Oh. Um." Jacen gave her a game smile. "We'll really work on figuring you out after this, I promise."

Jacen knew. This reaction soothed her as others hadn't because Jacen *knew* what it was like to have your own body betray you and not function as it should. It was not pity from him, but empathy, and a promise from one friend to another to help as much as possible. She inclined her head in silent agreement. "Let's focus here first."

"Right. Sarsen you said is coming?"

"He's going to probably arrive in the morning," Sevana confirmed. "He was a little farther out than you."

"Anyone else?"

"On that, we're not sure," Master responded, "as people were promising to help as much as they could, but some were being diverted to the mainland problems. But we're not to worry about the sea. The

Unda have promised to take care of it."

Jacen's eyes nearly fell out of his head. "I'm sorry, I can't be hearing you right. The fearsome, ruthless Unda, known for their dark natures, are quietly taking care of their own territory and not making any demands or using the situation to their advantage? Did I understand that right?"

Master chuckled and shrugged. "Correct."

"How did you negotiate *that*?" Jacen demanded incredulously.

Sevana raised a hand. "Me. Well, partly me. Aran did the initial contacting."

"Ah, Arandur," Jacen said in complete understanding. "I should have figured. That man can charm the devil into giving up his luck."

Sevana glared at him but couldn't deny it. "Let's just get to work. Jacen, grab something and follow me, I'll show you where to set up."

Jacen obediently grabbed a few wands, a tarp, and shouldered one of his tents. Sevana grabbed the other two tents and struck off, not really concerned if he were keeping up or not. He was, and fell into step with her, eyeing her sideways. "You want to tell me why your mood is so sour?"

"I had a goddess throw a tantrum and cause a volcano to go off, a shield that failed to completely work and threw some lava into an ocean, and the Queen of the Unda come after my blood all within the space of two days. On top of that I can't use my magic and am stuck with manual labor. You want to explain to me why I should be in a good mood?"

After contemplating this for a full second, Jacen ventured, "I don't think I should comment. It will likely get me killed."

"You're a good friend, Jacen. I promise to only maim you a little."

"Definitely not commenting," he decided with a vigorous nod. "What about the wildlife here?"

Sevana generously decided to let him shift topics. Coward he might be, but he'd live to see another day. "Due to Chi-Lin's efforts, about half of them were saved. Some of the animals dove into the sea, the ones that could swim, at least, and the Unda saved them. We still lost a good portion of them, unfortunately."

Jacen rubbed at a temple. "Sad, but understandable. I'm impressed you were able to save any. The isle is intact, though?"

"More than that, the lava was controlled enough to add onto the north-east tip of it."

"Well, that's a bonus at least."

"I should warn you that we're having strange things happen with magic up here. It's not just me, Master has noticed it as well. Sometimes when we're invoking a spell, the magic splutters or hiccups. Sometimes peters out completely before it activates. It's very strange. The magical fabric in this area is not reliable or consistent. So be aware of that."

Jacen stared at her as if she had just announced that the sun was not actually in orbit, it was all a hoax. "Are you serious right now?"

"You'll see for yourself shortly," she sighed. "Just keep it in mind. Sometimes you have to try a spell twice before it will work right."

"You're actually serious," he said in disbelief. "This job of yours is getting wonkier by the moment."

Sevana had no argument on that. She stopped on the only 'open' spot just off the docks, before they got into the crooked and narrow streets of the village. It was usually the market day area, wide enough for multiple stalls to be set up, but right now it was used as a gathering place. It was one of the few areas mostly cleared of ash, although there was still a buildup in the alleyways. "Here. Pick a spot, just leave this building and the one beside it open to traffic."

"Sure. Should I set up all three?"

Sevana didn't even have to think about that. "Yes. One for food, the other two for treatments. We're getting more injuries than I care to count."

Jacen didn't seem a bit surprised by this. "It's common in disaster zones like this. I take it the ash is responsible for most of the injuries? I thought so. Alright, I'll set that up first, so people have a place to go." Looking about, he seemed to verify something before stepping in a little closer and lowering his voice. "If my memory serves me right, there's quite a few saints, gods, and goddesses in this pantheon. I'm not seeing any of them, though."

"Some of them are here, have been since the beginning," Sevana denied. "I've been told that others have been notified and they're on their way. If you do see any of them, don't be shy in putting them to work."

"Really? I'll do that, then."

Satisfied that he was up to date enough on the situation, Sevana gave him an analyst's salute and went back to clearing ash. The sooner that was done, the sooner she could hunt down a certain goddess.

It might have been mind-numbingly boring, but the work did make time go faster. Sevana felt like she'd barely been at it any time at all when the light failed her and it was time to stop and eat dinner. She retraced her steps down the main street and to the tents Jacen had set up. For the first time in two days, she was able to enter a space that was completely clear of ash and sit down to a meal that wasn't contaminated.

A slight smile on her face, she took a corner seat and looked around. There were new faces here, magicians that had likely arrived while she was occupied, and at least two gods that she didn't recognize. It would explain why all of the streets and buildings were now clear of ash. With that much magical and divine help, of course the work would go a lot faster. Sevana might be freed from her obligations here sooner than she anticipated.

Master came in, pausing in the doorway to take a good look around the tent. It was magically enhanced so that it expanded whenever another person entered, but even so it looked crowded in here with half the village sitting down to dinner. Clearing his throat, he pitched his voice so that everyone could hear him.

"Attention for a moment, please! Thank you. First, I'd like to welcome and thank every magician and god that has come so speedily to the rescue. Truly, we'd be in dire straits without your very capable assistance. I'm happy to report that with the additional help of magicians and gods alike, we have officially cleared every building and street in the village of ash and it is safe to walk through this area again."

There was a loud cheer at this that brought a tired smile to

Sevana's face.

Master outright beamed at them. "Wonderful, isn't it? I ask that our helpers not go away just yet, however, as we have the rest of the isle to clear. Our next goal is the fields so that we can replant them. I'll divide you up in a moment and make sure everyone knows where they need to go and what they should be doing. I know we had two gods arrive this morning—do either of you have domain over plants or something of that ilk?"

Both of them shook their head.

"I apologize for my uselessness," the goddess apologized with a contrite smile. Her plain robes were streaked with ash, as was her pale skin, dark hair in a sensible knot on top of her head. If not for the divine power that she shone with, one would have thought her a village matron from the sensible way she dressed. "I am Guan-Yin, Artifactor. I am the goddess of compassion and caring."

Which would be why she was one of the first to respond. Sevana made a mental check in her head. Of course this goddess was perfect for this situation; she was basically victim support.

"Not at all, Guan-Yin," Master assured her. "I don't believe we've met, I'm Tashjian Joles. I'm very glad to meet you."

"Likewise, Artifactor Joles," she responded with a voice like smooth honey.

"I'm afraid I lost track of things partway through the day. Where were you spending most of your time?"

"The medical tents next to this one."

"That's perfect," Master assured her. "Stay there as we're terribly shorthanded in that department."

They truly were. Sevana had seen that for herself the few times she had helped someone hobble along to the tents for treatment.

Guan-Yin gave him a nod of consent, the movement entirely graceful.

"Well, if we don't have a god on hand that specializes in this sort of thing, then we'll make do with the talent we do have." Master shrugged as if this wasn't a big deal of any sort and they'd be fine. "In other news, has anyone managed to reach the Jade Emperor yet?"

"Oh, were you trying to reach me?"

The whole tent went deadly silent, the strain and quiet so absolute that it would make a graveyard look loud. Everyone's heads creaked around to stare in the corner where the voice had come from. There, looking quite innocent, sat a grandfatherly figure with a long white beard and mustache, white hair streaming along his shoulders, dressed in a plain robe that had seen better days. There wasn't a patch of hair, skin or clothing that wasn't covered in filth. He'd clearly been hard at work all day and did not look like some towering or imposing figure that was the head of a pantheon of gods.

Sevana's surprise kept her rooted for two full seconds and then she was on her feet in a split second, hands slamming against the top of the table with a bang. "You're the Jade Emperor?!"

"I am, young woman," he responded as calmly as if they were discussing the best types of tea. "Why are all of you looking for me?"

Her focus was so funneled on reaching him that Sevana went half-blind to her surroundings, so that she was almost rough as she pushed past people to reach him. Aran was quick to catch her before she could actually physically leap on the god, although her rage was intense enough that even he had to struggle.

The Jade Emperor regarded her with mild surprise. "You are very angry, young woman."

"You don't know the half of it," she snarled at him. "Because you stupidly put a phoenix on top of a dormant volcano, you threatened the lives of every living creature in this area! And then you disappear? We lost seven people! How thoughtless are you?"

Most of the villagers were now flat against the ground, and a few of them vocally winced at her confrontation, but Sevana was of the opinion that decorum could go hang itself. Someone had to take this man to task for being so stupid.

The Jade Emperor regarded her with a blank face for several, agonizingly long seconds. Then he bowed his head slightly to her. "You speak in anger on behalf of those that do not have the courage to confront me. You have my respect, young woman."

Sevana wanted to take that respect and shove it down his throat.

His next words stopped her from doing so. "Sealing Feng-Huang here was an error on my part. I was in too much of a hurry to truly think of the consequences. It is now a judgment I very much regret. I came as soon as I felt the seal break to help right the situation as much as I can."

A god that could apologize? Her anger cooled a notch, but not by much.

"Who are you?" he asked her gently.

Still too upset to answer calmly, she gritted out the words between clenched teeth. "Artifactor Sevana Warren. Sellion of South Woods. I am the person your gods called when they couldn't reach you."

"Ah," he intoned in complete recognition. "I know of you. And the man standing at your side?"

"Arandur of South Woods," Aran introduced quietly with a slight bow of the head. He had not released his hands on Sevana yet, which was probably for the best.

"You both have my thanks, and my apologies, as you worked hard to protect my people. This situation should not have happened and this destruction is inexcusable." The Jade Emperor sighed and most of the room flinched at the sound. "Rise, my people, rise and continue to eat. You worked long and hard today and you need to regain your strength." No one dared except the foreigners in the room, and even they did so hesitantly. The Jade Emperor's expression said he understood why so he continued in a gentler tone, "Know that while I am angry, it is not directed at any of you. You did very well handling a terrible ordeal. I will reward all of you as I am able, and I will not rest until this isle is restored to what it should be."

That, finally, did the trick. They timidly got back into their seats and at his silent encouragement, went back to eating. All of them stole glances at the Jade Emperor with awe sketched on their faces, as if they couldn't believe he was actually in their presence.

Sevana was too angry to be awed and kept at him. "Do you know who is responsible for this?"

"Tian-Mu, I believe." The Jade Emperor's mouth went flat in an angry line. "You are a witness to what she did?"

"I am."

"I see. You stated earlier that you have been trying to reach me. Why?"

"I have a promise to keep with a phoenix and a score to settle with Tian-Mu." Sevana crossed her arms over her chest defiantly. "Why do you think?"

He stared back at her with that blank expression from before. "You want my assistance in tracking Tian-Mu down. But what if I say that I will not cooperate?"

19

The whole room once again held its breath.

Unexpectedly, it was Aran that dared to step into the breach and continue the argument. "Jade Emperor, there is one thing that you should know before you make any decisions."

Those dark eyes shifted to Aran's face. "And what is that?"

"It is not just the mortals that have suffered here. The Unda territory took a huge impact because we were not able to completely shield the sea from the volcano's fury. They are very…upset." The way Aran said the word made it clear 'upset' wasn't even close to describing how they felt. "Their queen, Nia Reign, has vowed vengeance on Tian-Mu for the destruction of her territory. The only person she has agreed to share the vengeance with is Sellion."

The Jade Emperor wasn't quite able to hide a wince at this news. Ruler of the skies and gods he might be, but he still had to respect the territories of the other mythical races, and angering the queen of the Unda was an extremely bad move. Even if he had played no part in it, he was responsible, and it would be on his head to make amends.

Aran, seeing that he had found a chink in the armor, pressed on. "Nia Reign has enough on her hands that I do not think she would choose to hurry off and track Tian-Mu down." Everyone heard the unspoken words of, *At least for the time being.* "If you negotiate this with Nia Reign, I believe she will be content to send Sellion as her ambassador with you."

In other words, the Jade Emperor could pick his poison. Taking Sevana with him was definitely the more palatable option.

The Jade Emperor locked eyes with her for a long moment before sighing again, this time in resignation. "It is true that this offense is not listed in our laws, and so it does not have a punishment prescribed to it, which means we must call Tian-Mu before a counsel of seven to review her deeds. I will need a witness for that as I was not here to see her actions for myself."

That sounded like a 'yes' to Sevana.

"I will work here another two days, to renew everything that I can, and then we will make retrieving Feng-Huang a priority. At that time, Sellion, you will accompany me." The Jade Emperor paused and studied Aran for a moment before adding with a distinct twinkle in his eye, "Do not look at me in that way, Arandur. I would not think of taking her without bringing you as well."

Sevana twisted about to see for herself what kind of expression Aran had on his face. On the outside, he looked completely straight-faced, but she knew him well at this point. Internally, he pouted so hard he was likely to leave a depression in the ground. The Jade Emperor got points for being able to see past the surface.

In the past months, Aran had made it clear that she was not allowed to go into unknown or dangerous situations without him. Sevana reckoned it was half-guilt that motivated him, as she wasn't able to protect herself as well right now with her magic screwed up, and he was trying to keep her safe until things could go back to rights. The other part of it was that he was strangely fond of her and seemed to like being around her. For some inexplicable reason. So she wasn't surprised that he was in his own way insisting on going with her.

She was surprised that the Jade Emperor was going to allow it. And what did that gleam in his eye mean, anyway? It looked like he was plotting something.

Aran gave him a lower bow this time. "My thanks."

"For now, we should finish our dinner. I, for one, worked hard for it. After that, we will go and speak with Nia Reign."

And wouldn't that be a fun conversation. Wait, come to think of it, "Who put you to work? Or did you just join in?"

"Ah." Jacen tentatively raised a hand. "I did. I, ah, well, you told me to put anyone new to work...."

Sevana gave him a look of considerable asperity. Of course it would be the person that barely knew what was going on to make this sort of slipup. "You didn't ask for his name?"

"He did, and very politely," the Jade Emperor assured her with a sort of grandfatherly indulgence. "And I told him. Yu-Huang."

Rolling her eyes to the ceiling, Sevana started to pray for patience, and then realized she was doing so in front of multiple gods and stopped. Even if they were in a different pantheon than her own, they could likely hear her internal prayers. "Jacen. You don't remember this pantheon that well at all, do you?"

"Basically the bare bones of it," he admitted with a wince. "It's not exactly in my field."

That part was true. In fact, they were so far out of his chosen field that she might as well be asking a monkey for advice.

"Don't be harsh on him, Sevana," the Jade Emperor scolded with a slight chuckle. "He was polite, and I was happy to have a direction, as I wanted to work. I will depend on his kindness tomorrow as well."

Yu-Huang had become the Jade Emperor due to his wise judgement and benevolence, after all. It was to be expected that he wouldn't be upset with Jacen.

Master cleared his throat in a deferential manner. "Jade Emperor, if you don't mind, I'd prefer you come and speak with me tonight. There are a number of tasks that need doing but we have insufficient knowledge or power to accomplish them."

The Jade Emperor inclined his head. "Of course. I will speak with you after I have negotiated with Nia Reign."

"My thanks. I will be waiting."

Sevana went back to her seat and her cooling dinner. It took several minutes before people finally gathered up enough courage to go and speak with the gods in their midst. They did so tentatively, one brave soul at a time, and then in a steadier stream when it was apparent that the gods were actually happy to speak with them. The Jade Emperor was almost swarmed, and he beamed so hard that he leaked light out like a halo.

Watching him, it became obvious that his love of his people ran true and deep, and Sevana's anger toward him dissipated a little more. He had likely told her the truth—he'd made a snap decision concerning the phoenix and it turned out to be a bad one. Nanashi Isle was not the only place where his people dwelt and he had a rather large pantheon of gods to manage as well; it was understandable that his attention was diverted elsewhere before he realized how dangerous it was here.

Understandable, but still highly regrettable, as it all could have been avoided.

Even in this moment, Sevana knew that they wouldn't have been able to completely stop the volcano or keep it from affecting the isle. But they could have contained the larger part of it and avoided the complete disaster that they were facing now. Part of that blame could be laid at the Jade Emperor's door. But the lion's share of it was definitely Tian-Mu's, and Sevana was more than willing to divert her anger toward the goddess. Especially since the Jade Emperor was doing his best to make amends.

Aran seemed to read her mood and he gave her a slight smile. "No longer angry?"

"Not with him, anyway." Reminded, Sevana asked, "In all the madness and confusion, I lost track of our young dragon. He left?"

"He did, when the volcano started to blow. I sent him on so that he wouldn't be caught up here. He was also tasked with warning his clan so that they wouldn't try to fly this direction."

Smart of him to think of that. Sevana had been so busy trying to protect the people she'd momentarily forgotten about their young dragon. In fact, she hadn't remembered him until this morning.

"You're just now thinking of him?" Aran asked a little incredulously. "I thought you could keep track of multiple things without strain."

"Rule of seven," Sevana grumbled at him, only a little defensive. "I can remember six things at once and handle them all, but not a seventh."

For some reason this amused him. He smiled at her, head propped in his hand, his dinner completely ignored. "Do tell. Six things, hmm?"

"Shut up and eat, Aran." Sevana stabbed her fish with a little more force than necessary.

Chuckling, he did so. Although she was sure she hadn't heard the last of it; he'd use it to tease her later. It was as inevitable as the sun rising in the sky.

It took another hour before the Jade Emperor was able to wrench himself from his worshippers, and then they walked down to the beach. The half-cleared beach. At least around the docks it was clear, but they still had many miles to go yet. Sinking down to one knee, he put a hand in the water and called clearly, "Nia Reign. I would speak with you."

She couldn't respond instantly, of course, she had to travel to where they were. The Jade Emperor stood again to wait.

Seeing she had the opportunity to do some probing, Sevana took it. "How do we track Tian-Mu?"

"I can see her trail as she fled." The Jade Emperor turned and pointed to it unerringly. "Also, I can sense Feng-Huang quite clearly. Tian-Mu only broke the first level of the seal in order to take her from the volcano. She did not break both levels."

"Meaning Feng-Huang is still sealed?" Aran asked in interest.

"Indeed, young Fae. If she had broken free entirely, Tian-Mu would have had a fight on her hands. Feng-Huang is quite powerful in her own right. I do not believe that Tian-Mu will win an engagement between them."

Hence why Tian-Mu kept Feng-Huang sealed? That made perfect sense to Sevana. Carting around an unconscious person was cumbersome to say the least, but it was still easier than trying to kidnap a person who was equal in strength and fighting back. Sevana carried that thought a step further and winced. "I'm almost grateful, then, that she left her sealed. If they'd had a fight right there on top of the volcano it would have escalated beyond control. Our barrier wouldn't have been able to contain them."

"It would have led to the complete destruction of the isle," the Jade Emperor confirmed and there was a hard set to his jaw that spoke of silent anger. "I am glad as well that she chose what she did.

Otherwise she could never be forgiven."

"Will she be forgiven, then?" From the ocean waves, Nia Reign stepped out of the water and onto the gravelly beach. She was much calmer than the last time that Sevana had seen her, and this time she looked more like the ethereal Fae only a darker version, her hair lying wet and dark over one shoulder, robes clinging to her from the sea water. "Jade Emperor."

"Nia Reign." The Jade Emperor gave a long, low inclination of his head, possibly the deepest bow that Sevana had seen him make yet. "Many apologies for making you wait. Forgive this incident. I am entirely to blame."

If Sevana was reading the mood correctly, the Jade Emperor had given her the most humble apology that he could, while making no excuses.

"Your people have been my neighbors for centuries, Jade Emperor. I have found them to be good neighbors. They are respectful. For their sake, I will forgive you. But understand this: Tian-Mu is not to be forgiven."

The Jade Emperor raised his head only to bow again, this time a little deeper. "You are magnanimous, Nia Reign. I am not worthy of your kindness."

Snorting, she turned her face away, deliberately not looking at any of them. "Thankfully, this is your first offense. Do not encroach upon my kindness again."

"I will strive not to do so." The Jade Emperor seemed to realize that he was not on smooth ground just yet, that he had only passed through a rocky patch and was about to step onto another one. "It is my understanding that you wish vengeance upon Tian-Mu."

"That is correct."

"It is also my understanding that the only person you have agreed to share vengeance with is Sellion?"

Nia Reign exchanged wolfish smiles with Sevana. "She shares my bloodlust for that woman. Her anger is not any less than mine."

"In that case, will you send her as your representative?" the Jade Emperor asked with all the caution of a man walking on eggshells. "I must leave soon to track Tian-Mu down and retrieve Feng-Huang. I do not wish to take you from your people, as you are sorely needed here, but I do not wish to disrespect your interests either."

Nia Reign regarded him coldly for several moments. "I am not pleased to be absent from the chase."

The Jade Emperor was wise enough not to comment but instead spread his hands in an open shrug as if to say, *What would you have me do?*

This stand-off lasted for several moments before Nia Reign let out a sound of aggravation. "However, you are correct, I cannot afford to leave in the near future. Sellion accompanying you is…a compromise I can live with. As long as you understand that she speaks with Our voice and witnesses with Our understanding."

Sevana's ears perked at those official 'ours' and knew that Nia Reign had just entrusted her with the interest of the whole of First Moon.

The Jade Emperor caught it as well and assured her, "She will be treated as your ambassador and her words will be your words."

This satisfied Nia Reign and only then did she face Sevana. "Sellion, you will go and see properly to our revenge. Do not let her off."

Sevana had no problem with promising, "I won't."

"And after it is all done, come and report properly to me. I expect every detail."

"I'll capture it all in a crystal so that you can see it unfold for yourself."

Nia Reign's interest perked visibly. "Human magic can do such a thing? Excellent. I look forward to that. Jade Emperor, I will let Sellion be there through all of it, but I want an official notice from you on what Tian-Mu's sentencing is."

"I will make sure that a proper messenger is sent to you."

"Then I am content." Nia Reign shared another wolfish smile with Sevana. "Good hunting, Sellion."

"She will not escape," Sevana promised her, nearly purring with dark promise. "On that, you can rest assured."

20

If Sevana had not known better, she would have vowed that before becoming the Jade Emperor, the man was the Immortal Janitor or something along those lines. Never in her life did she see a cleanup as fast as this one. In two days, the village, docks, and rice fields were all clear. A good section of the coast was also clear, leaving half the isle in good condition, although it couldn't be said to be back in its original shape. Most of the animals that had survived the explosion chose to congregate there, as it was the safest place for them to be. Chi-Lin was riding herd on them to make sure that any natural predators were kept in check. He also worked out some deal with the Unda to help him feed everyone from the sea. Most of the cleanup work was done by the Jade Emperor, as he did not rest for more than a few minutes before applying his considerable divine power onto the problem.

Master had him help with the breach, the section of sea impacted most by the break in the barrier, with Nia Reign's blessing. Since it had spilled over from land and into sea, it took everyone's combined effort to fix the situation. Now the lava was back where it was supposed to be, the acidic water filtered, and it was safe to walk through that area. Sevana knew that it would take years before the place was habitable, but at least it wasn't dangerous anymore.

Early on the third day, she found the Jade Emperor poking and prodding at *Jumping Clouds* the same way that a child would a new toy. If memory served, the gods of this pantheon were used to riding palanquins during holidays and celebrations. From his perspective, perhaps *Jumping Clouds* looked like a massive palanquin? It had the same square shape, roof, and open windows to it that a smaller palanquin would.

Sensing her approach, the Jade Emperor turned and beckoned to her. "Is this yours? I have seen three devices like it but this one seems very different from the rest."

"Of course it is," she agreed, coming up to stand next to him. "It's the original. I created this. Everyone else copied my design. It's a flying ship, designed to carry cargo and passengers great distances."

Intrigued, he asked, "How far can it fly?"

"It's more a matter of how much magic it has to fly with. Other than that, it has no limit."

"Truly?" He regarded the ship from prow to stern once again. "I have been contemplating on how to bring both you and Arandur with me. It would be cumbersome to hold you throughout the journey after all."

A point that she had not considered until he brought it up. Now that he had, she started to worry about that too. Did she really want to be held by this god for days at a time? "You're welcome to use *Jumping Clouds*. It'll be a far more convenient way to travel, especially as we're bringing two more people back with us."

"That is so." Beaming, he nearly bounced on his toes. "I accept your offer. While we travel, you must tell me more about human magic. I have had little interaction with it and I see now that my ignorance is to my people's detriment. You have done much to help them, as have the other magicians you have called, and it would behoove me to gain a better understanding of such matters."

A god willing to learn? Sevana had respect for people that could not only acknowledge their shortcomings but work to overcome them. "I have no problem teaching you, Jade Emperor."

"I am glad. Then, I think we shall take this and leave soon. I believe that you and Arandur will want to pack provisions first?"

"Aran anticipated that you wanted to leave soon, so he's seeing to our food now. Jade Emperor, if you could make sure the ship is clean? I'll pack my tools and things and we should be able to get underway in the next hour."

Blinking, the Jade Emperor regarded her with mild surprise. "So quickly? I thought preparations for journeys would take longer than that."

"Not with us," Sevana denied with a shrug. "Aran and I both are used to traveling, as our occupations demand a great deal of it, and half the time we're leaving because of an emergency. We've learned how to pack the essentials quickly. I'll meet you back here in an hour."

Sevana was correct in that it took less than an hour for them all to meet back at *Jumping Clouds*. The bags of clothes, tools, and food were safely stowed before Sevana took the wheel. She had left the majority of her tools behind, as she didn't need them anyway and the people here might. But she took what she thought she'd need, if her magic decided to cooperate.

Without a word to her, Aran touched the main control pad and inserted his magic, starting *Jumping Clouds* off. This interaction, so quietly done, still did not escape the Jade Emperor's eyes. As they lifted up into the air, he watched their ascent for long moments before asking, "Is there a reason, Artifactor, that you do not use magic on your own machine?"

"I think you know there is," she responded a little tartly. "You said they went in a north-easterly direction? Precisely where?"

Aran pointed for her, then bent over her back to guide the ship around until the compasses were pointing in the right direction. It was a gesture he had done often, as they'd spent so much time together that physical contact between them had become a comfortable thing, although for some strange reason it was not like that right now. She was hyperaware of every brush of him against her back and every breath he took. "Here," he said against her temple. "Keep this bearing for now."

Sevana was highly relieved when he leaned back again. She felt strangely flushed from that contact.

The Jade Emperor regarded him with respect. "I have underestimated a Fae's eyes. I did not believe you could see their trail. It is several days' old after all."

"I'm a tracker," Aran explained simply.

"Ah, now I understand." Not to be put off, he inclined his head to Sevana. "Her magical core is fluctuating badly. I do not wish to pry, but considering where we are going, I do need to know."

Aran, as usual, spoke the words that left a bitter aftertaste in Sevana's mouth. "Sev nearly died several months ago. In order to save her, I put some of my blood into her, but in doing that it made her partly Fae. Her magic has been wildly out of control since."

Eyebrows arched, the Jade Emperor pressed, "Was that the only effect?"

"No, strangely enough, it did do several other things none of us were anticipating. It's increased her sense of sight, smell, and hearing by about thirty percent. It's also seemed to have an anti-aging effect. It hasn't halted her time, not like an immortal's, but it has decreased it. We believe that if she were to remain in her current state, she would live a good three hundred years." Candidly, Aran confided, "We don't wish to leave her in this state, of course, it's terribly inconvenient for her. But Sev is a unique case. We haven't had someone like her in living memory. We're thinking that we'll have to do some serious study and experimentation to solve her magic problems. Either that or turn her wholly Fae."

"I did not think you could do that to an adult…?" the Jade Emperor said slowly, thinking hard.

"We didn't either, but honestly, our lore suggested that putting Fae blood into an adult would be like poison. It would either strengthen them or kill them. I was taking a huge gamble when I tried what I did. It's why the results are so surprising. Not only did it save her, it also adapted to her, changed her into half-Fae. We're now starting to question a great deal of our lore and teachings because of her."

The Jade Emperor gave a sage nod. "I see why. Do keep me apprised of this, Arandur. I want to know the results."

"Many do. I'll add you onto the list," Sevana drawled.

Looking about, the Jade Emperor found a swivel chair and perched himself comfortably. "We will hold this course for some time, I believe. While we fly, I wish to learn more about your magic."

Taking that as an open invitation, Sevana gave him a crash

course on the basics of human magic. No surprise to anyone, the Jade Emperor was an avid student and his mind such that he retained anything told to him, so that she never had to repeat herself. Sometimes her explanations confused him, but Aran had gone through this same process, and he would rephrase it in a way more understandable.

This wasn't something that could be taught in a single afternoon, but she'd covered the highlights before they agreed to break for dinner. At that point, Sevana realized that they had a slight problem to work out. "Gentlemen, how do we want to do this? We can land, as *Jumping Clouds* is sea worthy and won't sink if we settle on the water for the night. Or we can take it in shifts and fly through the night. I have no preference."

The Jade Emperor lifted a single finger to call attention to himself. "Sevana, are you able to see their trail for yourself?"

"Not in this failing light, no." Even right now it was barely visible to her, only a faint glimmer in the air.

"Then I would need to stay up with you if we chose to fly through the night. Humans do not function well without sleep the next day, so I am not sure if this is a wise choice."

"I wouldn't need to stay up all night," Sevana explained patiently. "Aran knows how to fly the ship and can do it on his own. Actually, what we'd be doing is splitting the shift in half, four hours each. I would need you to stay up with me to navigate but then we can rest when he takes over."

Brows arched slightly, the Jade Emperor gave Aran an interested study. "You can pilot this on your own?"

"If you hang about her for the better part of a year," Aran responded with an amused shrug, "you learn how to do all sorts of things. I learned how to pilot this first as it was more convenient that way."

"He hasn't gotten us lost or crashed us yet," Sevana said cheerfully. "Which is more than I can say for some of my students."

"In that case, I am amenable to flying through the night. Who shall take first watch?"

Sevana lifted a fist toward Aran, an open invitation to play, and he readily held out his own. They did a quick game of rock-paper-scissors, resulting in Aran's win, so he chose the second watch. Sevana actually preferred that as she hated sleeping only to have to wake up and immediately work again. Her brain didn't normally shift gears that readily.

After dinner, Aran grabbed a quilt and pillow from a back cupboard and rolled into it, almost instantly falling asleep. Sevana made sure he was settled before regaining the pilot's seat and checking her instruments to verify they were still on course. "Tian-Mu's not deviated from this direction all day. But as far as I'm aware, there's nothing out here but ocean until you cross to the other end of Mander and reach the Kesley Islands."

"I am not sure if she is heading toward them," the Jade Emperor said slowly, stroking thoughtfully at his beard. "But I am concerned with her direction. She will have stumbled across both dragon and Unda territory if she does not deviate."

And that worried Sevana. Neither one of those races was lax about uninvited guests to say the least. "Jade Emperor, if we have to cross them, then it would be best to stop and explain ourselves to them, gain permission to cross their lands. I do have a few contacts near here that might help if we need it."

"That is good to know. I do not believe we will have that trouble, however. Tian-Mu is rash, but not stupid. She will surely avoid making more enemies this far from home."

One would think, but this was the same woman that had set off a volcano in a fit of rage, so Sevana wasn't holding her breath. She started making mental contingency plans for when things did go very wrong. She didn't have any gold on board—which now seemed like a very gross oversight—so going into dragon territory would be more than difficult. Outright dangerous. She would consider it suicidal if not for that fact that a god and Fae were on board. If anyone could talk them through it, it would be these two.

Sevana didn't even want to consider how to cross into Unda territory. Even with her elevated company, it might be suicidal to approach them.

"Sevana, if I may ask, how did your relationship begin with the Fae?"

It was a question that many wanted to ask and few dared to. Sevana saw no reason not to relate the story, as it would while away the time. "I'm neighbors with South Woods. That was the very beginning of it. I respected their territory, they in turn respected mine, and it stayed that way for many years. Then one day I brought them a human orphan. I did it more for his sake than anything else, but they were extremely grateful to me, and I promised to bring other orphans as I found them. I average anywhere between fifteen to twenty a year, just children that I stumble across in my travels. There is nothing that the Fae cherish more than their children. It fostered an extremely close relationship between us."

The Jade Emperor gave a silent 'ahh' of understanding. "That would account for it."

"That's mostly the basis. At the end of last year, however, a case fell into my lap that was rather heinous in nature. I discovered during the course of it that Fae ink had been used, and when I pursued the matter, I learned it had actually been stolen from North Woods. They were livid at the theft and grateful I had found the hole in their security. After the case was settled, and I was back on my feet, I went through South and North Woods' security systems and made sure that human magic couldn't defeat it. By that point, I'd become a daughter to them." She'd said it so simply, but Sevana felt the weight of all those memories and experiences as she relayed the matter. Becoming part of the Fae had nearly cost her life. "You wondered earlier why Aran is so protective of me? Because I nearly died during that last case, all while helping the Fae nation, and they are now anxious to avoid such a situation again."

"I do not think that is the only reason," the Jade Emperor demurred with a distinct twinkle in his eyes. The setting sun still gave her enough light to see that there was an enigmatic smirk on his face.

Knowing what he meant, she shrugged. "He's strangely fond of me as well, which I can't explain, as I know well that I'm a bear to live with sometimes."

Giving a noncommittal sound, the Jade Emperor let that be. "Arandur has mentioned perhaps the chance of you becoming truly Fae. Is this something you desire?"

"I have no idea," she admitted with a troubled frown. "It wasn't something I thought possible until I came here. He only recently mentioned the idea to me. I want to return home, do some research, and really think about it for a while. It would mean changing my entire lifestyle and I'm not sure if I'm willing to do that."

"It is wise to take your time and ponder. Once changed, it would be impossible to reverse and return to being human."

Which was exactly her worry. Actually, Sevana wasn't sure if she preferred being human over the possibility of being Fae. The Fae body was far superior after all. It was the *rest* of it that she wasn't sure what to think of. Her magic would change completely and all of her human ability in that department would disappear. She would be wholly Fae, magic included. Also, the Fae didn't live apart from each other, not even those like Aran who worked outside of the territory. They always returned home as soon as they could. Aran coming to stay with her was far outside of the norms, and even in his case it was only because she was considered to be Fae. He wasn't really living among humans per se.

Having lived most of her life traveling about the world at ease, would she be content always staying in the same area? Sevana highly doubted it. But if she became completely Fae, Aranhil would likely prohibit her from traveling about freely, for fear of her safety. It was not an idea that sat well with her.

"There's many potential troubles to take into account and I'm not sure if the benefits will be worth it," she said on a sigh. "But on the other hand, I might not have much of a choice if we can't straighten my magic back out. If I can't make a living as a human, I'll have no choice but to become a Fae."

"I do not think you will be forced into that. Your magic is unbalanced, not damaged. That much I can see."

Well that was heartening to hear. Sevana glanced down at her instruments, checking the bearings and the map that was tracking their progress, and frowned. "Jade Emperor, we're about an hour or so from entering Unda territory. Please tell me her course changed."

"It has not." The Jade Emperor stood and looked out, his features highlighted in the dying sunlight, making him look like a chiseled statue. "I fear we will have trouble ahead."

21

Aran had only been asleep about three hours, but the situation demanded that she wake him up anyway. Sevana did no more than touch his shoulder and call his name before he was rolling upright, eyes wide open. His ability to wake up in an instant was one that she privately envied on a regular basis. "What is it?"

"We have a slight problem. And by slight I mean massive. Tian-Mu's trail goes straight down into Unda territory."

He let out a groan and flopped back down. "That is so not good."

"If you have a trick up your sleeve on how to deal with this, I'd be very glad to hear it," she said hopefully, smiling down at him.

Staring back at her, Aran drawled, "Did I ever mention to you that the Unda of this area are even more ruthless than their northern cousins?"

"…You're just full of good news, aren't you?"

"You started it."

"It's my fault we're chasing after a stupid goddess with a mad-on? Who doesn't have the sense of a fruit fly?"

Contemplating this, Aran agreed, "You're right, we'll blame it on the Jade Emperor."

The Jade Emperor didn't groan but he did heave a long, drawn out sigh. "I did not anticipate that she would blunder into another's territory like this."

"People are not known to make sensible decisions when they're angry." Aran sat up again and threw the blanket off. As he folded things up and stored them away, he asked, "How close are we to Unda territory?"

"We're smack on the border of it, according to the map. We're hovering in place there."

Aran gave her a nod of approval and relief. "Good. It's close to, what, ten o'clock?"

"It is." Sevana would have suggested that they just land and anchor for the night except for one little fact: the Unda were nocturnal. They actually had a better chance of speaking to the Unda without rousting someone out of bed by contacting them now. Sevana was all for doing that instead of trying to negotiate with someone rudely yanked from sleep. "Well, gentlemen, who wants to do the honors?"

The Jade Emperor and Aran shared a long, speaking look. "How much experience do you have with these Unda, Arandur?" the Jade Emperor finally asked.

"Probably more than you do," Aran admitted. "I only come into contact with them about once a year. Sev, remember that group of kids we brought from Sao Kao? Two of them came to this territory."

Sevana snapped her fingers. "Right, I remember that. The Unda actually sent a representative and bargained for two of them. Jade Emperor, let's send in Aran first. We've got trade relationships with them after all."

He waved them on, not so secretly relieved that they were volunteering. Sevana maneuvered *Jumping Clouds* down so that it settled on the sea and anchored it to make sure it didn't accidentally drift into Unda territory. That would be very, very bad. When they were settled, Aran leaned over the sides and put his hand into the water, just holding it there for a long time before finally pulling it free again.

It took barely ten minutes before a head popped out of the water, that of a mermaid with glistening dark hair and large, liquid eyes set above sharp cheekbones. She blinked up at Aran and then beamed a siren's smile. "Hello, my handsome cousin."

Aran didn't seem quite sure what to make of this greeting and went with a neutral, "Hello. I am sorry to come and just knock on your door like this. I am Arandur of South Woods."

"Oh, the one that brought us children before?" Grabbing the railing, she lifted herself partway out of the water so that she was speaking on a more even level with him. As she did so, she of course saw the other two and paused, giving them a confused study.

"This is Sellion, also of South Woods," Aran carried on the introductions calmly. "She's actually the one that found the children to begin with. Our guest is the Jade Emperor."

The mermaid inclined her head to both of them, her flirtatiousness vanishing without a trace. "I am Kari. I am the sister of the second cousin's mother's best-friend that was gifted with one of the children you brought. We are happy with our son."

Sevana didn't even try to unravel that connection. Unda family relations could make dwarves' family trees seem simple. "We are very happy to hear it. Actually our business here has nothing to do with the children, but while I am here, I would enjoy seeing them. They are surely glowing as they change and grow into Unda."

This softened the mermaid and she gave a slight nod. "I will be your guide for that. But if not for the children, what brings you here?"

The Jade Emperor cleared his throat slightly. "As to that, one of my goddesses has kidnapped another and fled with her. We are afraid they have come straight through your territory."

At that, the mermaid's eyes flashed with anger. "That rude, destructive woman is yours?"

Oh that did not sound good. What had Tian-Mu done *now*?

Face completely impassive, the Jade Emperor said neutrally, "She is. I would like to speak with someone about retrieving her."

Kari regarded all three of them, mouth pursed. "I will fetch someone. Wait here." She dropped down in a splash and was gone within a second.

Sevana let out a low breath and dropped back into her chair. "This just gets better and better."

"If not for the fact that you're with two people that brought them children, they probably wouldn't have agreed to even speak with us," Aran informed the Jade Emperor. "This is more serious than we anticipated. If Tian-Mu had gone straight through their territory, it'd upset them, but we would have been able to negotiate our way around it. But actually doing something destructive in their territory? While they have two children here to raise?"

"I want to go home," Sevana whimpered, only half-kidding. "Nothing upsets the Fae or the Unda faster than bringing a threat near their children. I'll be highly surprised if Tian-Mu is even still alive."

"She's alive," the Jade Emperor disagreed solemnly. "I can feel both her and Feng-Huang clearly. Their powers are diminished at the moment, sealed, but still steady."

So they had somehow sealed Tian-Mu? Sevana wasn't too surprised by this; it's what she would have done in their shoes. Why leave a loose cannonball in your territory when it could be safely locked up instead? "Jade Emperor, I have a feeling that the only way we're going to be able to get in and out with our skins intact is to make them some pretty hefty promises. Now, I doubt this, as I know your people's culture well, but I'll ask anyway: how often do you have orphans among your people?"

"It's unusual. Even when it does happen, extended family takes them in." The Jade Emperor caught on quickly. "You think to bargain with children?"

"Nothing is more important, more cherished than children to us," Aran explained quietly. "Especially for the Unda, human children are hard to come by, which is why their numbers have always been so small. The two that we brought to them this past year were the first children they've had in fifty years."

"I have no compunction about giving either the Fae or Unda children as they are amazing parents," Sevana stated bluntly. "And often the orphans I bring to them are barely scraping by on the streets, so it's worlds better for them to become Fae anyway. In this case, if you don't have orphans to offer, then we'll work out some sort of payment between us. I'll promise to supply them with children." It was easily enough done, all she had to do was contact Kip, or two different kings that owed her major favors. "How much they will demand from us, that's the question. The rest is details."

The words had barely left her mouth when two heads popped

out of the water. One was Kira, the other a male mermaid with short hair and a trident in his hand. He looked bulky, strong, and extremely angry. His dark eyes took in both Aran and Sevana and he gave them an inclination of the head, barely courteous, before pinning the Jade Emperor with a glare hot enough to melt steel. "I am Taslim, Guardian of the Southern Border. I am here on behalf of my king, Curano, and I speak with His Voice."

In other words, he had full power to negotiate for the whole of this tribe.

The Jade Emperor stepped forward and gave a deep bow. "Taslim, I am the Jade Emperor, ruler over Tian-Mu and Feng-Huang. I am deeply sorry for the trouble mine have caused yours. I have come to make reparations as best I can."

Taslim didn't budge. "Your women have posed a danger to our children."

"It is a grievous offense," the Jade Emperor agreed promptly and with a troubled frown. "In truth, we are chasing them because Tian-Mu broke several laws in my own territory and then fled. Feng-Huang is an innocent party in this, being sealed, and I am trying to retrieve her to bring her home again. Tian-Mu I seek to punish."

Seeing this might be the right moment to speak, Sevana cleared her throat. "Taslim, I am Sellion of South Woods. I speak for Nia Reign with Her Voice."

That made both mermaids pause and stare at her openly. "You speak for Nia Reign?" Taslim asked, voice rising an octave.

"I do. It was in her territory that Tian-Mu caused havoc. She wishes vengeance upon her and I have promised to make sure that happens." Which complicated matters extremely, as now there were two Unda clans out for the goddess's blood, but it also gave them an additional bargaining chip. The Unda here did not want to upset their northern cousins. They would have to factor that relationship in to any choice they made. "Also, I have a vested interest in this matter personally. I am not sure if Kira told you, but Arandur and I are the ones that brought you the children."

Taslim stared hard at his counterpart, silently reprimanding her with his eyes. "No, she did not mention that part to me."

"You took off before I could get it out," she grumbled under her breath.

Mentioning all of this was the right move as Taslim became visibly more interested in actually talking instead of ranting. "Sellion, I am glad to report that our children are safe despite the danger that woman put them through."

"I am also very glad to hear this," Sevana responded in kind. "I will make sure her punishment is more severe for this offense."

That soothed another ruffled feather, but it still left many others that were prickly. "You said that she broke several laws in Nia Reign's territory? What did she do?"

Without any apology or sugar coating, Sevana gave him the outline of what had happened. She could see his ire build again and she could feel the Jade Emperor openly wincing behind her, but there was no getting around the truth. Even if she tried to skirt around it now, it would be pointless; word was bound to get to them eventually. She couldn't sacrifice trade relations with this clan just to get two goddesses out right now.

At the end of her telling, Taslim looked down, troubled. "This complicates matters. You do have the right to punish her on Nia Reign's behalf, but we must have say in this matter as well. I cannot speak for both of our clans. Wait here. I must confer with my superiors."

In an instant they were both gone and only then did Sevana draw in a proper breath. "Alright, this is going better than I thought it would."

"Truly," the Jade Emperor agreed. "I am correct in assuming that he was sent here to get rid of us?"

"You are," Aran confirmed. "He had the power to do that, or the power to decide that wasn't the right course of action to take. That we managed to convince him to hear us out completely was the first success of negotiations."

If they had failed that, Sevana really didn't know what they could have done. Pull rank and have Aranhil try? Although she didn't think pulling three different Fae and Unda clans into negotiations was a good idea in any sense.

This time they had to wait a long while. When there finally was movement on the water, it was a bulge in the sea, sending water in every direction as something massive surfaced. Sevana nearly swallowed her tongue as she realized it was a giant sea turtle, larger than anything she had ever seen before. On its back lounged three different people. One of them was Taslim, but the other two were unknown to her. From the elegant robes they wore, embroidered with tiny shells, hair in elaborate braids over their shoulders, and the small crowns spanning their foreheads, it was clear that these were highly ranked officials of the Unda. Sevana would bet her eye teeth she was about to meet queen and king.

The turtle maneuvered so that he was side by side with *Jumping Clouds,* and Taslim did a very elaborate roll so that he was close enough to them to offer a hand up. He did the motion with such grace that he didn't even look like a landed fish in the process. "Sellion, Arandur, Jade Emperor, you are invited to come up."

Sevana took his offered hand and levered herself up and out, gaining the back of the sea turtle. It was a hard, round, slick surface because of the water. Thankfully it had enough rivets in it that it gave her boots some purchase. Otherwise she would have disgraced herself by sliding right into the sea. Aran was close on her heels and immediately put a hand at the small of her back. She recognized the gesture for what it was—a silent declaration to the parties here that he would react at the slightest danger posed to her.

With the Unda, such statements were probably necessary.

The Jade Emperor took up position on her other side and gave a bow to the other two. "I am the Jade Emperor, ruler over Feng-Huang and Tian-Mu. I am deeply sorry for the trouble she has caused you."

Silently, Sevana applauded, as it was good to get the apology out there right off the bat. "I am Sellion of South Woods. I speak for Nia Reign with Her Voice."

"I am Arandur of South Woods."

Taslim did his roll trick again and ended up back on the other side. "I present King Curano and Queen Rane of Living Waters."

Oh, that was their clan name here? First anyone had mentioned it.

"We greet you, Sellion and Arandur," Rane said in a silky smooth voice. She actually sounded cordial, which wasn't too odd, as she was probably inclined to like the people that brought her children. "Jade Emperor. I am very grieved by what your goddess has done in my territory. She barged into our waters without greeting or permission, ran through our waterways and upset the tides, and then went straight into one of our Rooms and created havoc inside."

Sevana felt the urge to find a corner somewhere, put her nose into it, and cry. Tian-Mu's stupidity had just crossed into the Legendary Category.

Seeing a flash of confusion on the Jade Emperor's face, Sevana explained, although it felt like she was chewing on a rotten lemon while doing so. "A Room to the Unda is a very special storage facility, you could say. From the outside, they look like underwater caves, but they house anything between magical artifacts to treasures. It depends on what they're designated for. Tian-Mu apparently entered one like a bull in a china shop. The damage she could do in one is...." Words failed her at that point. Just her internal guesstimates of the price tag made Sevana want to throw up.

The Jade Emperor looked about ready to lose the contents of his stomach as well. "I plead ignorance on her behalf. Feng-Huang was sealed inside of a mountain in Nia Reign's lands. Tian-Mu was likely trying to find a similar location to seal Feng-Huang inside of."

"So we gathered from what she was screaming at us," Curano drawled. Waves of anger poured off of him. "Sellion, I am glad that you fully understand the damage she has done. It saves us time in our negotiations. Answer me this: did this woman cause similar damage in my sister's lands?"

"She did, although more grievous in a way, as she threatened the safety of the entire territory," Sevana answered promptly. "Nia Reign wants her blood and I have promised to see Tian-Mu punished as fully as possible."

Curano gave her a smile like a co-conspirator. "Then we are in one accord in that regard. This pleases me."

If Sevana had been on the receiving end of not one, but two Unda rulers wanting her blood, she likely would have had a heart attack and died on the spot. It was just as well Tian-Mu wasn't present during all of this, as her immortality might have been put to the test. "Curano, Rane, I understand that the damage that she did in your Room is likely priceless. I understand as well that more importantly than what you have lost in the Room, it was the danger she posed to your children that most upsets you."

"You are correct, Sellion." Rane's head tilted in a gesture of keen interest. "Do you have a proposal for us? What can you offer that will equal what we have lost?"

"I cannot replace what is gone," at least Sevana was pretty sure that was the case and wasn't about to try, "but what if I offer you something equally priceless?"

22

Rane was quick on the uptake. "Children?" she breathed hopefully. "You offer us more children?"

"I do." Sevana glanced at the Jade Emperor. "He and I will work out separate payment so that I'm reimbursed for the trouble, but that is what I am offering on his behalf: release Tian-Mu and Feng-Huang into his custody. I will bring you children within six months."

The Queen of Living Waters looked ready to agree on the spot. To her, she was coming out ahead in this deal. Her husband was a different story as he was still mad about the whole situation. Glaring at them both, he demanded, "Why, Sellion, would you aid this man in their release?"

"Because I want Tian-Mu punished," Sevana responded promptly, without batting an eye. "Curano, you have amazing power and ability, but do you have the power to punish Tian-Mu? Truly punish? I think your options are rather limited to either imprisoning her or killing her. That is not what Nia Reign wants at all. She wants Tian-Mu alive for many centuries so that she can feel the full weight of her punishment."

Curano let out a sound that might have been a curse or a growl.

The Jade Emperor cleared his throat. "We have our own process in punishing one of ours. I will have to bring Tian-Mu before a council of seven in order to obey the laws. However, I can safely promise you this: at the very least she will be stripped of her godhood, her powers, and relegated to that of a human. I will set her to the task of laboring for many centuries so that she has no rest."

Both of them understood that for a god, there was no worse

punishment than to lose all of your powers. This promise mollified Curano some and the pleading look in his wife's eyes did the rest. She was perfectly willing to boot Tian-Mu out if it meant getting her hands on children. The expression on her face made that clear.

Not willing to give up that easily, Curano pointed a grumpy finger at Sevana. "Three months."

Sevana had to bite the inside of her lip to keep from smiling. She had just won the battle. Now was the easy part. "That entirely depends on how many children you want. It will take me a while to find them and transport them down here, after all. Ten? A dozen?"

Rane leaned forward, eyes glued to her. "You can find a dozen children in three months?"

"I think so." Sevana turned to Aran, all casual in manner. "Remind me, doesn't King Bellomi and King Firuz still owe me children?"

"They both promised you some, yes." Aran played along beautifully. "We didn't have time to check in with them in the past three weeks, considering all that happened, but the last that I heard from them, they had found a few orphans they thought would be appropriate."

"Really? That will save me some time, then." Sevana blinked at her audience, all guileless. "If I find that I have more than a dozen waiting for me, should I just bring them all? Or do you just want a dozen? I can always take them to North Woods—"

"All," Rane commanded firmly. "Every child waiting for you, we will take."

Curano looked like he wanted to argue, just to maintain his ground, but even he was willing to put the priority on having more children. It shifted his stance so that he didn't have a figurative toe to stand on. "Sellion. You have traded with us before. You are Aranhil's daughter. You speak for Nia Reign. All of these things tell me that I can deal with you in good faith and you will not break the bargain. But I do not have experience with the Jade Emperor. What if he does not uphold his bargain with you?"

The Jade Emperor looked affronted by this, as well he should be, but these two didn't have a relationship with each other in any way. It was a valid point that Curano raised and he knew it. "I do not have a relationship with you, but I do with Nia Reign, and she has agreed that I can handle Tian-Mu's punishment."

"That is correct," Sevana verified. "Curano, I do not believe that the Jade Emperor will go back on his word. He is not a god that would do such trickery. But on the off chance something goes awry, rest assured that it will not affect my promise to you. I can ill afford to lose my trade relationship with you. Within three months you will have children, delivered by my hand."

That satisfied him. "Then the deal is made. Taslim, go and retrieve the women."

Taslim put a fist to his heart, rolled and dove off the turtle's back.

Curano wasn't quite done and he gave the Jade Emperor another glare. "Whatever task you set her, make sure that she never puts so much as a toe into the sea. If I feel her presence in the water, she will lose that limb."

Being a wise god, the Jade Emperor simply inclined his head in understanding.

Rane was satisfied with the matter and her mind clearly on other things. She held out a hand, gesturing for Sevana to come closer, and patted the area next to her. "Come, speak with me further about the children. You mentioned two kings. Where are they?"

Sevana crossed and settled comfortably, crossing her legs, and tried to wrap her head around having a nice, cozy chat with a scary Unda Queen. "One of them is Sa Kao, a desert land that doesn't see much water. The two children that I gave to you? They are from that country originally."

"Oh, more from there? I am glad to hear it, they are very good children. And the other?"

"The other country is Windamere, which is where I am from. South Woods is on their border. I know the king there very well, he and his queen, and they are always quick to give me any orphans they find." Partially because it kept crime off their streets. "My business partner, Morgan, is the one that keeps tabs on all of this while I'm on a job, as it's hard for me to stay in communication with them both.

I'll contact him the moment Tian-Mu's punishment is settled and get a headcount of how many children are available now. How shall I communicate with you when I have that information?"

"You raise a good question." From her throat, she unlatched a small conch shell that hung off a gold chain, and then reached forward to put it on Sevana. "I have the sister of this shell. It will let you speak directly with me."

Whoa! Sevana hadn't meant for something like this to happen and was a little floored that she now had direct access to the queen's ear when she needed it. "Rane, I am humbled by this gift."

"Do not be. It comes with a price." Rane's rebuke was softened with a smile. She nearly glowed with excitement. "I want regular updates, not only on my children, but also on that woman's punishment."

Which meant that Sevana now had two queens to report to. Lovely. "I understand. In order to use it, do I just lift it to my mouth?"

"No. It is perfectly understandable in this position. You must say my name three times. Then I will hear and respond. Try it now, to make sure that it will work with your magic."

Wise idea considering how her magic behaved these days. Better to break it now and be able to get a replacement than try it later. Sevana dutifully said, "Rane, Rane, Rane."

The shell lit up faintly on her chest and the sound of the ocean filled her ears.

"Perfect," Rane's voice said in a dual echo. "It works fine."

The shell's power faded and went still again. Sevana picked it up and stared at it with great curiosity. Interesting, her magic hadn't tried to flare out of control when she had used it. In fact, that was the smoothest interaction she'd had with another magical device since her injury. Now why was that?

Aran had caught this as well and tentatively stepped up to her side, also bending his head to look at it. "That worked amazingly well."

"Didn't it?" Sevana agreed, still staring hard at the shell. "I think this is the first magical object I've tried to use that wasn't human made. I wonder if that's the difference or if my magic is just behaving today?"

"It's a good question, and an easy one to test."

Rane regarded them both curiously. "I noticed, Sellion, that your magic is out of balance. There is a cause for this?"

Aran launched into the explanation, as he always did, and Rane listened attentively throughout. Curano just as avidly listened in, expression growing thoughtful. When Aran finished, he offered, "We have an expert here that likes to study human magic. He is one of our researchers. Perhaps, Sellion, you should speak with him when you return with the children. This state of fluctuation is not one that you should live in."

"I can agree with that whole-heartedly. I will be pleased to speak with him, Curano." Sevana glanced at Aran, wondering if this was one of the experts that he had mentioned before. Aran seemed to realize what she was wondering and he gave her a small shake of the head. No? Then that was all the more interesting.

Taslim returned with several others, all of them bearing the two goddesses wrapped in a clear membrane of some sort. They were tossed in front of the Jade Emperor with little care and both goddesses bounced once before settling. Sevana could feel their silent anger from this and the Jade Emperor hiding his feelings behind a stone mask.

With another bow to the two rulers, the Jade Emperor lifted both women and retreated back into *Jumping Clouds*.

Sevana had to make a few more promises of updates as soon as she had information before she could finally escape back into *Jumping Clouds*. Aran lost no time in lifting them into the air and turning the ship around before retracing their route. Only once they were airborne did Sevana take her first full breath.

"That went amazingly well. I was very afraid that you were going to have to sacrifice Tian-Mu to get Feng-Huang back."

"I also feared such." The Jade Emperor stood staring at both of his goddesses with a contemplative look on his face. "Sevana. Did you have the idea of bartering with children before we came here?"

"Not really, no. It's more habit than anything else, as I've become an adoption center for the Fae. I find them children all throughout the year and I have a list of clans that want children waiting for me. They usually pay in kind for my help by giving me rare elements. This is the first time I've used it in a hostage situation. I was going with the flow more than anything else. You object?"

His expression said that he did. "I find the idea of bartering with a child's life…discomfiting."

"You shouldn't. If not the Unda, the children I find will go to some Fae clan." Seeing that he wasn't sold, Sevana gave an aggravated sigh. "Jade Emperor, understand this: the children I bring are orphans that are not being taken care of. They literally have no family or means of support. Often they're street rats and thieves because that's the only way they can survive. I'd rather have those kids in a Fae or Unda clan, with parents and extended family, wouldn't you?"

"Well, I would, but…"

"And I can't work for free. Gathering all of those kids up, traveling with them to their new homes, all of that takes a lot of time. I incur expenses in the process. I have to be repaid somehow."

The Jade Emperor gave her a long look, his face blank so that he didn't show any emotion. "I won't win this argument, I see."

"Many have tried. But they also don't give me any other viable option. I find these kids good homes. My conscience is clear." Pointing a finger, she tsked him. "What you and I should be discussing is what you're going to pay me with. After all, the tab for this is on you. Not just for the considerable help I gave your people with the volcano, but also for this rescue mission."

He inclined his head in agreement. "That is true. We shall discuss it on the way home. First, however, I am inclined to release Feng-Huang. There is something that I must verify with her."

Oh? Sevana was interested to see this so she stepped aside and let him have the room he needed to approach. With a snap of the fingers, the membrane surrounding Feng-Huang disappeared in a flash, and then the seal around her broke as well. For the first time, Sevana could see the goddess properly.

She resided in phoenix form, red and golds and blues, beautiful in coloring. She shimmered as she moved, sitting up gracefully and half-unfolding her wings as she stretched and found her bearings. On seeing the Jade Emperor lean over her, she dipped her head gracefully forward. "You have freed me?"

"I have, to answer my question. When we were at the banquet, what did you say to Lei-Gong?"

Feng-Huang blinked up at him as if she couldn't begin to understand why that would be important or why he would be asking. "I asked him if he could pour me a cup of wine, I think."

Aran leaned in closer to Sevana and whispered dubiously, "That's it? That's not flirting."

"Not per se," she whispered back, thinking hard as she spoke. "But in this culture, pouring someone else a drink can either be a gesture of respect or a sign of affection, depending on the situation and the parties involved. It can be misconstrued as flirting if the mood is right."

The Jade Emperor pressed, "You asked him to pour you a cup?"

"Yes. He had the last of the wine sitting in front of him. Jade Emperor, forgive me, but why is this important?"

Clearly from her reaction, Feng-Huang hadn't done anything to be guilty of. She had asked another woman's husband to pour her a drink because he'd had the flask in front of him. So it was more a matter of convenience? Sevana groaned.

"Tian-Mu blew this completely out of proportion, didn't she."

Looking pained, the Jade Emperor let out a year's worth of sighs. "Feng-Huang, Tian-Mu accused you of flirting with her husband while drunk. That is the reason for your punishment."

Feng-Huang's beak dropped in shock and she transformed in a second into her humanoid shape. Her hair was still bright red, done up in an elaborate bun on top of her head, clothes red and gold and draped around a shapely figure. She was more beautiful than Tian-Mu, and Sevana saw in that instant where the jealousy had really spawned from.

"That woman accused me of flirting with her husband?! Who would want to be with that overbearing, judgmental man!"

That made the Jade Emperor sigh again and this time he looked beyond pained and maybe a little embarrassed.

Had he just taken Tian-Mu's word for it? He hadn't tried to investigate the matter himself? "Jade Emperor. Just how much in a rush were you that you didn't even ask the accused if the matter was true or not?"

"Very rushed," he admitted sourly. "We were interrupted mid-banquet with dire news and I literally had a few minutes to settle the matter before I left. Tian-Mu kept hounding me to see to Feng-Huang before I went."

And he'd done so just to get her off his back. Like a parent would a child that wouldn't leave them be? It sounded just like it.

"Feng-Huang, much has happened while you were sealed. How aware of events were you? I know that Sevana spoke to you through a dragon at one point."

Sevana let the Jade Emperor and Feng-Huang sort things out between them and retreated back to Aran's side. "Remind me never to get involved with a god of that pantheon. They apparently are too quick to make snap judgments."

"To think that this whole thing could have been avoided if the Jade Emperor had just asked Feng-Huang if it was true or not." Aran shook his head in wonderment. "Why do so many problems occur because of miscommunications?"

"And stupidity, don't forget stupidity. It's the leading cause of death and destruction in the world." Sevana would know, as she was called in to fix things after people made those stupid decisions. "Apparently even gods are not immune to this. Well. The Jade Emperor going to be paying through the nose for his mistake, so hopefully he won't repeat it. No matter what emergency is hanging over his head." Sevana had an idea that Tian-Mu's punishment just got worse, though. Men hated to be embarrassed more than anything else in the world. The Jade Emperor would not react well to her machinations.

Thinking ahead, Sevana requested, "Call Kip. I want a headcount and if it's short, we need to put him in motion. I'd rather get our repayment to the Unda out of the way quickly, if I can."

"He's likely asleep at this time of night," Aran pointed out. "I know there's a time difference between here and there, but you do realize it's after midnight? He's probably in bed by now."

"If I'm awake, he's awake. Don't worry, he's used to me rousting him out of a sound sleep and making unreasonable demands."

Aran stared at her for a long second. "Why is he friends you with again?"

"He's a glutton for punishment."

"That does explain it." Shaking his head, Aran pulled a Caller from his pouch and set it in front of her. "Morgan."

It took a long moment, some fumbling sounds, and a curse, but eventually the Caller came alive with Morgan's features. His hair stood on end and he had a robe barely on, eyes blinking rapidly as he tried to focus. "*Arandur. Sev. About time you called me with an update!*"

"Not just that, I have unreasonable demands," Sevana informed him cheerfully. "Kip, how many kids do we have for adoption?"

"*Judging from that scary smile on your face, not enough. I'm probably going to regret asking this, but...why?*"

Sevana settled in for a long conversation. This was going to take a while to explain.

23

Sevana had been in some very surreal situations before, but this one, well, this one took the cake by a long mile.

It might have been because she was surrounded by eight gods, including the Jade Emperor, all of them looking very majestic and resplendent in colorful robes. Or possibly it was because she sat with them, acting as ambassador for two Unda clans, which was mind-boggling in and of itself. But Sevana was fairly sure that the main reason lay in that for the past two hours she had been sitting quite comfortably on a cloud.

A cloud, mind you.

Sevana had seen many illustrations of the gods meeting and coming together in counsel in her lifetime, and they were always depicted being on clouds, but she had chucked it up to a gross misunderstanding on behalf of humankind. Or perhaps a blanket lack of creativity. Never had she suspected that it was actually truth until the Jade Emperor had kindly pointed her to the cloud near him and invited her to take a seat.

The only complaint that she had was that it felt a little airy, like wind was passing underneath her buttocks. Other than that, it was remarkably comfortable. It made the inventor in her wonder how she could duplicate it. Surely there was a way.

In the two hours she had been here, Sevana had been introduced, she had given her testimony of events—Aran had as well—and she had given a recounting of the very least punishment the Unda were willing to accept. That last part hadn't gone over very well. Tian-Mu had done a lot of wailing while Sevana tried to talk.

Then it was time for the accused to give her defense. For the past thirty minutes, Tian-Mu had been on a roll, justifying everything that she had done, pleading for leniency, the works. Her pleas more or less fell on deaf ears. Sevana had tuned her out two minutes in, Aran was actually napping while sitting upright, and the other gods were whispering to each other behind their hands. Being so openly ignored made Tian-Mu grow more shrill, which was harder to ignore, and Sevana glared at her. Wasn't this woman going to shut up?

"Enough," the Jade Emperor finally commanded, his voice ringing out like a bell toll. "Be still, Tian-Mu."

She choked to a stop, staring up at him with wide eyes, trembling hands clenched in front of her.

All of the whispering stopped as well, and the Jade Emperor looked from left to right, connecting to each god with his gaze alone. "You have heard all of the testimonies, arguments, defenses. What is your judgment?"

"Tian-Mu committed many mistakes in a very short time span," Yen-Lo-Wang declared slowly. As the God of Death and Ruler of the Fifth Court of Feng-Du, he cast a very dark figure. Black robes, black hair trailing down his back, a thin mustache outlining his mouth, dark eyes. For some reason, however, he wasn't a forbidding or frightening person. In fact, he was one of the calmest people in attendance and Sevana was inclined to like him for that alone. "I watched these events unfold, afraid that I would be overrun with souls that had lost their lives because of her rashness. It is only because of the mortals' efforts that we did not lose everyone. As it stands, we did lose seven of our people prematurely."

"This is very true," Guan-Yin observed. She had shucked her common clothing for the more celestial robes and no longer looked like a nurse that had spent a full day at a hospital. Sevana actually hadn't recognized her for a moment, the change was that extreme. "I saw with my own eyes the destruction that was caused. Our people are still suffering because of it and I expect that they will struggle for some years until the land around them fully recovers."

"I am especially angry regarding her conduct in the sea," Ao-Chin, Dragon King of the Southern Ocean, declared with an open flare of temper. "I am on good terms with the Unda, and she has nearly destroyed our relationship because of her thoughtlessness. It will take perhaps centuries to regain my balance with them."

That was likely true. Sevana eyed him sideways and made a mental note to catch him after this was done and speak with him. She might be able to work out a side deal to help him get back on the Unda's good side, which would result in some interesting trade between the two of them. She wasn't as good as Kip about spotting ideal moments for striking bargains, but this one was so obvious that even she could see it.

Zhang-Xian, God of Birth and Protector of Children, had both of his arms crossed over his massive chest and sported an expression darker than a thundercloud. He was also in black, oddly enough, and if Sevana hadn't known better she would have thought him the God of Death just from his expression. He certainly looked ready to whip out the bow at his side and shoot something. "Jade Emperor, I frankly don't trust Tian-Mu's judgment anymore. I do not believe that we should leave her powers intact."

Several gods voiced a 'second' to that and the Jade Emperor nodded instant agreement.

Tian-Mu slumped to the…ground? If clouds could be considered as such. She was splayed out in every direction, looking far from dignified, tears streaming down her cheeks.

Sevana was less than moved by the sight.

"I do not think that simply stripping her of her powers is sufficient, however," Guan-Yin argued. "She should work to undo what she has done. She must face the consequences of her actions."

The Jade Emperor turned and regarded Guan-Yi with a thoughtful expression. "I am inclined to agree. What would you have her do?"

"I think she should labor on Nanashi Isle. Should she not try to repair what she has destroyed?"

"Yes, let her work with her hands, as the humans do," Yen-Lo-Wang agreed with an approving nod. "Then she will understand the value of what she has destroyed."

"Immortality is not easily taken," the Jade Emperor observed to no one in particular, "and I am not inclined to strip that from you as well, Tian-Mu. However, I think it should be modified. I have heard the counsel and I agree with their consensus. Ambassador Sevana."

Sevana perked up instantly, sensing that things were coming to a close. "Yes?"

"It is the opinion of this counsel that for the crimes that Tian-Mu has committed, we will strip her of her powers as a goddess of lightning and command her to labor on Nanashi Isle. Along with laboring as a human, Tian-Mu shall be subject to the same perils of the flesh. She will suffer illnesses and injuries as they do. Only her life will be spared. Is this sufficient?"

From the way that Tian-Mu bawled, Sevana was inclined to think so. As a human being, it sounded a little harsh, but doable. But apparently to a dramatic goddess, it was the worst punishment imaginable. "Just one question. How long is she to labor?"

"A millennium," the Jade Emperor decided. "She is restricted from meeting any other gods during that time, including her husband." That made Tian-Mu actually scream in horror. Sevana, knowing how the woman felt about her husband, felt that was a nice touch on the Jade Emperor's part. "At the end of that term, we will revisit the idea of making her a goddess again, assuming—" here he raised his voice and his eyes cut to the woman sobbing hysterically on the floor "—that she shows proper remorse and has *learned from this*."

Tian-Mu choked back sobs and looked at him hopefully. "I can return to my husband's side?"

"Perhaps. But you have much to repay, Tian-Mu." *And your current attitude is not helping you*, his tone added.

Working with her hands for a straight millennia, without the escape of death, and without her goddess powers to help her, sounded like the perfect punishment to Sevana. She was inclined to think that the Unda would also find it fitting. "Jade Emperor, I cannot think of a more perfect punishment. There is one thing I would like to add, however." Turning, she addressed Tian-Mu directly. "I bear a message from Curano, King of Living Waters. He warns you to never put any limb into the sea. If ever he feels your presence, you will lose that appendage."

Tian-Mu stared hard at her and gulped.

Seeing that her message had gotten across, Sevana smiled at the Jade Emperor. "I will report your decision to the Unda monarchs. I thank you for your wisdom, and the guidance of the counsel."

Most of the counsel breathed a not so subtle sigh of relief. Tian-Mu had angered them, but she was still one of theirs, and they likely felt some urge to protect her. Sevana could have demanded more, but in truth she didn't think the Unda wanted to really destroy relations with them either. Better to keep things in balance.

"Then I declare this session at an end. Tian-Mu, follow me." The Jade Emperor ducked down enough to whisper to Sevana, "I'll take you down shortly, after I've dealt with her."

"I understand, I'll wait here." Sevana paused only until his back was turned before striding quickly for A0-Chin. The Dragon King of the Sea was about to disappear when she caught him by the sleeve. "Wait, A0-Chin. I have a proposition for you."

A0-Chin stopped mid-stride and turned to face her. "What matters do we have to discuss, Ambassador?"

"You said just now that you are very afraid that your relationship with the Unda will be damaged because of Tian-Mu. As you know, I am on good terms with them. I believe that I can negotiate between the two of you, smooth things over, so that you can be on good standing with them again."

His blue eyes narrowed slightly. "Do you."

"I have a sure-fire way of making them happy, you see. It's the very way I managed to get two goddesses out of their territory even though they wanted to lynch Tian-Mu."

"Is that so." A0-Chin stroked his chin thoughtfully. "I am inclined to listen, Ambassador. Assuming that your method really will work in my case."

"Oh, it'll work," Sevana assured him airily. She had to struggle to keep a shark-like smile off her face. "The question is this: what's it worth to you?"

"I can't believe you bargained with three different gods," Aran said for what must have been the fourteenth time. "Just how ruthless are you?"

"Extremely," Sevana said, puffing a strand of hair out of her eyes, "and will you get over that already? I'm a businesswoman, of course I'll take advantage of the situation." She sank back onto her heels and looked around her. The Jade Emperor had taken them back to Nanashi Isle, partially because she had left some of her equipment behind, partially because she had agreed to stay a little longer and tidy up the isle as much as she could before leaving completely. He was paying handsomely for her services so Sevana felt that she was getting the better end of the bargain.

After three days of working, she had declared an end to the matter, as there was nothing else that she could really do. The isle growing back and regaining its natural habitats and foliage would just take time. There was little that she could do to speed that process up. Besides, she had other things that were demanding her attention.

Three different gods had promised her a variety of very rare elements, all to be delivered to Big by the end of the week, and she needed to be there to receive them. Some of them were on the volatile side and would take careful handling and storage to preserve them. And to prevent Big from being blown sky-high. Plus she had fifteen children that were all ready to go to Living Waters, and from the desperate calls that Kip kept making, he was at his wit's end trying to manage them all. It would behoove her to get back soon and transport them to their new home before her business partner really did follow through on his threat and resign.

Sevana carried a crate of things to *Jumping Clouds*, moored at the docks. As she walked, she noted that Nia Reign was once again lounging on the edge of the dock, her feet in the water, eyes glued to a laboring Tian-Mu. Sevana glanced back and saw that Tian-Mu was still weaving nets to replace the ones damaged.

The former Goddess of Lightning had definitely fallen from grace. Her silken robes were gone, replaced with hardy cotton clothes that already looked a little ragged. Her hair was thrown up in a simple bun at the top of her head, strands of hair already escaping, and she constantly cried as she worked, silent tears that streamed down her cheeks.

Aran paused alongside Sevana, shifting the crate in his hands up a little more. "One would be inclined to feel sympathy for her, seeing her like this."

"Perhaps, but her tears aren't ones of remorse." That was clear even from here. "She's just feeling sorry for herself. She really hasn't learned anything from this. I now understand why the Jade Emperor assigned her to this state for a millennia. It's going to take that long for her to figure it out." With a shake of her head, she put the woman behind her and focused on loading up. "I've already spoken with all of the Unda monarchs, so that's done. When we get home, I have new inventory to sort through, and the children, of course, to deliver. After that, though, shall we go hunt up your experts?"

"I'll put out some inquiries as soon as we're back at Big," Aran promised, lifting the crate from her hands and storing it in one of the upper cabinets. "Aranhil wants his own personal update from you. You know that, right?"

"Of course he does," Sevana responded with an elaborate roll of the eyes. "When does he not? I swear I'm like a storyteller or a minstrel to him sometimes. He gets more enjoyment out of my reports than he should."

Aran shrugged as if this was obvious and understandable. "His contact with the outside world is somewhat limited, after all. It might be best for you to rest inside South Woods until we can contact the experts. It will be less harrowing for you, and you won't be dragged into another emergency that way."

It was a valid point. Sevana had put matters off this long because of people banging on her door and demanding immediate help. If she wasn't home, it would prevent that from happening. "I think I will. It's not like I can get the world to agree to hold off on the emergencies until I'm fully restored again."

Relieved his suggestion was taken so well, Aran openly beamed at her. "I'll send word home, then, so they're prepared for us."

"No need to do it that soon," she denied, "I still have a solid week's worth of work to do before I can retreat into South Woods."

Adding tasks up on his fingers, Aran's mouth pursed in reluctant acknowledgement. "Maybe a little more than that."

"See? But you might want to tell Aranhil that I'll be coming anyway. He'll be less grumpy that way."

"You did scare him rather badly, being kidnapped like this." The way Aran eyed her said she had done more than scare him. "Please, for the sake of my heart, try not to do this again. It was not fun tracking you down."

Arms akimbo, she demanded of him, "I ask you, who wants to be kidnapped?"

"You're an Artifactor, aren't you? Create an anti-kidnapping charm or something."

"Anti-kidnapping charm?" she repeated, blinking.

"You have an anti-theft charm, surely it wouldn't be too different."

Well, it probably wouldn't be, in principal. "I'm not creating that. Seriously, it's not like I get kidnapped all of the time." The way the man was carrying on, you'd think she was in danger on a constant basis. "Quit this nonsense. Help me load up the rest of my tools. If we're quick enough, we can leave for home today."

Aran dipped his head in agreement. "Let's go home."

Sevana came blearily awake. A strange, medicinal taste rested in the back of her mouth, and her head rang, which told her that she had not been naturally asleep. As she blinked her eyes open, she saw a bright, white ceiling above her head.

It didn't look at all familiar.

The last thing that Sevana remembered was leaving Living Water's territory after delivering fifteen children. There had been quite the celebration, but she had only stayed for part of it, as she had no desire to party for a week straight. She'd called Aran, said she'd be leaving on *Jumping Clouds* soon, and…it was a blank after that.

Worried, she sat up more fully and tried to get her bearings. She was in a rather nice bed, white sheets and blanket, all of the walls also white, and the floor a very soft grey stone. It reminded her of a research room she had been in before, years ago, as it had that sterile quality to it.

She had absolutely no memory of entering a place like this. Which could only mean one thing. Sevana gave a dramatic flop back on the bed. "I've been kidnapped. *Again*."

What was wrong with this year? It was just one thing after another.

The door slid open and a man with a very bushy mop of hair and round glasses stepped through. He wore the protective white jacket that most Artifactors or researchers wore and there was a variety of tools sticking out of his front breast pocket. He blinked at her and then gave a satisfied grunt. "You're awake. Excellent."

Sitting up again, she swung her legs off the side but didn't try to sit up just yet. Her head spun a little from the movement and that told her it would be prudent to take any movements slow and easy until the drug was completely out of her system. "I am. Now, who are you and why have you kidnapped me?"

"I am Richard Nath, Second Head of the Cope Research Foundation. You are currently in the Foundation's dormitory."

Cope Research Foundation? Sevana's ire was abruptly shelved with excitement. She had heard of the Foundation of course, who hadn't? It was a think tank for magical theory, *the* place to go if you wanted to do serious research. Sevana had tinkered with the idea of applying for a while, and probably would have, if not for her near-death experience. That had put a halt to such plans. Only the very best came here.

Trying not to become a giddy fangirl, she made her voice stern. "And why am I here?"

"Don't you realize how many problems you've been causing?" Nath responded in aggravation. "Your magic is such that it's snarling all of the magical eddies every time you use a spell. I'm half-convinced that you breathing is wreaking havoc in the magical fabric!"

Sevana blinked at him. Was she really? It was entirely possible, on a theoretical level, as all magic that was used eventually dispersed and re-entered the magical fabric of the world. It was like the condensation cycle of water. Exposed to open air, it would eventually evaporate, turn into some other form of water, and then collect and release again into a physical form. Such was the case with all nature, really.

His statement had one flaw in it that she could see. "Just me? I'm creating problems?"

"Your magic is partially Fae, of course you can cause significant problems!" he snapped back.

Holding up a hand, she requested, "Wait. Let me understand this. You kidnapped me to *prevent* more problems developing?"

"That is correct. We had no choice in the matter. You were running all over Mander creating glitches and it's been extremely difficult trying to nip everything before it could escalate into a major disaster." Fuming, he shook a finger at her. "Why didn't you solve your own magical core before this?"

"I was actually on my way home to do just that." Sevana shook her head, feeling a mother storm of a headache coming on. "I just got kidnapped and rescued not one month ago, which made a lot of my inner circle very angry, and now you do it again? Don't you realize what kind of trouble you're bringing down on our heads?"

"I had no choice," Nath maintained stubbornly. "You were endangering more than you realize."

"Oh, I realize. You're the idiot." Sevana rubbed at her temples and sighed, long and loud. "They're not going to want to let me out after this."

"You're correct, we don't," Nath snapped at her.

"Not *you*," Sevana corrected absently. "You're the least of my worries. I need my Caller—" which would hopefully work "—so that I can make a quick call. Otherwise a world of trouble is going to come down on our heads."

"Haven't you been listening to me?" Nath demanded, turning alarmingly red in the face. "You have to stop using magic!"

"Fine, then you make the call, but either way we have to contact Aran now. *Now*," she repeated with growing urgency. "He's already on the lookout for me, if I don't arrive when I say I will, he's going to go ballistic."

Nath stared at her with hard, angry eyes. "Why is this more important? Damaging the very fabric of magic doesn't mean anything to you?"

Sevana returned his stare and realized with dawning horror that he had not really done his research on her. Oh, he knew what effect she was having on the world, but he didn't know who he was dealing with. "Nath. Who am I?"

"Artifactor Sevana Warren, why are you asking me stupid questions?"

"Who else am I?" she pressed.

Losing all patience, Nath snapped, "A magical menace."

"You complete idiot." Sevana felt like strangling him. "Don't you realize that I'm an adopted daughter to the Fae?"

"No, you're not," he scoffed.

Sevana stared into that face of complete disbelief and almost felt pity for the fool. Pulling a pocket watch from her vest, she checked the time and realized with a sort of inevitability that she had been unconscious for six hours. That meant she was now an hour overdue for arriving home, Aran would have already become completely panicked, and since he was so close to home, would have already informed Aranhil. And Master, likely.

"I give it twenty-four hours, max, before your front doors are assaulted by some very angry Fae," Sevana predicted. Her heart felt like lead in her chest. "Nath, you were far too rash and impulsive. Because of you, we're both going to be in serious trouble."

Nath studied her face for a long moment. "You really believe the Fae will fly to your rescue."

Sevana gave him a twisted smile. "Remember: I warned you."

It didn't take a prophetess to guess what would happen next. Unfortunately, the building she was sitting in likely wouldn't survive the experience. Not to mention she would never, ever, live this down.

Perhaps Aran had a point about that anti-kidnapping charm.

Dear Reader,

Your reviews are very important. Reviews directly impact sales and book visibility, and the more reviews we have, the more sales we see. The more sales there are, the longer I get to keep writing the books you love full time. The best possible support you can provide is to give an honest review, even if it's just clicking those stars to rate the book!

Thank you for all your support! See you in the next world.

~Honor

Honor Raconteur is a sucker for a good fantasy. Despite reading it for decades now, she's never grown tired of the magical world. She likely never will.
In between writing books, she trains and plays with her dogs, eats far too much chocolate, and attempts insane things like aerial dance.

If you'd like to join her newsletter to be notified when books are released, and get behind the scenes about upcoming books, you can isit her website or email directly to honorraconteur.news@raconteurhouse.com and you'll be added to the mailing list. If you'd like to interact with Honor more directly, you can socialize with her on various sites. Each platform offers something different and fun!

Other books by Honor Raconteur
Published by Raconteur House

♪ Available in Audiobook! ♪

THE ADVENT MAGE CYCLE

Jaunten ♪
Magus ♪
Advent ♪
Balancer ♪

ADVENT MAGE NOVELS
Advent Mage Compendium
The Dragon's Mage ♪
The Lost Mage

WARLORDS (ADVENT MAGE)

Warlords Rising
Warlords Ascending
Warlords Reigning

THE ARTIFACTOR SERIES

The Child Prince ♪
The Dreamer's Curse ♪
The Scofflaw Magician
The Canard Case
The Fae Artifactor

THE CASE FILES OF HENRI DAVENFORTH

Magic and the Shinigami Detective
Charms and Death and Explosions (oh my)

DEEPWOODS SAGA

Deepwoods ♪
Blackstone
Fallen Ward

Origins

FAMILIAR AND THE MAGE

The Human Familiar
The Void Mage
Remnants
Echoes

GÆLDORCRÆFT FORCES

Call to Quarters

KINGMAKERS

Arrows of Change ♪
Arrows of Promise
Arrows of Revolution

KINGSLAYER

Kingslayer ♫
Sovran at War ♫

SINGLE TITLES

Special Forces 01
Midnight Quest

Crossroads: An Artifactor x Deepwoods Crossover Short Story

Printed in Great Britain
by Amazon